Chapter One

Counting the number of seconds she was late as she burst through the doors of Maine PR was not helping with her stress levels. With a bundle of today's newspapers in one hand and half a latte in the other, Alicia Simpson ran through the corridors, ignoring the "oh-shit-you're-in-trouble" look Sarah, the receptionist, pinned her with.

She was late. Six hundred seconds late, to be exact, and that was the last thing she needed on the day she was pitching to the highest profile client she'd ever been given a shot at.

As she burst into the boardroom, panting, her colleague Kenny was shaking hands with the man she'd spent the better part of the week researching. The man who'd made the front news – again – which was why she was holding a stack of newspapers and her jacket was stained with coffee.

One glance at Mr Maine's murderous expression had her fighting the urge to scamper out of the boardroom. Her stomach was a flutter of nerves and her heart rate exuberated like she'd had a shot of adrenaline injected straight into it.

Pulling herself together, she threw a quick smile at Collins, dumped the papers on the table, and whipped off her jacket. She only hoped she didn't have sweat marks, but what was worse? Pit stains or a frothy brown mark down the front of her grey coat?

'I stopped to pick up the news. Mr Collins, you're on the front page of them all.' She didn't glance his way, only stared down Maine until he nodded to acknowledge she was late for a reason.

'Shit,' said a voice that sent a shiver down her spine.

She turned in time to see him flip over the daily rags and catch a glimpse of his headshot on the front of each – but it wasn't this story that threatened to make cleaning up his reputation harder than stuffing Hitler's skeletons into a closet that caught her attention.

It was the man himself. He was tall, more built than he looked on television, and his dark curly hair had grown out, resting on wide shoulders.

The ground seemed to sway under her, like her father's yacht on a windy day. Alicia clasped the edge of the table for support. But this was just the stress of being late and a week of sleepless nights putting together her pitch. She needed to get over it quick if she wanted to convince Collins she was the woman for the job. No wilting wallflower would stand a chance with a project like this.

Neither would an earl's hapless daughter who had always been outshone by her sisters. This pitch was step one of leaving that shadow behind. And she'd get this bad boy tennis player to sign with Maine if it was the last thing she did.

Collins dragged a hand down his face and turned to them. Dark circles underscored his eyes as if to highlight the hint of anguish, but he wiped it away with an easy grin as Mr Maine introduced her. When Collins stepped closer, she had to crane her neck. Refusing to shrivel, she met his dark eyes with a smile.

The way he beamed back made her stomach flutter. Alicia's pulse raced as he clasped her hand in a shake that went on for too long, but she couldn't find the strength to break the connection.

'Ms Simpson, I can't wait to hear what you have in mind.'

He really didn't. Right now she was wondering what his lips tasted like and whether his chest was as defined

SCANDAL

Aimée Duffy

What had she done?

Published by Accent Press Ltd 2015

ISBN 9781783757534

Copyright © Aimee Duffy 2015

as it looked beneath his polo shirt. Tension curled low in her stomach and she snatched her hand back. Cleared her throat.

She reminded herself that he meant her pitch. 'I'm sure someone at Maine can help you.'

Great. Just flipping fabulous. First she was late, and now this! She should have said *she* was capable of helping him.

Collins' grin only got wider. 'That's why I'm here.' He winked, then turned back to Mr Maine. 'Let's get this thing started.'

As Collins made his way to the chair at the opposite end of the table, Alicia was glad to be able to sink into her seat. Her legs didn't feel strong enough to support her, especially when she got treated to him walking away. Those wide shoulders led down to a narrow waist. The polo clung to his lean muscles like a second skin. His jeans hugged his rear so tightly that she flushed imagining him without the clothes and her over-excited body went from hot to scorched in a heartbeat.

'Kenny, carry on,' Mr Maine instructed.

She didn't hear a word of what Kenny said, too horrified at herself for gawking at Sebastian. It had been so long since she'd allowed herself to look at a man like this. Not since she was sixteen, in love, and then destroyed in the worst possible way – by a sportsman who could convince any woman to drop her knickers with a few well-placed lines.

She wasn't that crazy girl anymore. The one who had indecent thoughts and urges for guys who could make her want to wrap her legs around their waists. They did her no good and, more importantly, were not suitable suitors for a Simpson.

Pit ten seconds spent with Collins and that part of her came roaring back.

Kenny seemed to speak in some sort of monotone. Even so, Collins nodded at what she assumed were the right places. Still, he had a frown between his brows like he'd expected more from them – or at least a mention of the latest scandal robbing the headlines.

Or maybe he just didn't want to be there. After flunking out of the Australian Opens, he'd partied it up instead of going straight back into training. The media had deemed his head wasn't in the game, and his management company claimed the stress of Collins' break up with Kiss-and-Tell Mai was the reason he'd lost focus on the court.

By the pictures printed in the news over the last week, his head and focus had been in the knickers of half the women in Melbourne. That couldn't be blamed on the stress of a break-up three months earlier.

Alicia wiped her damp palms along her skirt. Challenge? This was going to be as difficult as an expedition to the South Pole wearing a scanty bikini and flip-flops.

His gaze snagged hers, as if he'd heard her disparaging thoughts. Collins' frown smoothed out and her heart sped faster. What was it about those eyes that made her forget the whole room around them?

Then it came to her. He was a player with a capital P. He could probably melt any woman he wanted with no more than a sultry look. Well, she wasn't falling for his charms – she'd had enough of that to last a lifetime. Plus, she'd dug up enough dirt on him to bury the Isle of Wight. This was about climbing the career ladder, nothing more.

So she turned to Kenny, which was like turning from the sun to stare at rainclouds. His speech droned on, but she couldn't make out a word with her mind full of Collins.

Damn.

Giving up the pretence, she shuffled through the papers on her clipboard, wishing she had practised her pitch delivery a little more. In front of shirtless posters of

Collins so she could have bored herself of this annoying urge to ogle him.

When her colleague was finally done, Mr Maine said, 'Great work, Kenny. As always.' Turning to Collins with a smile, he continued, 'Are you ready to hear more, or have you made a decision?'

Collins looked at her with a raised brow. 'Are you here as a pretty face, Blondie, or did you have a pitch ready too?'

Her eyes narrowed. Blondie? No doubt he thought she'd be as useless or boring as Kenny and his monotone speech. She had to bite back the urge to tell the arrogant sod exactly what she thought of him. Antagonising a potential client this big would have her P45 slapped on her desk so fast she'd barely have time to finish a rant filled with words a lady should never use.

'I do.' Alicia pushed away from the table. 'And I think you'll want to hear what I have planned, especially after that.' She pointed to the newspapers spread over the table.

Collins didn't glance at the desk. He just leaned back on his chair, folding his arms across his chest like he couldn't care less what the media were slinging at him.

The smile teasing the corners of his mouth only made her irritation grow. It was obvious he was mocking her. He probably didn't believe she had anything worth pitching, but seemed he was playing along for his own amusement.

Irascibility won out over nerves. Alicia straightened, walked over to the whiteboard, and turned it around. The previous day she'd bullet-pointed her three-step action plan.

'It isn't just the UK media stringing up your reputation and hanging it out for a beating.' She turned to face him, but pointed at number one on her list. His attention zeroed in on the board with a deeper frown, like her words had pissed him off. Funny, she didn't care too much if she'd offended him.

'Your number one priority is making sure your sponsors don't drop you. That means an image clean-up. Not just here in London, but worldwide. We need to give the media another angle to work with and win back faith from your supporters. That's where point two comes in.'

Collins held up his hand. '"Clean up" as in prove innocence, you mean?'

He met her eyes with none of the cheeky sensuality he had earlier.

'No,' she said.

'Alicia.' Mr Maine's voice was layered with warning, but she barrelled on regardless.

'Your management company tried to deny allegations that you were partying every night of your trip to Melbourne and look how that turned out.' No one had believed it. 'They dug deeper because they smelt a cover-up, and they weren't far off the mark if today's news was anything to go by.'

His shoulders stiffened. 'Pictures can be deceiving.'

'Maybe.' She doubted that. 'But the truth doesn't matter as much. People believe what they want to believe, and your sponsors will be cautious about investing in you. Making it up is the right way to go here.'

He cocked an eyebrow. 'You think I'm guilty, Blondie?'

The low, seductive way he asked spurred more than anger. Her blood sizzled and she had to grind her teeth to keep from losing her cool. Sportsmen, it seemed, were all the same. Players, liars, and self-assured bastards.

She forced out a non-answer, trying not to sound breathy. 'Like I said, that's irrelevant.'

Keeping an easy grin on his face was tough, especially since Sebastian knew there and then she believed every word the press had printed about his break up with Mai.

6

Just like his sponsors. And they wondered why he'd almost gone totally off the rails. It had only been months of slander and false accusations, after all. That would cause even the most innocent guy stress.

He should walk out of there. The first pitch was an extension of what AIG had done for him and he knew he was up the creek this time. He needed a miracle, and no one at Maine seemed up to the job.

Blondie turned back to the board and his mind took off on a little holiday. The drab grey pencil skirt hugged her backside like a second skin. With a fizzle running through his veins and his throat suddenly dry, keeping up the casual act got tough.

'Step two,' she said, pointing a finger at the writing on the whiteboard.

Instead of walking like he should, Sebastian found himself saying, 'I'm all for charity work, but I'm stuck in England until the French Open.'

Alicia turned back to him with a smirk, like the joke was on him for doubting her. Still, he cocked a brow to show he wasn't convinced and the smirk slipped. Point one for him.

'I'd thought of that. I also know that you have acquaintances all over the world who play tennis, and your father did too. You don't need to leave London, but free lessons or some volunteer work at a club could go in your favour. Plus if you unite with a few other sportsmen and convince them to spend a little of their time doing the same under a program, you're hitting it worldwide. As long as your name's thrown in there, you're going to get the right media coverage.'

The idea was tempting and he should give her a point for her smarts. Maybe he'd underestimated her. But …

Shaking his head, he said, 'I don't have the kind of time to organise all that. Training is gruesome before a tournament and I'm not willing to miss any.'

He'd missed enough, got sloppy, and made a public

spectacle of what was left of his reputation. No more.

'You don't have to,' she said. 'That would be my job. All I need is your contacts and a few hours a week from you.'

This time he had to give her credit where it was due. One point each. He could squeeze in a few hours a week. His manager Tony would kick his backside up and down the court if he didn't do something to stop the sports companies pulling their funding. Savings only went so far. He didn't fancy picking up a shift or two at a bar to stay in the game.

'I could spare a few hours, and I know some people who might be interested in something like this.'

Alicia smiled like he'd just given her a diamond necklace. The curves of those lips had him remembering her other curves beneath that hideous suit. Even with her hair in some kind of fifties up-do, there was something about her that caught and held his attention. Kept him in the chair, even when that guy's pitch had him ready to walk.

Even when it was clear, just like everyone else, she believed the worst about him. A cold sweat broke out on his forehead, but he refused to swipe it and give himself away. Instead, he took a deep breath, willing himself not to get sucked back into the spiral of the last few months.

What she thought about him didn't matter. Not if she could back up her words and turn things around for him. Especially after the latest kiss-and-tell, this time from one of the women he'd fallen into bed with *after* he got back from Australia.

'Step three.' Alicia pointed to the word scrawled in red.

'Rebuild?' he asked with a frown. 'Is this a twelve steps to sobriety pitch?'

She scowled and he couldn't hold in a burst of laughter. From the corner of his eye he could see her boss gaping at them, and the first guy to pitch sat with his hands folded and shoulders stooped. He knew Blondie was on to the win.

'Three.' The angry burn in her eyes and clenched jaw made it seem like she wanted to say more, but she kept her voice cool with a slightly prissy edge that made his lips twitch. Sebastian couldn't help but be impressed by her control.

'Like I said, cover up is pointless at this stage. It won't earn respect. If you put your hands up, admit you made mistakes, and prove that you're trying to rectify them, people will sympathise. Denial will lead to disaster. There's too much evidence out there and too much hype around your split with Mai. The best way to go is to *prove* to the world you're sorry and show them how much you've grown.'

Now it was him struggling to keep his irritation in check. Sorry? Yes, he was sorry alright. Sorry he'd met the media whore in the first place. Sorry he'd trusted her when there wasn't a decent bone in her perfectly buffed body. Sorry he'd been too much of an idiot to see that sooner.

Sebastian had sworn to never make those mistakes again.

His career was what mattered, and though he was tempted to let Blondie sweat or make her work harder for this sell, it was stupidity like that which had landed him in this position in the first place.

'You're right.' As far as her action plan went, at least. 'At this point, covering up is tacky and pointless considering the evidence.'

He rose from the chair, then stuffed his hands in his pockets. Her gaze dropped down to his hips and a flush scored her cheekbones. His blood rushed south, and if he wasn't careful she was going to get an eyeful of a part of him she hadn't bargained for.

When her gaze met his again, she was blinking as if trying to hide her reaction or wake up from a dream. As his blood simmered he pictured what it would be like to unpin that golden hair to let it fall through his fingers and he made the first mistake of the day.

'Just one question.' Sebastian turned to Mr Maine. 'When does Miss Simpson get off for lunch? I'd like to discuss her pitch in more detail.'

Chapter Two

Blondie was not happy to be going to lunch with him.

After claiming she had a meeting with a client, Maine pulled her aside and mumbled something to her. Her peach skin turned a deep pink – probably with irritation – and her angular jaw tightened like she was biting back a refusal that would have gotten her in serious trouble.

Why this made Sebastian grin, he had no idea. But as her heels clattered staccato on the pavement beside him and with the way she clutched her file and handbag so tight the circulation in her fingers must have cut off, he couldn't help it.

As was the norm for England before the spring, rain drizzled down, turning the streets a muggy grey. His sports jacket was waterproof, but her suit didn't look water resistant – the soaked-in stain on the front proved that. She had no umbrella, and instead her golden hair caught the water and turned it a few shades darker.

There was a chill in the air and he didn't want to have to go too far from Maine PR in case the weather got worse. She probably would never forgive him if he was the reason she ended up with the flu, and that was hardly conductive when he'd pretty much made up his mind to sign with Maine.

'Baxter's good for you, Blondie?'

Those flaming green eyes turned on him like rat poison-tipped daggers. 'My name is Alicia.'

Then she tripped. He reached out, grabbed her by the waist, and pulled her to him. The second her slender body hit his, heat stirred in the pit of his stomach and his grin slipped. Her damp hair smelled like strawberries and he had to wonder if her lips would taste as sweet, especially coated in that clear gloss that reminded him of smeared honey.

Her file and handbag hit the pavement with a clatter. He didn't let her go so much as she shoved out of his grasp. Her face was rosy now, but not in the way women who were attracted to him blushed. Alicia briefly scowled at him before crouching down and collecting what she'd dropped.

Sebastian tried to help, but she batted his hands away. 'You don't like me much, do you?'

She mumbled something that sounded suspiciously like, 'Well spotted, genius.'

As they rose, he asked, 'Why?'

The fact that her dislike grated on him was a surprise. After months of judgement and slander, he thought he'd be over caring what others thought by now.

'Why what?' she called over her shoulder as she strutted away.

The way her bum moved beneath that tight monstrosity of a skirt was way too distracting. 'Come on, you're dying to tell me. Have been since you started your pitch, I'll bet.'

The only reaction he got was her shoulders tensing.

In three easy strides he caught up to her. 'Go on, I promise I won't tell your boss or pull as a client.'

'You haven't signed yet.'

Her attention was on the pavement in front of her, like she didn't want him to have to catch her again. And if he was thinking more about his reputation than the way she felt pressed against him, he'd be inclined to agree having her in his arms was a bad idea.

'And if I said it wouldn't affect my decision?' he pressed.

She stopped outside the restaurant and turned to him with narrowed eyes. 'I'd find it hard to believe you.'

She'd pretty much called him an idiot and a liar in less than five minutes, and all Sebastian wanted to do was ruffle those prissy, professional feathers to loosen her up. He *was* an idiot, pure and simple. When she burst into the boardroom and he saw how she withered under her boss' glare, he'd been hit with a pang of sympathy.

Striking a deal with him was obviously important to her and it hadn't been her fault more of his shit was covering the daily rags. So he'd tried to lighten her up by flirting a little. The more worked up she got, the more he teased her. It wasn't fair, not when she was trying to be professional. But she hadn't looked anxious since. Instead it was like a fire had lit behind those big green eyes and it made her all the prettier. Even with the drab suit and outdated hairstyle.

He moved forward to open the door for her. 'OK, how about we start again? I promise not to tease you through lunch.' He may have crossed his fingers behind his back, but she didn't notice.

'Good. That's … good.' The doubt in her eyes said she didn't believe him.

Smart cookie.

He grinned. Lunch was going to be more fun than he'd hoped.

Mai's feet might ache from strutting around London in a pair of Gucci slingbacks, but her mood was higher than it had been in months. She had a cheque in her pocket for more than she expected and a contract with *Taylor Made* to do a series of in-depth interviews on her relationship with Sebastian.

It seemed the more he screwed up and slept around, the more people wanted her to have her say. Who knew having such a public relationship with an up-and-coming tennis star would do wonders for her own career?

And the fact *Taylor Made* had taken her suggestion and titled the series *The Beginning of the End* just added to her joy.

Her first instinct when she left their offices was to call Jack, but he was busy with his script and she didn't want to throw Sebastian in his face any more than she had to. Sure, he was the reason she broke up with Jack all those years ago but back then, money and the potential to become a celebrity mattered more than love.

She was just lucky he'd taken her back after the affair. Luckier still that he encouraged her desire for revenge. It made her realise how important love was. Jack's kind of love, the love that saw them through the rough times and then brought them back together.

Instead of calling him, she was set on hitting the Tube and Oxford Street. The money was only going to burn a hole in her bank account and right now she was in the mood to treat her man to something that would take his mind of his silly script. Luckily, she knew just the shop to visit.

Mai turned the corner, only to jump back into the shadows and lower the umbrella to cover her face. What the hell was Sebastian doing *here* and with a woman who looked frigid enough in all those layers to be a nun?

She stayed where she was until they passed, but the sound of his laugh still hit her like it had the first time, heating her blood and making her want him. The craving was lust of course, which was all they ever had, but she still missed it. She still missed *him* at times. Even now, when she hated him more than she'd ever hated anyone.

When the oddest couple in the city had gotten far enough away, Mai poked her head around the corner. Sebastian had his arms wrapped around the woman's waist with a big, stupid grin on his face. The same grin he'd given Mai once. The same grin that still had the power to steal her breath.

She darted out of sight and used the dirty alley wall for support. This time that grin squeezed at her heart until she bled with misery. Her eyes welled but she blinked the moisture away. Vengeance made more sense than tormenting herself. Revenge was sweeter than wondering if he'd left her for having a big arse or small tits. Payback for this would line her pockets and give her and Jack the life Sebastian never could.

Mai walked onto the street and saw him leading the frigid bitch into a restaurant. She pulled her mobile out, snapped a picture, then searched her contacts. This one would be a favour for old time's sake, but it served that bastard Collins right. He would soon learn he couldn't destroy her life and get away with it!

Sebastian guided Alicia through Baxter's with a hand on her lower back. The place wasn't overly flashy, though the berry coloured walls with black and chrome décor did make it feel a bit more gothic romance than he was comfortable with. But all he cared about was not bumping into the ex from hell. Or the press. Neither should expect him to visit here when he was supposed to be training.

Or maybe they did, going by his actions in Melbourne. As he glanced around at the uncovered windows, he breathed out a curse. He really should have thought this lunch thing through.

They were seated at the far side of the building, right next to a huge window with nothing but a purple, see-through veil covering half of it. Sebastian was about to insist they had more privacy until he noticed there were no other tables free.

Given his father had drummed good manners into him all his life, he pulled out a chair for Alicia. She stared at it with parted lips, like the gesture was the last thing she thought he'd do.

'Didn't you expect a ladies' man like me to be a gentleman?' He winked before sliding into his own chair.

Pink tinged the tips of her cheekbones. 'Thank you.

What else would you like to know about my plan?'

All business. He sighed. 'If we're going to be working together, don't you think it'd be a good idea to get to know each other?'

Alicia shook her head and he frowned. Her reply was cut off by a server asking them what they'd like to order.

'Just lime and soda for me. This won't take long,' Alicia said.

He quirked an eyebrow at her then turned to the waitress with a grin. 'I'd like to see the menu.'

After the woman gave him a flirty smile, she left to get what he'd asked for.

'If we're going to work together to save your sponsors, you might want to tone the flirting-in-public-places thing down a notch or ten,' she said in the most prim English tone he'd ever heard.

'Jealous?' he asked, resting his elbows on the table and leaning forward. Her eyes burned again. He fought back a laugh.

'Don't be ridiculous. It's my job to make sure you stay out of the newspapers for the wrong reasons.'

He couldn't fault her logic, but it wasn't like he'd invited the server for an afternoon sweat fest at his flat. 'A little flirting's great for both parties. Don't women love the compliment? Why else would they ask if their bum looks big in clothes if they don't want to hear nice things so they can feel good about themselves?'

She sighed and massaged her temples. 'This is going to be harder than I thought.'

Alicia hiked her bag onto her lap and he frowned at the top of her head. What was with this woman? It was like she'd been born without the humour gene.

The waitress came back, handing over a menu and eyeing him like she wanted to say something else. He was too intent on the blonde fussing around in a bag taller than her midriff to do more than give the girl a dismissive 'thanks'.

Alicia's hair was pulled back tight and twisted into some kind of coil at the back. How long did those pale locks fall when let loose? Down to her shoulders, or long enough to cover her breasts?

His heart pounded at the thought and he shoved the image aside. She wasn't his type; too highly strung and clearly not even interested in him enough to pretend to laugh at his jokes like most women did.

Not that he should consider her anything other than his publicist. This lunch might have been a spur of the moment decision – probably due to the fact he liked the way she'd checked him out – but he did need to know more about this plan of hers. After all, there were a lot of rumours going around about him lately. Most were ugly. Some were downright insulting, the worst coming from Mai.

'Lost something?' he asked, because she was still fumbling around in her handbag.

'My pen,' she mumbled.

'Blondie, stop worrying. You don't need to take notes, and I'll go by the office tomorrow to sign. Right now, I want to eat and hear more about how you're going to try to straighten me up.'

She looked at him, the fire in her eyes reminding him he should ditch the nickname and use Alicia. Such a pretty name too, but he liked the way she glowered when he didn't.

'Of course,' she said, then clenched her teeth.

He pressed his lips together to keep from grinning. A bit of teasing never hurt anyone, and it was about time Miss Prim and Proper learned that.

Alicia should have known better than to believe a man like Collins. The promise not to tease was broken before they'd been served a drink.

Not to mention the flirting. Would she have to keep an eye on him twenty-four seven to make sure he kept what he was packing in his boxers? She couldn't do that, not with her other clients and the way he riled her up. It would be *her* headlining the news next. She could imagine the headline – *Earl of Cumbria's daughter slung up for murder*, or worse, *Playboy of the Year Screwing for the Title*.

Alicia shuddered.

Sebastian looked at the menu and she had to force herself not to tap the table and give away her impatience. Her stomach was on the verge of growling but she couldn't have that. She needed this to be over and done with so she could get back to work. Away from him. Maybe he ate quickly. She could only hope.

He placed the menu down and asked, 'What's good here?'

She was about to say 'everything' just so he'd pick something until she remembered what he did for a living. 'I thought you'd be on a special diet.'

Sebastian shrugged.

She thought he gave a damn about his career. More than likely his management company had forced him to come to Maine. That at least explained the way he had looked like he couldn't care less in the boardroom.

Well, it was her job to make him look good in the public eye, which meant he had to appear focused – if he ever signed. What would a sportsman need? She wished she'd looked into that. Surely protein. Probably refined carbs, too.

'The salmon is nice, with brown rice and steamed veg.'

'Good to know,' he said and waved over the pretty brunette waitress.

The woman subtly slid her hands down her stomach, then tucked her shirt in tighter so it emphasised her breasts. A burning sensation flared in Alicia's temples. She did her best to ignore it – after all, what did she care if a woman flirted with him? If he signed, she'd have to put up with that sort of thing daily. It was better she got used to it now.

'I'll have the salmon with brown rice and steamed vegetables, please. Oh, and the grilled chicken without seasoning if you can, with salad?'

Her eyes narrowed at Collins. Surely he didn't need all that.

'What would you like, miss?' the girl asked.

'Just the lime and soda.' Her voice dripped with her growing irritation.

Before the waitress left, Alicia asked for a loan of her pen. The other woman obliged and she turned to Collins, her suspicion rising. 'Hungry?'

Collins shook his head. 'I can't eat all that. The salmon's for you.'

'I'm not –' but her traitorous stomach grumbled.

He laughed. 'Figured as much.'

Without thinking, she snapped, 'Why are we here, anyway? We could have discussed my pitch at the office.'

Collins relaxed back into the chair with that easy grin and hint of amusement in his eyes that drove her bonkers. Her blood simmered at the thought he was laughing at her again and she considered getting up and walking out the door. But that would just put her back on desk duty, coming up with new campaigns for small, going-nowhere businesses, wouldn't it?

Combined with her late entrance earlier, her bottom would bounce off the pavement on her way out of Maine for letting Collins slip through her fingers.

She shuddered as she imagined the heavy disapproval in her father's glare when she was forced to go crawling back. One he used only on her. Time and time again.

She never wanted to return permanently to the cold brick and stone building she'd grown up in, with parents who were cooler than the concrete. An overnight visit once every other month was more than enough.

'We're here because we're hungry and there's more I need to know before I sign,' he answered, snapping her focus back to the conversation.

His voice, low and rich, did *not* make her heart pound faster. No, that was the thought of losing the first job she'd ever had and having to go running home to her father's country mansion.

'What do you need to know?' she asked, putting her irritation aside. Or trying hard to. It bubbled under her skin, making her want to say things she shouldn't.

'Why did you get into the PR business?' he asked.

'I don't see why that's relevant.'

Leaning forward on his elbows, he grinned in a way that made her heart flutter and skin tingle. He shouldn't be allowed loose on the female population. She scowled to hide her reaction.

'It is. I need to know that you love your job, that you have the drive to do it right. Otherwise, what's the point hiring you?'

Collins was seriously testing her patience. She'd worked hard to win the right to prove she could salvage his reputation. She wasn't going to let his cocky attitude or flirting or whatever he was trying to do ruin this for her.

Humouring him was the only option she had.

'I've always wanted to help people get out of trouble, and I'm very good at bringing out the best in my clients.' Alicia unclipped papers from her board. 'This is Maine's standard contract. After you've read it over you can sign on the last page.'

She placed the document in front of him with the borrowed pen on top. Collins didn't even glance at it.

'And you think you can bring out the best in me?' he asked with a smirk.

She had to take a deep breath so she could speak calmly. 'Yes, although I admit it will be challenging. All you need to know is what I'm going to do for you and how. The whys are irrelevant. Understand?'

'I don't know … the whys say a lot about people.'

Was he playing her for his own amusement? It seemed so, the way his eyes lit up and his lips pressed together as if to hold back a laugh. The thought of having to go into work this afternoon and tell her boss he'd walked away from the deal filled her empty stomach with dread.

She had a sinking feeling that it was inevitable. Hadn't she already been over this, with a man who made her crazy with lust, passion, fear, anger, and worst of all, love? He'd strung her along until she actually needed him. What had he done then? He'd walked out on her when something shinier came along.

Collins wasn't trying to take her virtue or flatter her with pretty words and irresistible promises, but she knew he was not going to sign. He'd probably invited her to lunch because he thought she was easy, or he was looking for a way out of his responsibilities with his management company.

Alicia picked up the contract and pen, determined to leave Baxter's with a shred of pride. After all, she was a Simpson and if her father had taught her anything, it was that no one played her family for fools. 'This is pointless.'

She made to get up, but he caught her wrist. His rough palm made her skin tingle and she met his eyes on reflex. They weren't laughing now. Determination made him look more serious, like he did when he was on the court.

'Relax. There's no rush. Sit down.'

The teasing tone slipped and though he spoke softly, the words were laced with command. Temptation to pull her arm free and storm out of the restaurant was strong, but then she'd lose everything – not just her pride. What was that worth when the alternative meant moving back to Cumbria?

She settled back into her chair. 'I don't appreciate being strung along.'

He released her and held up both his palms, the serious expression making him look older than his twenty-eight years. It was odd, she'd never thought of him as someone who could be what he needed to be, only someone who might be able to fool his fans and sponsors for short intervals. Now …

'Blondie, if I was leading you on it wouldn't be to sign a deal, if you catch my drift.'

The wink, followed by a decadent grin, stole her hope. At least Darrell had pretended to be a decent man. He even took the time to make promises he would never keep. Sebastian couldn't even use her name!

But she shouldn't be comparing him to her ex, and she certainly shouldn't let him affect her mood this much. After their meals were served, she decided to ignore the teasing and get back to business, giving him a more in-depth rundown of what she had planned, all the while he shovelled his chicken and salad between lips she couldn't stop peeking at.

Halfway through his lunch, he interrupted her plan of attack. 'You're hungry, you should eat.'

Alicia looked down at the healthy, unappetising fish and boring rice with a wrinkled nose. 'I don't really like this. I just guessed what a sportsman might need.'

He grinned. 'I thought you didn't care about me?'

'I care about your image – something *you* don't seem to have much interest in – because that's my job.'

The easy-going smile slipped and he skewered another slice of chicken with his fork. 'I care.'

His shoulders seemed rigid and the teasing glint had disappeared from his eyes. Fearing she'd offended him, Alicia scrambled for something to say. 'Why don't you show it?'

She bit her tongue. Crap, she was just making this worse.

But his smile reappeared and he wiped the corners with a napkin, then left it on his empty plate. 'I'm not about to disclose the whys when you won't.'

Frowning, she said, 'Fair enough. I'll get the bill.'

Collins caught her wrist again before she turned to wave over the waitress. His thumb rubbed lazy circles, making her tingle in places she shouldn't. She was about to tell him off, but got caught up in his eyes. His concern was highlighted by the slight line between his brows.

'We should get you something else if you didn't like it,' he said.

She snapped out of whatever spell he had her under and gently wrestled her hand back, instantly missing the connection. This was bad, she had to get out of there.

'I have a sandwich in my drawer and a client to see soon,' she lied.

Collins didn't call her out or push for anything else. Instead, he picked up the contract.

She'd done it.

She'd gotten him to sign.

Excitement zipped through her, making her even more jittery.

Until he folded the papers in half.

'What are you doing?' she asked.

Collins grinned. 'You didn't think I'd sign before having it looked over properly, did you, Blondie?'

The disappointment clogging her throat was so great she didn't take offense at the nickname. He could still say no. Alicia pushed the thought away. He would *not* say no. She hadn't gone through a week of sleepless nights and two hours of torture for nothing. If he didn't appear at Maine with a signed contract soon, she'd just have to track him down.

'Of course.' Alicia left the pen on the table. 'It was a pleasure to meet you, Mr Collins. I hope we'll get to work together soon.'

He laughed, probably at the false sweetness she'd

forced into her voice, then rose too, throwing a few notes onto the table. After swiping up the mints, he led her out of Baxter's with one hand on the small of her back, resurrecting those inappropriate tingles.

Outside, Collins handed her a mint. Then, in a move too quick she didn't see it coming, he kissed her cheek – so close to her lips she could inhale his breath. Her skin sizzled, and her stomach melted. All she needed was for her knees to get all wobbly and she'd be a walking cliché.

'I'll come by tomorrow with the contract. It was lovely having lunch with you too, Ms Simpson.'

Alicia couldn't help but smile at the formal way he addressed her, and felt hopeful that she'd scored the client of her career, so much so that she let the inappropriate kiss slide for the moment. After all, it was chaste. Not his fault that she reacted the way she did. 'See you tomorrow, *Sebastian*.'

His eyes darkened when she said his name for the first time. Alicia knew her voice was a bit too suggestive for a business deal. It resembled the tone her little sister, Sylvia, used to get more wine in her glass.

As long as it got him to sign on the dotted line, that was the main thing. It had nothing to do with how his lips felt against her skin.

Before he could say anything else, she turned and headed toward the Maine building, with a grin she couldn't seem to wipe off her face.

Chapter Three

So close, so bloody close, was Alicia's thoughts when Mr Maine called the next day demanding an immediate meeting. The rage in his voice had her stumbling on shaky legs all the way down the long, grey corridor. It felt like more like walking on death row, not the building she'd known for years. The sides seemed to close in around her.

Since she'd seen the front page of the newspapers on her way to work this morning, she knew this was coming. She'd briefly considered calling in sick, but that wouldn't make any of this better. She was done with wallflower Alicia, and going into the office proved that, if nothing else, she was growing a backbone.

Still, she'd rather dip her toe into a pool filled with piranhas than face Mr Maine's wrath.

She knocked his door once, then entered when he grumbled something. His elderly face was raw, contrasting with what was left of his salt-and-pepper hair. Air puffed his chest out and she couldn't look at him without trembling. There were newspapers scattered across his desk, all with various pictures of her … and Collins. She'd glimpsed the captions earlier. Saw what the media had come up with.

Alicia clasped her shaking hands together.

'What's going on here, Alicia? The truth.' His voice was low and laced with steel. Just like her father's had been the first time he'd given her a lecture. The first time she'd really made him angry by coming close to dragging his family's reputation through the mud. A cool sweat broke out across her forehead.

'I've no idea, sir. I didn't know there were photographers there. We had lunch, discussed my pitch in more detail, and as I told you yesterday, Collins took the contract away to have his people look at it.'

Far from mollified, Mr Maine scowled at her. 'You do realise there's no way in hell he'll sign now. His manager at AIG has already been on the phone chewing my ear off. He recognised you from the picture on our website – which I've had to remove. The last thing Collins needs is to be linked to another woman, even if you are the daughter of an earl.' He ran a hand over his jaw with a sigh. 'Not to mention our strict rule about getting involved with clients.'

Alicia gasped. 'We're not involved!'

His brows furrowed and his jaw tightened. He tapped his finger against the picture of Collins kissing her. She moved closer. It was like looking at a different woman. Her eyes were big and bright. She remembered only too well the shiver that went through her when he'd leaned in. Remembered the fiery scorch of skin on skin that smouldered right down to her bones.

With her face burning, she was about to launch into another denial but it was pointless. Wasn't she the one who said people believed what they wanted? Mr Maine was obviously no different. Tears pricked her eyes as she imagined what came next, but she wouldn't break down here. That could wait until later.

'I'm going to have a think about what to do with you, Alicia. You've never given us problems before, but this crosses lines I've put in place for a reason. You've risked our reputation.'

He shook his head, and she could almost believe he didn't want to do what was clearly coming. She'd be sacked. Without a chance to prove the pictures were not what they seemed.

Collins signing would be the only thing that could save her job now, but if his manager was angry at Maine, there was no doubt he would be too. As she walked back to her office, her shoulders stooped with defeat and the corridor seemed more claustrophobic than before.

A flurry of noise down the hall caught her attention. She kept going until she got to the reception desk. A large man, tall and wide, was causing the fuss. Making angry demands, if the way Sarah shied away from him was any indication. His voice was growling words so fast they were difficult to understand.

She was about to turn and look for security when she noticed who the big guy was with. Her breath stilled.

The man who could have cost Alicia her career before it even really got started lounged in one of the chairs, his arms folded across his chest while he looked at the bigger man with an amused glint in his eyes.

What on earth was *he* doing here?

Collins turned to her and his grin made her heart pound. Before she could give into the urge to run, he said, 'Told you I'd be back, didn't I, Blondie?'

Watching the colour drain from Alicia's face made him feel like a first class-shit.

Seeing Tony turn on her like an angry pit bull made the feeling worse. Sebastian hopped out of the chair and was at his manager's side before he could say a word. With one hand on the guy's arm, he muttered, 'Let's wait until Maine comes down, then we can all air our grievances.'

He understood the questioning look Tony threw him, the suspicion glinting in his manager's eyes. Since Tony gave him a wake-up call the grim reaper would have feared, he'd stuck with denial all the way. Besides, this time the media had it so wrong it was almost funny, but it had given him an idea. Which is why he'd insisted coming to Maine PR with Tony instead of letting him thunder on alone.

Nothing to do with the fact he wanted to see

Blondie's eyes flare up. Though at the moment she was all wide eyes and pale skin. That was his fault for being careless, and there was no doubt her boss had already given her hell. Unleashing Tony's fury on her was the last thing any of them needed.

He mouthed 'go' and she backed away.

But then footsteps sounded down the hall. Before she could disappear, Maine was at her side. Sebastian cursed under his breath. He didn't want her anywhere near this meeting. Tony and Maine erupting could get messy, and she looked scared enough without having them throw insults her way or talk about her like she wasn't there. He'd known from the nightmare that had been his life since the split how horrible slander could be, and he wouldn't even wish it on his ex. Though after Mai's latest bullshit kiss-and-tell, it was tempting.

'Perhaps we should do this somewhere private? Alicia, ready the meeting room,' Maine instructed.

She disappeared in a flash and he had to lock his knees to keep from running after her to offer help. Or at the very least give her the massive apology he owed. That said something. He wasn't the kind of person who had regrets until Mai came along, so apologies didn't come easy.

At Tony's grunt of an agreement, they were led through the building at a slower pace. Sebastian didn't pay much attention to the plaques on the walls or potted greenery every few feet. He was focused on how he was going to save Blondie's pretty little self from losing her job, all because he couldn't resist kissing her.

When they got to the conference room they'd visited the day before, his attention zeroed in on Alicia. Her hands shook as she put a fresh filter in the coffee machine. He took a step towards her but Tony gripped his arm. He caught his manager's scowl and decided against arguing. Tony was on the verge of dropping him as a client after Melbourne, and he didn't want to push his luck.

They both slid into chairs across from Maine, but his gaze was on Alicia fussing with mugs in the corner.

Maine didn't waste any time. 'I apologise for the turn of events on behalf of Maine PR and Ms Simpson. The pictures are unfortunate, and I assure you we will do everything we can to prove the allegations are false and that Ms Simpson is not dating you, Mr Collins.'

'Too little, too late,' Tony snapped. 'The evidence is already out there, and my client hardly has the best reputation.'

Alicia dropped a mug. It clattered on the counter then rolled over the side. She made a grab for it, but missed. The porcelain smashed when it hit the floor.

'Leave it,' Sebastian said. 'We've already had coffee.'

His blood simmered at the thought of her being treated like the help. She was too smart, too good at what she did to play servant to the sharks.

She made her way to the table, her eyes never meeting his. She looked everywhere except directly at him. He gritted his teeth, his frustration growing. He liked her gaze on him, especially when it was fiery and scolding.

As she slid into a chair across the table, she focused on Tony and visibly wilted. Turning, he caught the look of bloody murder on his manager's face and elbowed him. With a grunt, the man dialled the rage down a notch.

'I'm … sorry. Of course nothing is going on between Mr Collins and I. Disproving the allegations is the first thing I'll do when –'

'You think we're signing now? Are you insane?' Tony boomed.

Mr Maine cleared his throat. 'Miss Simpson's indiscretion was unfortunate, and we have both apologised.'

His manager and Alicia's boss argued until their rage just about replaced oxygen in the room. Sebastian tuned them out and instead focused on Alicia. Moisture made her eyes shimmery and that hit him in the chest harder than a wayward serve. This was his fault. She'd been more than professional, had sold him on her pitch, and hadn't taken any of his shit at the restaurant. There wasn't anyone else he wanted to hire. How was he going to convince Tony?

Lots of words, insinuations, and insults were volleyed back and forth between the two hotshots at the table. Alicia kept her chin dipped, hoping to appear remorseful when in truth her hackles were rising with every verbal slap she took from Collins' manager.

It wasn't *her* fault his client couldn't keep his lips to himself. It certainly wasn't her fault they'd been snapped in such an unfortunate pose. And if Collins didn't sign, then surely that couldn't be pinned on her?

If only the slither of guilt in her gut would believe the logic.

Something tapped against her foot and she jerked her head up. Collins had that look of concern again, and she tried to convince herself the leap in her pulse was rage. If anyone should be on trial here, it was him.

Don't worry, he mouthed. *I'll think of something.*

She'd passed worry the second she'd stepped into Maine PR. Now she was running on terrified.

Don't, you'll make it worse, she mouthed back. The traitorous sting in her eyes highlighted the fact she'd lost all hope. He hadn't said a word since she'd sat down. If he really wanted to help, why wasn't he jumping to her defence?

Because even though Collins wasn't Darrell, they had more than one thing in common. Neither of them could man up when she needed them to.

'Of course, she'll be disciplined.' Mr Maine's words

shocked her out of her thoughts. She closed her eyes to hide the tears collecting there. 'I can't promise more. Until now, her performance and behaviour have been exemplary.'

Seconds, minutes, maybe hours passed, and the hurt overcame the anger. She'd been disciplined as a child and a teen, but never as an adult. Certainly not since she'd left Cumbria.

'You're both missing the obvious.' Collins' voice had her snapping out of her pity party. She stared at him, along with the others. He couldn't actually be coming through for her, could he?

'Which is?' Tony asked.

Sebastian gave Tony a run-down of Alicia's plan to help save his career, and though his manager's face paled to a healthier shade of pink, he shifted in his seat like hot coals lined the chair's padding. Her heart raced with hope, but the terror Collins would screw this up dampened her forehead.

Tony frowned. 'So the girl has good ideas. Doesn't explain why you felt her up on the street.'

Oh, so now it was *his* fault? She was tempted to ask why he'd put her first in line to be shot at.

'Alicia doesn't only have good ideas, but she's from a well-respected English family.'

Both Mr Maine's and his manager's expressions were blank, expectant. Alicia wondered where he'd dug up that information. He threw her a look that said 'go with the flow'. Her expression froze and so did her spine. She had a bad feeling about this.

'Dating an earl's daughter is one way of showing I'm getting my act together, and the press don't know she works here. They assumed we were on a date when really it was a meeting.'

She gasped and all eyes were on her. Collins' foot connected with hers beneath the table and she swallowed back the insta-refusal. Under the scrutiny of her boss and the huge, rosy-faced man next to Collins, she ran the idea over in her head.

Denial was pointless. The papers had what they considered 'proof' along with several spins. All she could do now was give them a positive angle to work with. That was her job.

But at this cost? Alicia didn't know. Using her family's reputation meant her father would ... Acid bubbled in her stomach and she rubbed a hand over her waist, trying to soothe the discomfort there. She couldn't think about what her father would do. It was clear Tony had come for blood and wasn't leaving until she was out on her backside or he was satisfied with their new plan. Her job was the priority, wasn't it?

When it all came down to it, she didn't really have a choice.

'He's right. My family's reputation is untarnished.' Or it would be, until she started officially dating the Playboy of tennis. 'I could be his undercover publicist while showing the world he's turned over a new leaf.'

Why was she even agreeing to this madness? A glance at the huge, angry manager who was all but puffing out his chest sent a shot of icy fear down her spine.

'By dating the honourable Miss Simpson.' Sebastian grinned and blood rushed to her cheeks.

She wasn't honourable, far from it, but nobody other than her family knew that and she planned to keep it that way.

Mr Maine frowned at her. 'Why didn't you tell me about this idea of yours?'

Collins jumped in, diverting that cold stare from her. 'My idea. It's the perfect way to start her plan, and it means we can hide the fact I hired Maine. The press will think I'm making the changes by myself and will hopefully get off my back.'

Tony clapped him on the shoulder. 'Good thinking. It

wouldn't have killed you to tell me, though.'

'Mr Collins, I'd like to point out that this is not standard practice.' Mr Maine's expression turned serious. 'We have strict rules about our staff getting involved with clients. However, I will make an exception this once since the relationship is a ruse.'

Alicia heard the warning in Mr Maine's cool tone and didn't doubt Sebastian had, either. She was still reeling, not allowing herself to think of what would happen in the days and weeks to come.

'I hear what you're saying and appreciate your concessions,' Sebastian said.

He pulled the contract from his pocket and smoothed it out on the table. In black scrawl across the bottom was his signature. It was the most amazing thing she'd ever seen. She sagged back into her chair and released the breath she'd been holding.

Tony rose with Sebastian and they headed for the exit. For once, she used the distraction of his body to take her mind off what she feared the most. It worked, but not in the way she hoped.

Her skin flushed and her hands itched to trace the muscles beneath his light blue polo.

Collins turned at the door and winked at her, lighting up a libido she'd long thought extinct. 'I'll be in touch, Blondie.'

What had she done?

Alicia closed the door to her flat a little after seven. She was exhausted, right down to her bones. Not to mention shell-shocked. Her worst nightmares couldn't even compare to what had happened today. All because she'd been determined to score the almighty Sebastian Collins as a client.

She laughed once, but it wasn't because she found this situation funny. Quite the opposite.

As she trailed through her home, leaving the lights

off to ease the buzzing in her head, her phone beeped, reminding her she had close to twenty missed calls from her father. She couldn't bear to face the lecture she'd get. His middle child, the disappointing one, trailing his precious family name through the mud.

Again.

She threw her handbag down on the coffee table and headed straight for the wine rack.

This was like the incident in high school, but made public. And if she wanted to keep her job, it would be even more public than the first soul-crushing 'spectacle'. No, she couldn't face anything right now except a huge glass of red.

After the first went down too quickly, Alicia poured herself another. She felt a bit braver, even pulled out her phone to see there were three voicemail messages. No texts, but her father didn't have a mobile. He preferred to call from his country manor, like some Lord of the Realm. Not a man who'd inherited a fortune and a title from his ancestors.

Ancestors who had brought him up to be the cold aristocrat he was today.

Her phone started ringing. A number she didn't recognise flashed across the screen. Alicia prayed it was Daria or Sylvia so she could have them test out their father's mood before she returned his calls. But they'd call from their phones, and both were at opposite ends of the world at the moment.

Stop being a wimp.

Taking a deep breath, she answered.

'Evening, Blondie. Do you miss me yet?'

Her hand tightened on her phone until the plastic creaked.

'Haven't you annoyed me enough for one day?' she asked.

His laugh shuddered through the speaker, but she was too mad to let the rough sound affect her. There was no reason for Collins kissing her yesterday, and she had no defence for not stopping it. Well, she'd learned her lesson. Really bad things come from being associated with him. With her job on the line, she didn't have much choice other than to go along with his plan. But that didn't mean privately.

'I thought you'd be nicer after I saved you from a spanking.'

Her face flamed and the tingles drove through her, shooting straight to between her thighs. Gulping down half the glass didn't help, but it gave her time to remember who she was. Or more importantly, the kind of person she refused to be again. 'What do you want, Collins?'

'Straight to business. Do you ever take ten minutes for fun?'

She could hear the mocking in his tone, could imagine the slow smirk and twinkle in his eyes that said he was laughing at her. Irritation fizzled under her skin, raising her temperature again but for a better reason. A reason she could accept.

Then again, she had to hope he did a one-eighty fast, and that the press bought into his turnaround. Otherwise she was stuck in Hades on earth with a man who was going to be the end of her.

'Mixing business and pleasure is a bad idea.' Even she cringed at her haughty tone – it was too much like her mother's. Picking up her glass, she drained it. The wine curled around her stomach, sending a warm glow throughout her body.

Collins laughed again and her skin broke out in goosebumps. She refilled the glass.

'Maybe you're right, but business is always more fun when you mix it up a little.'

Was he *flirting* with her? She blinked to clear the shock, then took another gulp to calm the flutters in her stomach. 'This isn't about fun. It's about saving your career.'

His heavy sigh sounded in her ear, but she didn't think he'd give up that easily. 'Now we're officially a couple, we should go over your plan again and make the adjustments. Plus, you still need to get my contacts for the charity program.'

Alicia gritted her teeth. 'It's late and I'm off the clock.'

'Think again, Blondie. The deal with Maine makes you mine all around the clock.'

Her mouth dropped open, but nothing came out but air.

'I'm training tomorrow, but you could swing by with a protein shake at twelve. The press usually sniff around, so it'll be good fodder. Then I was thinking we could do a proper press release, come out as a couple, you know. And –'

'Sebastian, stop!'

Her heart was beating so hard, mimicking the pounding in her skull. This wouldn't work. She couldn't imagine spending all that time as his girlfriend. He'd drive her to violence, or worse –into his bed. Putting the heat thrumming through her veins down to the wine, she forced herself to think of more realistic problems.

Like the public shame she'd bring down on her father, one who was no doubt considering disowning her after one picture.

'What did I say?' he asked, his cautious tone suggesting he could sense her panic.

'There has to be another way to do this.' After all, getting ahead in her career was only going to kick her further down the social scale – not that she really cared; since she'd moved to London she'd managed to avoid that circle.

But her family still cared.

He took a long time to answer and she spent it playing with the stem of her empty glass. At last, he said, 'Alicia, I'm only trying to do what's best for us both. Maine was threatening to discipline you and my manager was about to give the contract to another company. Convincing the world we really are a couple is the only way to go, or we both lose out.'

Gratitude was the last thing she wanted to feel, especially toward him. Especially imagining what her father would say. But Sebastian had done everything he could to keep her from a disciplinary, still winning her the contract.

She'd just have to find a way to deal with her father.

'OK, I'll be there at noon.'

He whispered something like, *two to me,* then said louder, 'Catch you later.'

'Wait,' she said, unable to let that slide.

'Shoot.'

The cockiness in that one word loosened her tongue, or maybe it was the wine. 'Don't expect me to be your slave, Collins, because it's not going to happen. Tomorrow I'm laying down the rules, and you're going to stick to them.'

She disconnected, unable to keep a grin off her face. He'd signed, and pulling from the contract would be harder, but she didn't think he would anyway. He needed her help, maybe more than she needed her job, so she wasn't going to bow down to his demands.

The feeling of triumph only lasted until she glanced down at the blinking voicemail message on the screen of her phone. She wanted to crawl into bed and hide, but for the first time in a long time she felt brave. Still, she poured another glass of wine and took a deep breath before she called her father.

Time to get this over with.

Chapter Four

The sun had long since set, but Juliette stayed in her chair in the drawing room, gazing out of the window with a glass of wine in one hand and an almost empty bottle on the table next to her. She'd always wondered what life would be like if she hadn't been raised the way she had, married a man with a title who was colder than the marble lining the dining room floor. A man who expected her to have the same disposition he did.

If she could live again, be young just for a little while, would she be here, surrounded by riches that could never hope to warm the chill in her heart no matter how vast? Juliette didn't know, but what she did was that dreaming of another life, a life like her daughters had in front of them, was the only reason she was here. If she had to live with no escape from the hard reality by days and nights, she would have swallowed one of the bottles of Prozac their family doctor had been prescribing her for years.

Washed down with a bottle of something stronger than Merlot.

Being her father's daughter meant her future had been written for her before her mother had even given birth. She would grace the arm of a noble earl, bring great respect to his family, and have children by the dozen who would inevitably inherit his fortune.

She'd had children. Children she'd fought hard for so they could have a reasonably normal life. She'd had to force herself on many occasions to seduce a husband who had no more interest in lovemaking with her than she had with him. An heir to his title was the only reason he chose to procreate. The bitter memories left an awful taste on her tongue that Merlot couldn't dissipate.

Her fantasies were more attractive than the cruel reality that was her life.

The drawing room door flew open and Arthur stormed in with all the grace of a raging bull. 'She won't listen to me, but when has she ever? I can't even force her hand this time. I don't know why we didn't put her up for adoption at birth!'

Every nerve ending in her body thawed under the heat of the anger boiling in her blood. She didn't turn to face her husband, instead she watched her own reflection in the window carefully, making sure not one twitch or frown uncovered her rage.

'She's your daughter.' The words were delivered with too much ice for a lady, but after what Arthur had put her through on returning from their honeymoon, as far as she was concerned she was entitled to the occasional slip-up.

'My daughter,' he scoffed. 'Are you certain she is? No daughter of mine would shame the family like this. And so publicly!'

'Darling.' She forced the words out past others a lady of her upbringing would never dare speak. 'You know what you're accusing me of –'

A sigh cut through her verbal attempt to castrate him, making the hairs stand up on the nape of her neck.

'That was inexcusable,' he said – which she accepted as the most she would get by way of an apology.

His hands landed on her shoulders and her muscles automatically stiffened. He wrapped a loose strand of her hair around his finger. 'Dear Juliette. So kind, so generous. I wonder sometimes if you are, in fact, not adopted yourself.'

Though she could see him in the reflection on the glass, she dared not meet his gaze. He could surely read every shred of hatred she had for him in that moment. It never seemed to please him when she did or said something that showed she was not as cruel as her father. She took another sip of wine. Arthur sighed.

'Another bottle? This is becoming more than a habit, darling.'

If only he knew about the bottle of rum she kept in her private suite for after he'd retired for the night. She'd hidden her 'habits' from him since their youngest daughter had left the house. It hadn't been difficult. A long time ago, she'd learned from him exactly how to cover up scandal, and over the years she'd earned a degree in it.

A lady never shrugged. A lady never argued with her husband. Juliette had no choice other than to do what she'd always done – put the night to the back of her mind with the other memories best not spent dwelling upon.

'I opened this bottle on Monday.' She had opened a *similar* bottle. What her husband didn't know was that the gardener brought her another every day and quietly disposed of the evidence.

'Hmm.' Thankfully, he released her and moved so he was no longer reflected in the window. 'I have things to organise. If you need me, I'll be in my study.'

I have never needed you. She never would. All she had left was to count down the days until death freed her – at this point she did not care if it was hers or his. 'Darling, do not overreact to this rumour. I'm sure the press are exaggerating. He could be her new client.'

His footsteps halted. 'Alicia confirmed it when I called. She is tainting the Simpson name with that sorry excuse for a man. I will not let it continue.'

Sweat slicked Sebastian's back and chest as he tore across the court. He swung the racket, lobbing the ball back to his trainer's side, watching it bounce once before it shot over the line. James' swing was half a second too late.

The thrill of the win drove the adrenaline higher, until he almost shook with it. They were both breathing hard. They'd been at the gym for hours and Sebastian was just getting into his stride. A week of early nights and constant training was paying off. James barely got a win past him the last few days.

Grinning, he said, 'Need a time out, old man?'

The look James shot him only made him smile wider.

'I whipped you on Monday, or are you choosing to forget that?'

Frowning, Sebastian made his way to the bench. Yeah, he chose to forget Monday, and the month before. Instead of answering, he pulled the cap off his water bottle and chugged half the contents. James took the same desperately needed drink from his own bottle.

Sebastian glanced at his watch for the fifth time in the last hour. The minutes seemed to creep by, mocking the ridiculous anticipation he had to see Alicia. After she promised to lay down the law in her strict, Lady of the Manor voice, he'd wanted to find out exactly what she had in mind. Just so he could see if he could make her bend her rules.

'Best out of three?' he asked, trying to take his focus off the blonde.

Accepting the challenge, James picked his racket up and they both headed to the court.

'You can't have built up all your endurance after a month off, Collins. I reckon after the sixth you'll lose your stride.'

Maybe, but he had something he didn't have much of before – incentive. Now he was facing what slacking off could do for his career, Sebastian was more determined than ever to get back to where he was before it all went to shit at Wimbledon. In fact, scratch that. He needed to be better. The sport was all he had, all he could trust, and there was no one to mess it up other than himself.

'How about you serve and find out, or are you worried your talk's nothing but hot air?' Taking position at the far corner, he prepared himself for a sneaky shot from his trainer.

'Guess we'll see.'

James' serve was like lightning, but Sebastian was ready and hit the ball back with everything he had. They both played as if they had something to prove, like their life depended on the win. Blood and adrenaline coursed through him, the feeling as addictive as winning. The challenge James presented made overused muscles feel fresh, the breath sawing through his lungs exhilarating.

His trainer stumbled to the right, guessing Sebastian's next move. Seeing his chance, he bolted across the court, swinging his racket with calculation, and was rewarded with a wide-eyed look from James as he swung wildly and missed the ball.

'What was that you were saying about my endurance?' he asked, swiping the sweat from his forehead.

'It won't last. Not through three more sets.'

'You're on, old man.' Sebastian went for another ball, but a figure in the doorway caught his attention.

He turned all the way around, his mouth dropping open at the sight. Blondie wore a purple top that barely encased her breasts and flashed a hint of pearly skin above low-rise jeans that were so tight they could have been painted on. Her hair fell in loose waves down to her elbows. So much better than he imagined it would.

With his mouth feeling like someone had stuffed it with grit and his mind stunned to blank, he could only gape.

James' whistle from behind him made her cheeks tinge pink. That snapped him back to reality. 'What the hell are you wearing?'

She looked down at herself and the colour in her cheeks darkened. 'What's wrong with what I'm wearing?'

She stormed toward him, clutching a bottle of what looked like a shake from the local supermarket. The fire was back in her eyes. He couldn't tell if the blush was anger or embarrassment.

'Since when do you invite your women to training?' James asked.

Sebastian gritted his teeth. 'Take ten. I need to speak to Alicia.'

James grunted something under his breath, then headed out through the door Alicia had walked through, his T-shirt in one hand and water bottle in the other.

He waited until his trainer was out of earshot, then rubbed his eyes to make sure this wasn't a dream. The adrenaline hadn't eased up, and now it was spurred by something different, almost predatory.

Kind of sexual. Most likely dangerous.

What the hell was Miss Prim playing at?

Alicia tried really hard to hold on to some form of annoyance as she closed the distance between them. She'd spent hours raking her wardrobe for an outfit that Sebastian Collins' girlfriend would wear, but it was seriously lacking – something she'd never cared about until now. She had to dip into the clothes Sylvia had left at her flat just to find something with colour, which was just depressing, really. And he had the cheek to look at her like she had a screw loose?

But the emotion didn't stick. His body was tanned, rippling with lean muscles, and the tribal tattoo covering his back and upper arm made her mouth water. There wasn't much hair on his chest, but as her gaze took an intrusive trip down his abs, she noted the darker trail arrowing south from his navel.

'Why are you dressed like that?' he asked, and for the first time she heard something other than humour in his voice.

She snapped her gaze to his and forced a frown. It was hard, especially when the image of the sweaty indentation of his hips was still burned into her brain.

'What's *wrong* with my clothes? Would you rather I turned up in a suit? That would give us away.'

'They're not you,' he said, placing the shake down on the bench and picking up a towel. 'They're a bit –'

'Don't you dare say what I think you're going to say.' They were *not* slutty, just a smidgen small.

His grin was easy and the annoyance seemed to fizzle out of his tone. 'I have no idea what you're talking about.'

Sebastian proceeded to wipe his face dry with the towel, then he went to work on his chest. She had to fist her hands to keep from hauling the cotton out of his reach. She liked him sweaty – his scent was delicious and musky and made her heart hammer against her ribs.

Shaking away the thought, she conceded any woman would want to ogle all that powerful male flesh while inhaling what must be pheromones. And that was why she was here, because Sebastian Collins couldn't resist the female attention thrown, or came, his way.

Not that she'd given him any indication she wanted him to kiss her.

'Sit down. We have to go over the rules.' She probably should too, since her knees were about to give out watching him assume a casual position on the bench, but she had to get the upper ground for this.

His gaze dropped to her stomach, and she tugged the material down. Last time she'd slipped into Sylvia's clothes, she'd had more wiggle room than this.

'Rules?' he asked, his voice thick with something she chose to ignore. He didn't rush to meet her eyes, instead he paid too much attention to the bits in between her stomach and face. 'Why do you think you need rules?'

She folded her arms and went for a serious expression. 'I don't need rules. They're for you.'

The quirk of his lips scrambled her thoughts. 'What makes you think I'll follow them?'

Finally, an answer she'd anticipated. After the horrific phone call with her father, she threw herself into her three rules for him, preparing for any protest he might have. It was either that or wallow in the anger and condemnation her father had slung at her.

She smirked. 'Because like you said before, you care about your career.'

A career he was good at, if the five minutes she spent watching him were anything to go by. They'd clearly been training all morning, but Sebastian had moved lightning fast, playing with so much focus he hadn't realised he was being watched. She'd briefly wondered if he put that much effort into everything he did, especially with all those women he'd bedded, and had to pull her thoughts out of the gutter as a flush swept over her body.

He leaned back, resting an elbow on the higher bench behind him and giving her a very unwanted and unobstructed view of his sensational torso. 'Let's hear them.'

Careful to keep her attention on his eyes, she laid out the rules, ticking them off on her fingers. 'One, no kissing. Two, no sleeping with any women during this farce. Three, no talking to the press or anyone else about our relationship unless you've OK'd it with me first.'

Two and three were a must, or her father would never speak to her again. She'd spent the entire conversation trying to convince him Collins had turned over a new leaf. Her father wasn't, but she'd managed to get him to agree to give Sebastian time to prove himself.

One because ... well, she couldn't kiss him and not want what he gave so freely to every other woman in the world. Which was one of the many reasons *that* wasn't happening.

'About rule one.' He frowned and she had to hide her

surprise. She thought he'd be more concerned about the second rule. 'How are we supposed to convince people we're together if no one sees us kissing?'

'That's the point, Collins. The fact people don't see us kissing will mean you respect me enough to keep intimate times private.'

He didn't look convinced, and neither was she, but kissing was *not* an option.

'I better let you get back to training. I'll write a press release to announce our "relationship" this afternoon and we can go out to dinner tonight to let the world get used to the idea we're together.'

Alicia turned to leave but he caught her hand and pulled her closer. His chin was inches away from her breasts and heat crept up her neck, even though his gaze never left hers. He grabbed her hips, his thumbs skimming her bared stomach, making her shiver and her breath hitch.

'There are more important things to do this afternoon. Meet me in the coffee shop at the top of Oxford Street at three.'

'OK.' She'd agree to anything just so he would release her.

He stood up. His big, sweaty body way too close and distracting. She wanted to slide her hands up his arms, feel the muscle flex beneath her fingers. Hell, she wanted to lick the beads of moisture from the indentation in his collarbone.

'And Alicia, wear something a little less scandalous.'

'What do you mean?' She was in jeans and a long-sleeved top, for goodness' sake. She wasn't wearing a skirt that flashed her knickers.

He stood and leaned close to her ear, his breath tickling her neck, right above her racing pulse. 'Look down at yourself.'

She did, her attention snagged instantly by her nipples straining against the too small top. A flare of heat set her face on fire.

Avoiding his eyes, she turned and rushed toward the exit, her forearm covering her crazy reaction.

'Oh, and Blondie, don't be late!' he called.

She had no comeback, not with mortification carrying her out the door faster than she'd ever moved.

There were a million things Alicia would rather be doing at the moment. Pushing her way through the crowds in the busiest street in London to face a man who'd seen how hard her nipples could get in his presence didn't even make her shortlist. The burn in her face told her she had a long way to go before the embarrassment eased.

Her mobile chimed and she scrambled in her handbag for it. As soon as she saw Daria's name on the screen, she hit answer.

'Where have you been? I've left you messages!' All night, before and after the conversation with their father.

'I'm in Paris – I had a show last night. Guess what?' Daria squealed.

Alicia dodged a commuter, then ducked into a wide shop front so she didn't crash into anyone. 'What?' she asked, letting her annoyance shine through.

'I'm engaged!' Daria screamed.

Her chin almost hit the pavement. 'You're kidding? Daria, you've only been dating Blair a month.'

'I know, isn't it romantic? He popped the question when we got back last night. The room was full of pink roses and illuminated with candles.'

Ignoring the dreamy tone her big sister used, Alicia tried to get her head around it. 'You barely see each other – you both travel the world for work!' She couldn't imagine having a relationship with someone she had to schedule time with. How could her older sister, the level-headed one in the family? 'Do you even love him?'

'What's not to love? He's the perfect match.'

'For who, you or Father?' she asked, hating that she

sounded bitter.

Daria deserved to be happy and Alicia worried she tried to be in a way that made their father proud. Just like Alicia had tried to for years, though she never would. Not after …

The scar in her heart that had never fully healed threatened to split. She refocused on the conversation and buried that awful memory.

'For me, silly. He travels a lot, sure. But so do I. We love the arts and his company is endorsing my designs. We make sense.'

Daria sounded too excited for what she'd just said. To Alicia, she was describing a logical business deal. Not a marriage filled with love like they'd all craved as children.

'And Father approves,' she grumbled.

'Of course he does, and that's why I'm calling. Mother's throwing us an engagement party in two weeks at home, and you have to bring your new boyfriend. Father wants to meet him.'

She bet he did. Her heart took off and sweat beaded at her nape. She couldn't let her father meet Sebastian. He'd already driven her brother away to God knows where and she suspected her mother was miserable being trapped in that house with him. One meeting with Sebastian and who knew what would happen.

Going by past experience, she'd lose everything that mattered to her. And then some. 'Daria –'

'No excuses. You're both coming. I want to know how you scored the bad boy tennis player.'

The tease in her sister's voice didn't loosen the knot in her stomach.

Daria went on before she could get a word in. 'I think you'll need help convincing Dad that Sebastian is the one for you.'

It was on the tip of her tongue to tell Daria he was most definitely not the man for her, when Collins appeared in front of her with one of his tummy-flipping grins.

'There you are. Come on, we haven't got all day.' He tugged her arm and her tongue froze.

'Is that *him?*' Daria whispered in her ear.

'I'll phone you later.' Alicia ended the call and dropped the phone in her bag.

His smile got brighter and raised her suspicions.

'What's the rush?' she asked.

'We only have a few hours and this is important.'

He didn't elaborate, just entwined his fingers with hers and tugged her back onto the street. Wearing a baseball cap and sports jacket, he didn't look half as good as he did shirtless and sweaty, but the connection humming through their clasped hands told her that didn't matter. Her hardening nipples remembered only too well.

'Sebastian, what are you doing?'

Looking down at her without missing a stride, he winked. 'I'm taking you shopping.'

Chapter Five

Alicia tugged his arm so hard the overused muscles in his shoulders groaned in protest.

Sebastian stopped and turned to look at her. She hadn't changed her clothes, but she'd put on a frumpy raincoat, hiding those curves that had nearly driven him over the edge earlier. Especially when he'd witnessed the proof of her attraction to him. It would've been impossible for her to hide it in that top, even if his eyes hadn't been level with her breasts.

'You're not taking me shopping,' she said. Affront was clear in her gaping mouth.

'Why? It's not like I'm breaking any of the rules.' Yet.

'You're not buying me clothes.' Her tone was firm, final.

Like that would stop him. 'It's for work purposes; besides, Maine's chipping in.'

He tugged her hand again to get them moving, but she didn't budge. 'Who you're paying a fee to, so technically, you *are* paying.'

OK, so his diversion didn't work as well as he'd hoped. Blondie was smart, he shouldn't forget that. 'Let me rephrase. We need to look like the perfect, respectable couple. Elegant, stylish, maybe even care a little about our appearances. Wouldn't you agree?'

A cute line formed between her brows. 'What do you mean "we"?'

She'd like this part. 'Now I'm officially dating the daughter of an earl, I need to look honourable.'

Alicia burst out laughing. All the seriousness was

wiped clean from her expression and the prim woman who drove him nuts disappeared. His heart thrummed as his smile widened.

'Something funny?' he asked.

'You.' She covered her mouth with her hand, trying to reign in the fits of giggles. 'I can't picture you in stuffy, boring clothes or a suit.'

'I look handsome in a suit,' he said, feigning a hurt expression. 'My mum said it makes me look dashing.'

The giggles continued. 'It's a mother's job to lie to her children.'

'I should make you pay for that.' Sebastian eyed her lips, curved up into a grin, and a few ideas on how to punish her flashed through his mind. All he'd have to do was lean in, kiss her into a frenzy, then pull away just as she hit desperate.

But heat burned low in his groin at the thought of kissing her and he figured doing that would punish them both.

'OK, we'll shop.' The look in her eyes and flush on her face said she knew exactly how he'd wanted to punish her.

What he didn't expect was the disappointment he felt at her going along with him to stop him catching her in a lip lock. Though what did he expect after she'd given him rules to follow and the no mouth to mouth action had been at the top?

Instead of commenting, Sebastian took her hand and led her through the crowds. 'First, let's get us something for dates.'

Seven shops and twelve carriers later, Alicia had a whole new wardrobe. She hadn't meant to get so carried away, but for the most part, everything she bought was from the high street. Well, other than the few dresses with designer price tags. Still, she had made a huge dent in her savings account. But hopefully, with the commission from landing Collins, she'd get a massive bonus.

After all she was doing to save his rep, she better.

They were in Jenners' men's department now, Sebastian promising they were almost done after he picked up a few shirts. She wondered if she should broach the engagement party with him, in case she couldn't find a way out of it, but figured she had lots of time to try. Plus, watching him pick up shirts and stand in front of the mirror with a screwed-up expression was kind of fun.

'Try that one,' she said, nodding to a shirt on the rail above him.

He shook his head. 'I'm not *that* desperate to fit the ideal.'

She giggled again. Actually giggled. It'd been so long since she'd felt this carefree. It was a lovely distraction from everything that had happened that day. She'd worry about Daria later. Or maybe never. Her sister was twenty-seven and sounded happy. Why couldn't Alicia be happy for her too?

'This, I can work with.' Sebastian pulled a black shirt off the hanger that looked far too small. Without disappearing upstairs to the privacy of the dressing room, he removed his jacket and then pulled his white polo shirt over his head, exposing his ripped stomach.

'What are you doing?' she whispered, turning her back to him as heat flushed into her cheeks. She caught the gaping eyes of the other customers. 'You're supposed to be acting low-key.'

'I'm trying on a shirt,' he said, his tone suggesting what he was doing constituted reasonable behaviour.

'People can *see*.' The whole shop could, and Alicia was sure the sales assistant in the far corner had drool on her chin.

'So what? They've seen it all before if they saw me at Wimbledon last year.'

She whirled on him, ignoring the tanned flesh on

display as he buttoned up the shirt. 'You're not playing tennis and, in case you hadn't noticed, people use the changing rooms to try on clothes.'

He rolled his eyes. Actually *rolled his eyes* at her.

'Relax, you're too uptight. No one here cares where I try on the shirt.'

'You should! You should care about what people think, how your actions speak for you. It isn't just your reputation on the line now, Sebastian.'

'I know,' he said, focusing on buttoning the cuffs. 'But the only one causing a scene here is you. You're totally overreacting.'

There was absolutely no talking to the man. She gritted her teeth as annoyance burned into something else. Something that made her *want* to raise her voice and really cause a scene. She knew he was going to be hard work, had known from the second he riled her at the pitch, but the new Alicia could handle him. She just had to figure out how.

'So,' he said, holding his arms out for inspection. 'What do you think?'

With an orange cap from one of his sponsors, the too-tight shirt that clung to every delicious inch of his torso, and a pair of well-worn jeans, there was only one word she could use to describe him.

'You look ridiculous.' But still sexy, dammit.

His grin was swift and dragged out hers. He winked. 'Perfect.'

He started unbuttoning the shirt but she dove forward and grabbed his wrists. She could smell his expensive cologne mixed with the unique hint of him that had made her body react at the gym. The effect was no different now, but she pushed on past the haze her mind was suddenly clouded in.

'*Please* use the dressing room, Sebastian. I've told my father you've turned over a new leaf, and he's already mad that I'm dating you. Pictures in the papers tomorrow of you trying on shirts in the storefront will make this a hundred times worse.'

His hands wound around her wrists until her pulse hammered out a mamba. 'He's mad at you for dating me?'

Alicia bit her lip and focused on the collar of his open shirt. 'Mad' was the understatement of the century, but it wasn't as bad as before. Back then, he'd made her do something so terrible that some nights she woke up in tears. He'd never shown any compassion either, insisting it was for her own good and one day she'd thank him for it. She was still waiting for that day.

The worst part wasn't even that he'd grounded her afterwards for three months until she learned what being respectable meant. She'd been happy to hide away from the world while her heart had time to heal. Her hands trembled against the awful memories and the pain threatened to break her in two all over again.

Sebastian let go of her wrist and tilted her chin.

'Is he always so uptight?'

She forced a small smile.

'You could say that.' Ruthless, brutal, and fiercely protective – of himself – were better ways to describe him.

'Then I'll try to not make this worse for you.'

Sebastian grabbed his polo and headed for the staircase, leaving her blinking at his retreating back. She'd never expected him to be understanding or care about anyone else except himself. Could some of what she'd found be made up, exaggerated? Or *was* he the man Mai claimed he was? Alicia wasn't sure, but the more time she spent with him, the more she wanted to find out the truth behind the stories.

'What are you doing here?' she squeaked as she opened her front door.

Sebastian looked like a different man. His hair was

still wild, but the suit he wore made him even more delicious-looking. His mother hadn't been lying at all.

She hid behind the door, far too aware of her blue sleep shorts and white vest. Oh, not to mention her braless state. Her face burned at the glimpse she'd given him.

'Taking my girlfriend to dinner,' he said, like that was obvious. 'Didn't you mention dinner earlier?'

'I'm not dressed.' It was the only thing that popped into her head. Did she suggest dinner? She'd been too distracted by her humiliation in the gym to remember the specifics of their conversation.

'Well, you'd better hurry. I made reservations.'

'I need to work on the press release.' He looked too good in his form-hugging suit. And she'd already spent way too much time with him for one day.

Sebastian crossed the threshold. 'That can wait. Come on. You've got new clothes to show off.'

'But –'

He closed the door, exposing her undress to him. His dark gaze dipped down, taking in her bare legs and scorching a flush over her skin. Shut into her small flat with him was stifling, and knocked up the temperature to uncomfortable.

'Quick, before I change my mind and break the first rule already.'

The threat had her bolting through to her bedroom, heart racing and breath coming too fast. She slammed the door closed, raced to the wardrobe, and pulled out the first dress she could get her hands on. Stripping and dressing in record time, she fumbled through boxes in the bottom of her dresser and grabbed a pair of shoes. At the mirror she snatched her lip gloss, smeared a little on, and then freed her hair from the twist.

Ruffled, rumpled, and plain would have to do. She needed to get him out of there fast, because after their afternoon together she'd spent way too much time googling him and his ex, wondering what accusations were true. The more she read the more she couldn't match to the man she'd spent the day with. Not to mention the hold he had on her libido.

A libido that should have known better than to want him after what had happened the last time she gave into reckless attraction.

She pushed the mistake and the three months of hell that followed out of her mind. Probably for the hundredth time since she met him.

After slipping on the heels, she gave her hair a final ruffle then opened the door. He was in the lounge, sitting against her leather sofa with the first draft of the press release in his hands. It was weird seeing him in her personal space, looking relaxed and as if he belonged there.

But he didn't belong there. Not ever.

'Ready,' she said to distract herself.

His attention flitted to her and his eyes became rich and melting. He took her in, all of her, and Alicia couldn't remember the last time a date had looked at her without the usual polite reserve. There was nothing polite about the way Collins' gaze lingered on her breasts, her waist, even her legs.

He laughed, snapping her out of the fantasy that he found her attractive.

'What?' Were her nipples out again? She folded her arms just in case.

'Alicia, you look stunning, but I don't think you'll want to wear those shoes.'

He crossed the room as she looked down to see what he meant. There, plain as day on her feet, was a pair of black court shoes she hadn't worn in forever. If it wasn't for the great big scuff and talking soles she could have got away with them.

'Need a hand?' he asked.

She swallowed back the embarrassment. 'I'm useless

when it comes to this stuff.' She pulled at her dress. 'My sisters would have a heart attack if they saw the inside of my wardrobe before today.'

'Come on.' He took her hand and led her to the bedroom.

The suffocating feeling got worse, especially when he glanced pointedly at the bed with a wicked grin. So what if it was pink? The sheets were the only thing in her life she was brave enough to douse in colour. The hues in her bedroom were the only thing she got to pick in the manor too – though she guessed that was because her father never went into her room there.

'Where are your shoes?' he asked.

Alicia nodded at the foot of her wardrobe and took a seat on the edge of the bed. Sebastian got on his knees and rummaged through the footwear that probably had more place in a pensioners closet.

'I want to look respectable,' she said, defending her choices even though he hadn't attacked them. 'I just can't figure out how to do that and keep things … elegant.'

He looked back at her. 'Your family are that uptight?'

'Among other things. My father is very strict and demands respect. He thinks we should be just like him.'

Of course she wasn't, she was the disappointing child – or at least, the 'other' disappointing one. She doubted Jonathan would have been shunned if he'd made their father proud. If it hadn't been for her mother fighting for her, she'd have been thrown out long ago and banned from having contact with the rest of them.

Exactly like Jonathan.

She'd wanted to leave once, after the 'incident', but she loved her sisters and mother too much. The only option she'd had was to stay, try to win back her father's approval, and count down the days until she could leave Cumbria for university.

But having to live up to her father's expectations had

never stopped. She didn't think she'd ever be able to.

'That sounds rough,' he said, and she saw the understanding in his eyes.

Before she could ask what happened that he could understand having a control freak parent, Sebastian reached blindly into the cupboard. He pulled out shoe box after shoe box, in all shapes and sizes, but he only glanced at the contents then set them aside.

'Most kids would've rebelled,' he observed.

'I'm not the rebelling type.' Not now she knew the consequences.

The pain it caused her: Jonathan's exile. It seemed better to be the kind of daughter a father would be proud of than a woman who lived her life without caring about the latest scandal or the Simpson reputation.

A flash of light blue caught her eye as Sebastian pulled another box out of her closet. Her palms got damp, her heart paused for a beat then took off double time, and scolding blood boiled up her neck.

She dived for the box but he was faster, pulling it out of her reach. She slammed into his chest, grabbing his shoulders for support, but he'd already clocked what she was desperately trying to hide. This had to be the most embarrassing moment in the history of the world.

Sylvia was going to pay.

'Now this is more like it.'

She grabbed for it again but he moved it further out of reach, shaking the blue vibrator's box at her like a kid who'd just found the secret cookie stash.

She groaned. 'It's a gag gift from my sister, it's only –'

'An eight-inch deluxe with five stimulating features,' he read from the box out loud.

Alicia covered her burning face in her palms. 'It's not like I wanted it!'

She heard something clattering on the floor, then he tugged her hands away. She didn't want to look at him, but would the new, improved Alicia cower and hide like this? Determined not to show him how affected she was, she met his gaze.

'Why?' Sebastian looked more like she'd just told him she didn't like ice cream than she didn't want a vibrator.

'Because it's … it's …' She couldn't hold eye contact as a wave of mortification washed through her. 'Inappropriate.'

'To who? There's nothing wrong with having this. It's kinda hot, actually. Don't all women have one?'

Her mouth opened but no words came. Maybe if she squeezed her eyes shut and wished really hard, time would go back and she could pick out a pair of decent shoes so Sebastian wouldn't have to come in here and find … that.

Alicia tried again. 'Not women like me.'

Watching Alicia kneel in front of him, unable to meet his eyes, made Sebastian wish he'd toned down the teasing. Her parents had obviously been way too uptight, making their daughter too embarrassed to even want something as basic as pleasure. It pissed him off that someone as fiery as Alicia could be was forced to stifle all that passion.

Though he suspected there was more to it. Growing up in the home of an earl with a reputation as clean as a whistle meant he either had deep enough pockets to buy silence, or was ruthlessly strict with his family. Part of him wished it was the former. The thought of a younger Alicia having to deal with her father's wrath didn't sit right with him.

'Come on.' He got to his feet and held out his hand.

She frowned at him. 'Sebastian, I don't feel like going out.'

'How about some Dutch courage and a takeaway instead?' Her eyes widened and some of the pink seeped out of her face. 'We can work on the press release. What you have is great, but you don't have all the details of how we met hammered out. I can help with dates.'

'Um …'

He took her arms and pulled her up. Alicia stumbled closer and he wrapped his arms around her for support. Not the wisest move, considering her hips now pressed flush to his, spiking his blood flow with a shot of arousal.

'It's fine. You don't have to be embarrassed. I'm the one who's slept with half the female population, remember?'

A smile twitched up the corners of her lips. 'In your dreams, maybe.'

Stepping back to regain a little control, he slapped a hand over his heart. 'You wound me.'

'I've a feeling it would take more than that to put a dent in your ego,' she said, her grin widening and her shoulders relaxing.

Sebastian didn't mind letting his ego be the focus of teasing if it helped her get over him finding the unwanted gift. 'You've caught me.'

He pulled his mobile out, then tugged her close to his side.

'What are you doing?' she asked.

Loading up the camera, he said, 'We need to let the world get used to us together, don't we? *I* know we're staying home but no one else has to know. Instagram will fix that.'

She frowned as the front camera came on and captured their heads. 'But –'

'Say cheese,' he said, then snapped the photo.

He entered the caption: *Finally get to take my stunning girlfriend, @AliciaSimpson out for dinner. #GoodTimes,* then hit send.

'Sebastian, I wasn't ready,' she protested.

He showed her the picture and said, 'You're

beautiful, don't worry. Now where do you keep the takeaway menus?'

Mai flicked through the pages of her diary from the previous year. What started so great, so beautiful, had ended so cruelly that she sometimes wished Sebastian would come down with something awful – like malaria.

Other times, like tonight, she just felt sad and unloved.

Skipping to February, she remembered her birthday. Sebastian had trained so hard for almost a month. She'd barely seen him. He'd taken the fourteenth off, arranged for them to fly to Paris that morning, and they'd had a very romantic dinner with the Eiffel Tower in full view. The champagne flowed all night and when dessert came, she found the seven-carat diamond ring that had given her hope that things would get better between them.

She'd realised then that she was adored, cared for. He'd shown her just how much, telling her how beautiful she was, but she knew he was just being nice – the winter had taken her up a dress size and she hadn't been feeling great about her new size ten figure.

But that night in Paris, she'd forgotten her worries as he'd made her feel sexy, loved, and like the only person in his world.

A tear dripped onto the paper and she wiped her eyes, not wanting to ruin the ink that described her last perfect day. After all, she'd only agreed to marry him for financial security – something she'd never had growing up in different foster homes around the UK. Plus, she had liked the attention, the way he treated her like she was precious. She couldn't remember a time she'd felt that cared for. Maybe if her mother hadn't been a smackhead she would have been cherished growing up, and would have seen Sebastian's bullshit for what it was sooner. A scheme used by men who thought they could stick their dick in anything that moved, no matter who was at home waiting for them to return.

Mai slammed the diary shut with a shriek. Jack was the man she needed. Someone who loved her for who she was and always would. She should start appreciating him more. After all, who took her back after she left him when Sebastian seduced her into false security?

Jack wouldn't have led her on, made her care about him, and then dropped her so hard the bones in her legs shattered. Jack wouldn't do that at all.

She heard the front door of the house open and glanced at the clock. It wasn't anywhere near his local pub's closing time, but he was back, and she was going to show him exactly how much she appreciated him.

After hiding her diary in the cabinet next to the bed, she stripped, letting her clothes fall to the floor. He was in the doorway before she'd taken a step and the gleam in his blue eyes along with the way he swayed a little told her he'd had a good few drinks, but not too much to not make love to her.

Mai sat down on the bed with her legs open, her gaze never leaving his.

'You gonna let me fuck you hard, babe?' he asked, his words a little slurred.

Anticipation throbbed in her pulse points. Passion was uncontrolled, and that's exactly how a man who was crazy about her should make love to her. None of that slow, sensual shit she got with Sebastian.

'Hard as you like. If it's not rough it isn't fun, right?' So said Lady Gaga, anyway.

Jack pulled off his coat then unzipped his jeans. He didn't take them off, just pulled his cock through the zip. She frowned, seeing she had her work cut out for her. It was always like this to start with. She'd have to blow him first just to get it hard enough to enjoy.

When he came closer though, she tipped her chin and let him shove it into her mouth. With impatience making her clit throb harder, Mai went to work like a Dyson, bobbing her head and moaning like having his dick in her mouth was the most erotic thing she'd ever experienced. It worked: in minutes he grew enough that he was thrusting into her throat, past her protesting gag reflex.

When her eyes started to stream, she pushed at his hips until he pulled out. 'I want you to make love to me now.'

He pulled her off the bed, turned her around, and wrapped an arm around her lower stomach. She bent over to give him better access, propping herself up on the bed and made a strangled noise when he pounded into her like he couldn't wait another second.

That was just the beginning. Jack swung his hips wildly, screwing into her over and over again. She could feel the pressure building at her core, the delicious swirl of heat gathering between her legs. The sting on her ass from where his skin slapped into hers only heightened the sensations.

Fisting his hands in the hair at her nape so hard her eyes watered again, he pulled her back onto his cock over and over again. She loved it when he got all ferocious and powerful in bed. Sure, she'd hurt for days but the orgasm steadily building would keep her going for longer.

Since he was holding most of her weight she reached a hand toward her clit, but he slapped it away.

'You'll come on my cock with *just my cock.*' His growl was what did it.

She tumbled over the edge as a full-blown orgasm pulsed through her. It was so epic she barely felt him withdraw, but she *did* feel it when his dick breached her anus.

Mai couldn't help it. She acted on reaction and tensed her muscles. That only made the discomfort at being penetrated hurt more, but Jack pounded away, seemingly oblivious to her pain. She gritted her teeth, resolved to do this for him after what he'd given her. After everything he'd done for her, how could she not?

But silent tears streamed down her face as his thrusts became harder and harder. The way he was holding her hair hurt instead of heightening her pleasure. A moan escaped her throat but Jack mistook the reason.

'You love this, babe, don't you? You love me in your arse.'

She couldn't reply, not without releasing a sob. Instead she tried to relax. When his thrusts got so fast and the agony so severe she thought he might have ripped her insides, she was about to scream.

But one last jerk of hips was all it took for him to go over the edge. The shudder that racked through him told her he'd found his pleasure, then he pulled out. Collapsing onto the bed, she kept her face away so he wouldn't see the dampness on her cheeks.

She heard him undress, then he was in bed beside her. Normally she'd curl up next to him, but there seemed to be a canyon between their bodies and she was raw, physically and emotionally.

Jack built a bridge across the distance and pulled her close. She stiffened in his arms, then ran a few curses through her head. What was she doing? This was the love of her life, not some bastard stranger.

'Babe, you OK?' he asked.

Tears turned into sobs that racked through her. Jack gasped, pulled her around, and she could see the pleasure ebb from his expression as shock took its place.

'I hurt you?'

She nodded. 'I wasn't ready ... I didn't ...'

Cursing, he pulled her into a hug. She melted into him and cried into his neck, probably ruining the shirt he'd left on to sleep in. Today had been too emotional, too much to handle, but with him holding her like this – like Sebastian used to – she felt protected.

'I'm so sorry.' Though his words were slurred, the

sincerity was there.

'I know, babe,' she said between sobs. 'I'm sorry too. For everything.'

Chapter Six

Alicia sat at the opposite end of the sofa from Sebastian with a stiff spine and her chin in the air, showing what little dignity she had left. Still, with every sip of wine she had waiting for their Italian takeaway to arrive, her inhibitions were loosening and the last of the embarrassment was seeping away.

Sebastian may be right, women might own toys for their own personal pleasure, but she never had. Not until Sylvia had picked one up at a charity evening at work to give Alicia as a gift. Daria received one too, a little less gauche and scary-looking. Until now, it had been thrown in the wardrobe and forgotten about.

The new Alicia didn't use things like that – and neither had the old Alicia.

'Earth to Blondie, you there?'

Sebastian's voice had her head doing a one-eighty. He'd removed the suit jacket and tie, rolled up his sleeves to reveal tanned forearms, and was lounging on her sofa with the computer in his lap, looking more at home than she felt.

'Sorry, I spaced out.'

He didn't comment, but she could sense the cogs working in that beautiful head of his.

'Scoot over and have a read,' he said.

After placing her glass on the side table, she did just that, careful to keep some space between them. Sebastian had refused a drink since he was training and now it looked like he was refusing that space she'd kept between them as he shifted so close their sides touched.

'We don't have much to work with since I was

pictured a few weeks ago.'

She focused on his changes to the press release rather than worry about the stab of jealousy at his reminder. Still, she remembered the pictures well. One in particular. The brunette and redhead he'd spent a night with might as well have been glued to him in that bar. It was the day he'd flunked out of the Australian Open, and instead of keeping a low profile, he'd been caught up in a threesome scandal that AIG had vehemently denied.

'Looks good to me.' She found it hard to force enthusiasm into her voice. Her father was right. She'd look like one more notch on a bed that was probably whittled away to a toothpick.

'Look, for what it's worth, nothing happened.' Sincerity shone from his dark eyes.

'Excuse me?'

He worked his jaw, glanced at the screen then blew out a breath. 'That night in Melbourne with those women. I got too drunk to do more than pass out on the hotel bed. No one came back to my room with me.'

Her throat dried up and she reached for the wine. That would make sense. He'd pretty much messed up his career, which would be enough incentive to drive anyone to drink to forget for a while. Wine had been her friend time and time again when she didn't want to deal.

Worse, she believed him, and she really didn't want to believe him. It was better when he was the womanising pig she'd thought he was. 'Why are you telling me this?'

He shrugged. 'I get it looks bad for you to be dating me after all that happened, but I wanted you to know that I didn't just hop out of their bed.'

A flutter assaulted her chest as cool fear lined her stomach. She didn't know whether he was flirting or making it clear if she gave into how she felt around him then she wouldn't be taking the twins' sloppy seconds. And he had to know she wanted him – the evidence almost had his eyes out earlier.

Not for the first time, she looked at his mouth. Those ever-smiling lips set at the peak of his squared jaw were relaxed now. Maybe even soft. Rule one flashed into her mind but it wasn't enough to stop her – especially when the thought of breaking it sent a thrill through her.

Sebastian leaned closer and picked up a lock of her hair, just above her breast, and she swayed forward, unable to take her gaze off his mouth. Blood rushed through her veins, making her mind fuzzy. Or maybe that was the wine. All she knew was it had been so long since a fire had burned at her core longing to be fulfilled, and he hadn't even touched her yet.

His breath brushed against her lips and that's all it took to snap the last of her resistance. She gripped one side of his open collar, intent on finding out if that delicious scent translated to taste. Sebastian cupped her face, his thumb slowly rubbing along her lower lip and sending little jolts straight between her thighs.

He went in for the kill. The pressure was soft, barely there, but not enough. Alicia leaned in closer. The sound of the door chapping hardly registered as her lips met his.

Her body disconnected from her mind and before she could stop it she'd shoved the laptop to the side and straddled his hips. He grabbed her waist, pulled her closer, and then his tongue was in her mouth and the fire burning through her morphed into an inferno. Using his shoulders, she pulled herself closer still until his erection pressed into her centre, sending a stab of need between her legs. She ground her hips, trying to get more friction, and moaned when another teasing rub was all she managed.

A loud rap made her wonder what she'd knocked over, but it wasn't enough to pull her away. Sebastian did, holding her shoulders and pushing her back an inch. She gasped for air and stared at the flush beneath his skin, his dilated pupils, and a chest that rose and fell as quickly as hers.

Alicia couldn't help it. She went back in for more.

'Wait,' he said.

She blinked at him, wondering why on earth he wanted to wait for anything, then a louder rap sounded. Oh God, someone was at the door. She scrambled off his lap, trying to right her dress in the process.

'I think our dinner's here,' he said with an ease that made her cheeks burn with shame.

Sebastian left to get the door. *Her* door. All she could do was sink back into the sofa. Last night she'd spent so much time worrying he wouldn't stick to her rules and publicly humiliate her when she should have been worried about her own self-control.

With the last of her working brain cells, she concluded wine and Sebastian Collins together in the same room were a very bad combination.

Despite what the press might think, that was definitely the first time he'd had to readjust his trousers to answer the front door. As he paid for the food he digested the new-found knowledge that Blondie's cool outer shell cracked after a glass of wine, revealing the fiery passion he'd glimpsed before.

Which presented another problem.

He'd promised himself, her boss, and his manager that he'd keep his mitts off his new publicist. At the time he was confident he could – regardless of what she threw his way – because contrary to universal belief, he *did* have control over his hormones.

After hearing she'd pretty much been raised to think outlandish, sexy, or even pretty clothes were a no-go, and to shy away from the basic pleasures in life, he found his promise harder to keep. She was going above and beyond for him – even risking her family's wrath. Would it be wrong to return the favour and help her see there was more to life than refinement?

When he returned to the lounge to see her lying back, her skin flushed and eyes closed as she caught her breath after that too brief but mind-blowing kiss, he knew asking for more was wrong.

Didn't stop him considering taking the expressway to Hell though.

'Do you want me to grab the plates?' he asked.

Her eyes snapped open and she straightened. 'I'll get them.'

After kicking off her shoes, she darted into the kitchen. The sight of her hips swinging under the dress he'd picked for her, a dark blue silk that hugged her curves to perfection, didn't help with the growing bulge in his trousers.

He followed her into the small kitchen and sat in one of the chairs at the table, watching her open the cupboards with too much haste, banging plates as she went. Resisting the urge to tease her took more effort than he'd put in at training. He liked knowing he could make her lose her cool, so much it was becoming an addiction. But he also liked kissing her, having her on top of him and demanding more with her hips.

Thoughts like that were definitely not helping with the problem in his trousers.

'I should probably apologise,' he said instead of giving in to the urge to stop her rushing with another mind-blowing kiss.

Alicia turned to him with a raised brow. 'Why?'

OK, that he didn't expect. There was no flush of embarrassment, no fire. In fact, it was like she'd shut herself down again and let little Miss Prim lead the way. 'For breaking your rule.'

She shrugged, then brought the plates and cutlery to the table with less haste. 'You weren't the only one. It was a blip, a mistake. We just have to be more careful next time.'

More careful? Alicia was too busy serving up their dinner to notice him frown but it gave him time to pull himself together. She was right, it was a blip in terms of the plan they had to stop his sponsors from walking, but the brief kiss also put a chink in the untouchable armour she wore which had to be a good thing.

He couldn't imagine how awful it had been growing up having to stifle every emotion or worry about what her actions would do to her family's reputation. His parents left him breathing space to do what he wanted with his life. They'd always been loving, caring, and outgoing. An anomaly that he now knew they were lucky to find with each other.

'Next time what?' he asked.

She sat too straight in her chair, showing off her perfect table manners as she nibbled on her pasta. It took so long for her to answer he dug into his own meal, though it was dry and unappealing but the only thing he could have ordered this far into training.

'The next time anything like that happens ... it can't. You know that, don't you? My job is to help you keep your sponsors,' she said.

Sebastian let his cutlery clatter on the table. 'Say it, Alicia. Tell me what *that* was.'

Her cheeks flushed a pretty pink and her eyes glazed over. 'It was our libidos getting overexcited. We can't let that happen.'

'Our libidos.' If he sounded incredulous, he didn't care. 'You're putting the attraction between us down to misbehaving *libidos*?'

She cleared her throat. 'That's what it was.'

'And I suppose letting your libido have what it wants isn't right or proper?'

She squirmed in her seat, and he knew he should stop pushing but he couldn't. No woman had ever put attraction down to an unwanted itch she refused to scratch.

This was the most ridiculous conversation he'd ever had. 'Well?'

Alicia's throat was so dry she wished she'd topped up her glass with wine, but it was still empty and in the living room. Those weren't her words, not even her beliefs, but the speech her father had given her all those years ago. She shrugged, hoping Sebastian would drop it.

Unfortunately, he was relentless.

'At least tell me you know how crazy you sound. The way you're talking, it could have been *anyone* next to you on the sofa. Does your libido play up around Maine? Tony?'

His eyes were hard, his jaw tense, and she'd take a guess his hands were probably fists beneath the table. Then it struck her; she'd dented his ego. It had nothing to with him being hurt because she didn't want him. The thought stung as it burst the fantasy that a man as virile and gorgeous as him would find her more attractive than the usual women he slept with.

Not that she should want him to.

'Does it matter? We're working together, not getting involved with each other.'

He actually snorted. 'If you think we can ignore the spark between us without wanting a taste of each other, you are crazy.'

Alicia's breath caught. There was a spark, but she'd thought it'd been one-sided. Now she knew it wasn't, a wild image of her swiping the table clear and crawling over it to get to him flashed into her mind. Her heart beat too fast as her lungs stuttered and her every pulse point tingled.

This was bad. Really bad.

She'd smothered this part of herself a long time ago and after a couple of days with Sebastian her 'wild side' had clawed its way back to the surface. Kicking it back down was a reflex she'd developed over the years, and it wouldn't fail her now. Not when everything she wanted for her career was finally happening, when she was becoming the new and improved version of herself that would make her father proud to call her his daughter, not the 'troubled one'.

Pulling out her well-bred accent, she said, 'Then perhaps I am. We will work together and nothing else. Keeping our distance unless we're in public will help.'

Sebastian shook his head, a small smile playing on his lips, and she almost rolled her eyes. The dented ego had obviously bounced right back.

'You can't hide behind that façade forever, you know.'

He leaned closer, resting his elbows on the table as he did. She really hoped her mother's engagement party plans didn't involve dinner because she didn't think teaching Sebastian table manners would go down well, or be any easier than keeping her hands off him.

'I don't know what you're talking about. This is me, it's who I am.' She drove the point home with a glare.

Sebastian rose, the smile still in place, then cleared his plate. After scraping his barely touched meal into the bin, he returned to tower over her and tilted her chin so she had to face him.

'You and I both know that's not true. We're going to finish this, there's no other option.'

Alicia recalled the conversation before she'd lost her cool and climbed onto his lap. Her resistance had snapped when he admitted he hadn't hopped out of the twins' bed and straight into hers. But what about the latest kiss-and-tell? That was apparently after Melbourne and he hadn't brought that up when they were talking about dates, had he?

She jerked out of his hold and stood to face him. 'You're trying to use me to deny the latest scandal, aren't you?'

His eyebrows shot up. 'What?'

If she hadn't been so flustered finding him with the vibrator she would have paid more attention. 'That woman you bedded when you got back to the UK. It was supposedly after our first date. You want me to lie and say we were dating then. You want me to make a fool of myself in front of the whole world – another poor woman you cheated on. You can forget it! I'm revising the dates.'

'Shit, Alicia, it's not like that. I didn't think about her at all and I didn't cheat on Mai either!'

He stepped forward as if to touch her but she couldn't let him. The spark was still there despite this confrontation and she didn't think she'd be able to fight it again. 'You're telling me you forgot, just like that? Are women so disposable to you?'

She didn't bother to call him out on the other lie. His kiss with his partner at Wimbledon on live TV while his fiancée had watched on from the side lines was proof enough.

'No.' His voice was hard. 'She was a night of fun, that's all. It was what she wanted and I bet the reason was so she could make a mint off her story.'

'But you wanted to lie and say you were taken at the time! Did you think you could convince everyone you didn't sleep with her just because you were with me?'

'Alicia, I didn't think about her. We can change the dates, that's not the issue here.'

He took a step towards her but she retreated until she hit the wall. Her heart hammered with more than anger until she was in danger of believing him. In danger of picking up where they'd left off.

But he was lying. Staring straight into her eyes and telling her what he wanted her to believe. Just like Darrell had done over and over when he told her he loved her, when he promised they'd be together forever.

'I want you to leave.' She'd aimed for stern, but breathy and pathetic was all she managed.

His jaw clenched. 'You don't, you're just terrified of taking this further.'

Maybe, but she'd never admit that to him. 'Get out, Sebastian. There's *nothing* going to happen between us. We're working together, nothing more.'

He shook his head and forced a wry smile that didn't show in his eyes. 'I'll go, but if you think this conversation is over, you're not as smart as I thought you were.'

She gritted her teeth and folded her arms to make sure she didn't find something heavy to throw at him. True to his word, he left. Maybe he'd get bored of whatever challenge he thought she presented and give up, because the alternative that he wore her down and turned her into another night of fun he could easily forget wasn't something she'd let herself become.

She had to find a way to keep them apart but still do her job. Alicia sighed. Well, hadn't she thought at the first meeting he'd be a challenge? But this was more than she'd signed up for.

After a sleepless night, a morning in the office working on her other clients' files proved to be the best distraction. Sebastian didn't try to get in touch, and they hadn't made plans to see each other again, which was just fine by her. Time away to get her priorities straight and work out a plan that would keep them together enough in public to be convincing, but apart the majority of the time so she could keep temptation off the radar, was exactly what she needed.

Come break time, she'd finished up her other work and was about to tackle Sebastian's file when a knock sounded on her door. Sarah came in a second later with the usual grace and style of what seemed like every other woman except Alicia herself.

'Wanna grab a coffee?' Sarah asked. When she got a good look at Alicia, she frowned. 'Are you OK?'

Not even a little, and the concealer she'd slapped under her eyes obviously wasn't doing its job. 'I've not had a lot of sleep. This Collins case is harder than I thought it would be, and with the new spin of me playing his girlfriend, its worse. I need to work on everything, but now we have to be seen together and there's not much time left over.'

It wasn't a lie, just not the whole truth. The lack of time was a problem.

Sarah slid into her chair across the desk. 'You're forgetting the fact he's like chocolate for the eyeballs.'

She laughed. 'That's not the problem.'

She wasn't a Christian, but the lie made her feel the need to visit confession. His delicious body was like caviar, champagne, *and* chocolate for the eyeballs. It's just a pity he was a lying cheat who assumed anyone in a skirt would fall into bed with him after a few well-placed lines.

'Mmhmm. If I were you I wouldn't take up professional poker. Anyway, that's not why I'm here.'

Now it was Alicia's turn to 'mmhmm'. Sarah loved gossip, probably as much as she loved her fiancé.

'Really,' she said with a grin. 'David's brother Sam is a freelance photographer who could use some extra cash. You wouldn't even have to pay him. Just tell him where and when you and Collins are together, he snaps a few shots, and sells them to the press, maybe even with an anonymous statement about how cosy and loved-up you two are. That solves one of your problems.'

It did, and Alicia was surprised she hadn't considered finding a freelancer to do just that. 'He won't tell them anything we don't want him to?'

Sarah nodded. 'And he may even get a regular job with one of the papers so it's win-win.'

Her time with Sebastian would be limited. They wouldn't need to worry about press coverage, merely set a night or two a week to be seen together and call the photographer to do the hard work for her.

Oh, this was good. Very, very good.

'Thanks, Sarah. I'll definitely give him a call.'

She handed over a card. 'That's Sam's digits. So, about the other problem …?'

Alicia smiled, hoping to hide the fact her stomach was in bits thinking about the more pressing issue. 'It isn't a problem. We're professionally pretending to be together, nothing else.'

And if she kept telling herself that, she might eventually start to believe it. Now if only she could convince Sebastian …

'I don't know how you can work with him and not want to jump his bones. He's the hottest guy I've ever seen in the flesh.'

She couldn't disagree, every part of his flesh screamed out to be nibbled and licked. *That* was her problem. She was done with guys who could make her gaga. What she needed was to fall in love with someone like Daria's fiancé. Blair was respectable, successful, and completely scandal-free.

She wished she didn't find that idea so unappealing.

Forcing herself back to the conversation, she smiled and said, 'Does Dave know you perv on guys?'

Sarah's grin was wicked. 'I can look, just not touch. What's your excuse?'

'Not that I need one, but Mr Maine has a very strict policy on dating clients.' One that hadn't popped into her head in days. Yet another reason to stay out of Sebastian's bed.

Rising, Sarah shrugged. 'What he doesn't know won't hurt him.'

Alicia scowled until the door closed behind her. She didn't need to find a loophole in one of the few flimsy reasons she had for keeping her hands off Sebastian. At least now she had a way of limiting her time with him. She just had to claw the professional distance back.

Chapter Seven

To: Sebastian
From: Alicia

Sebastian,
I've attached directions to a charity function tonight.
Meet me there at 8pm.
Alicia Simpson
Publicist, Maine PR

No matter how many times Sebastian had sworn he wouldn't re-read her email, whenever he and James took a water break he'd pick the thing up and try to read between the lines. There wasn't anything to find – just a straight-to-the-point email from his publicist, which was exactly what Alicia was aiming for.

The email only added to the pissed-off mood he'd been in since leaving her flat. After the kiss last night, how could she expect him to just forget and start a professional relationship with her? And it wasn't even him who'd made the first move – that had been Alicia and her 'misbehaving libido'. He muttered a curse and put his phone down on the bench.

'Come on,' he said to James. 'I want to get a few more sets in before this party.'

A party that would no doubt filled with the kind of cold, privileged people Alicia had grown up with. A party he'd rather stab himself in the thigh than go to. But she was clearly all about his reputation clean-up now and if he was thinking with his head rather than his dented ego he'd agree it was a good idea to be seen there. After all, showing up to a charity function put on for supporting homeless children and making a donation could only make him look better in the public eye.

'Look, I'm all for you getting back into the swing of things, but we've been training for hours,' James said.

His trainer didn't get up from the bench after he emptied his water bottle. He looked exhausted and by rights, Sebastian probably should be too. But anger and frustration seemed to kick his adrenaline into gear until it felt like he could go on for hours. He had to burn it off before he saw her tonight, or who knew what would come out of his mouth.

Who knew what he'd do to her scrumptious mouth.

She'd even accused him of cheating on Mai! When it came down to it, Alicia was just like everyone else. One overexcited woman who'd won her first game at Wimbledon playing doubles with him and suddenly he was caught up in the biggest scandal of the century. And as he should have expected, Mai had gotten her own back and then some.

'One,' Sebastian pleaded. 'C'mon, old man. You can do it.'

As he anticipated James stood and threw a scowl in his direction. 'God forbid you ever turn thirty.'

Sebastian grinned. 'No way, twenty-nine will do. And I plan on winning every game on the way – including Olympic gold.'

Because that was all that mattered now. Not a wife or a proper, grounded home or a woman who refused to loosen up enough to have some fun. Those were pipe dreams. Winning was all he could make happen. That way the only person he had to rely on was himself.

'We'd better keep going if we're going to have a hope of getting you anywhere near the Olympics,' James shot back.

He pushed all other thoughts aside and concentrated on the win. There was only one more game to get this right, to burn off the anger that had boiled over since Alicia's email had hit his inbox. He just hoped James wasn't too knackered to keep up with him.

Alicia hadn't received a reply from Sebastian and her stomach was a ball of nerves waiting for him to show up at the party. She was familiar with some of the faces – they were in the circle her father deemed appropriate to associate with. The only reason she'd even considered bringing Sebastian was because she'd called her mother to make sure they were staying in Cumbria. Having to deal with Sebastian and her father in the same room was something she was planning to avoid for the remainder of his contract with Maine – her sister's engagement party be damned.

Though she'd still not thought of a way out of it and her mother's near excitement about her bringing a boy home made it harder. For as long as she could remember, her mother had never been excited about anything. On the outside, anyway.

Another anxious glance around the room told her he wasn't there yet. A waiter stopped in front of her with a tray topped with glasses and she took one. Downing champagne at a party like this was probably frowned upon, but a sip wouldn't ease the worry that the ego-bashing followed by her impersonal email would make Sebastian stay away – maybe even try to get out of his contract.

The event was hosted in a townhouse in Mayfair by a couple who had founded several charities. From overhearing conversations between her mother and father, the hostess was famous for her indiscretions and her husband took more interest in golf than his wife. She couldn't understand why people would stay together if they weren't happy – but to be married in this circle was usually for mutual gain. Divorce was as abhorrent as not having the latest Bentley. Apparently it was better to look happy and act like everything was OK while you were dying inside.

Alicia knew that feeling.

And true to these events, the place was over-decorated to the point of being gauche. Sure, everything was expensive and sparkly but carrying the theme of the chandeliers into side table decorations just made it look a little tacky. She preferred her cosy flat with dodgy plumbing to this. It was just so ... cold. A bit like the parties her parents hosted – but at least then she could escape to her bedroom and wait it out with her sisters.

She wandered into the hall and tried not to roll her eyes seeing the sparkles carried out through the house. The air was filled with so many fragrances from the flowers it had grown cloying. When she reached the front sitting room, she pulled the curtain covering the window back to see if Sebastian was almost there. It was just after eight, and she was losing hope that he'd even show up.

A dark figure across the street caught her attention. It looked like a man, but she couldn't be sure. Shadows surrounded him and when she opened the curtains wider, he started to back away quickly. Her heart pounded as she thought it was Sebastian leaving her but when he walked under a streetlight, his hair glinted gold. She squinted to try and make him out but after a second he was gone.

'Didn't anyone ever tell you spying is rude?'

Alicia spun around. She was relived Sebastian had shown up, even if he was late. But now he was there, she was more than a little pissed off that he had kept her waiting. 'I'm not spying. There was someone lurking about in the shadows across the street. Where have you been?'

He smirked. 'So you thought you'd have a nose and see what they were up to? I'd call that spying.'

She gritted her teeth and took a deep breath though

her nose to help calm her down. It didn't help so much as the lungful of his spicy aftershave, and then it only worked in a way that was almost as bad – or arguably worse. Her skin prickled and her feet almost carried her towards him without permission. She dug her heels in and folded her arms.

She would not touch him.

He let loose the full power of his grin. 'If you must know, I was training.'

She snapped her focus back to the conversation. 'Until now?'

If she sounded incredulous she didn't care. All evidence pointed to him not knowing what honesty was.

'Relax, Blondie. I'm here now.' He ignored her scowl and looked over her outfit. His eyes darkened and her heart raced despite her irritation at the nickname. 'You look pretty. The shoes match and everything.'

Her cheeks burned. 'I had help from a friend.'

She probably shouldn't have admitted that she had to get Sarah to help pull together an outfit for the night – but he knew how hopeless she was. This time she'd stuck the vibrator in the bin before anyone got there to save further embarrassment.

'Your friend did a good job.' He looked over her shoulder, but the curtains had fallen closed. 'So who were you peeping at?'

'I wasn't *peeping* at anyone! I think I saw a man but he disappeared. It could have been someone planning to rob the house.' The guy had looked shady …

He didn't mock her like she'd expected, instead he walked around her then opened the curtains. 'But he's gone now?'

'I think so. He took off when he saw me.' She stood next to him and pointed across the street. 'That way.'

He met her eyes then. 'Do you think we need to warn the host?'

She shrugged and looked out of the window. It was a

strange feeling being taken seriously by him, especially when a minute ago he'd been teasing her. 'I'm not sure. Maybe he was just curious about the party. There are a lot of people arriving. I should probably mention it to security.'

He turned to her. 'Good idea.'

She went to do just that but he caught her wrist. 'Before you go, we should talk about last night.'

Her spine stiffened but she couldn't help it. 'Sebastian, I don't think –'

'I know.' He sighed and his gaze dropped to her lips.

She couldn't hide the flush that spread across her cheekbones, couldn't even stop her tongue from popping out and wetting her lips. But she refused to give into this … this … lust. She had more control than that. And who knew how many women he'd had in his bed since he got back from Australia? The girl who sold her story could have been one of dozens.

She broke free of his grasp. 'Let's tell security what I saw and then we'll make an appearance. I don't want to take the tube home too late.'

Alicia walked away, and this time he didn't try to stop her.

She dragged Sebastian around and introduced him to almost everyone. He'd never been in company so dull he could easily fall asleep standing up. It amazed him that Alicia looked enthralled when men droned on about their family wealth, new yachts, and cars the Queen would envy. He couldn't believe she was actually interested in any of it. Especially after seeing how being brought up in her family had affected her.

He reckoned she was just pretending to be fascinated by all the boasting – it wasn't *her*. He'd caught a glimpse of the passionate woman beneath all the reserve and knew she wasn't as stuck-up as the rest of them – despite that Lady of the Manor voice she'd used on him when she told him off.

And he'd been wrong earlier. Now he had to concede that the only way to get Alicia out of his head was to burn out the spark between them once and for all. If only he could convince her, and fast. Every night he was too keyed up, even after hours on the court. It had been the same way since she'd stumbled into the board room at Maine, and now he recognised what it was – sexual frustration. And despite what she might think, it was all for her. Not some woman he'd met once and wouldn't see again. None of them could turn him on wearing a shapeless suit and a scowl.

She was driving him crazy. The built-up tension had even driven him to push James too far, which resulted in his trainer's knee almost giving out.

Which meant he had to train with machines for the next few days. Just another thing to be pissed off about – and this party wasn't helping either.

After a particularly stifling conversation with the host, Alicia picked up what he guessed was her third glass of champagne and took a sip that drained almost half the flute.

He'd been right, she must hate being here as much as he did. Still, he had to give her credit for scoring them access. There were a few journalists from high-profile magazines who were there taking photos and logging donations.

Hopefully being seen at places like this instead of bars would make his sponsors stay put. And maybe now Mai had made enough off her kiss-and-tells to keep her in Prada for a while. Though he doubted one appearance and a new charity would fix the mess he'd made the last few months, he could hope.

'There's someone else I want us to speak with,' she said, then took a step away from him.

Sebastian caught her around the waist and pulled her close. It felt so natural, so easy, and not at all like he was

85

putting on a show. Alicia's spine stiffened and she kept as much distance as she could when their hips were pressed together. He wondered what it would take to melt the ice surrounding her and be reintroduced to the woman who straddled his hips last night.

She pulled away, walking into the crowd, but he took her hand and kept up with her fast pace for a few steps. Then he slowed their footsteps as they made their way around groups of people enthralled in what Sebastian assumed were boast-fests. 'If I have to meet one more guy bragging about how big his yacht is I can't be held responsible for asking him if he's overcompensating for something.'

'Will you keep your voice down?' she whispered, but her lips twitched like she was holding back a smile.

He stopped them and leaned closer, sliding his hands to her hips, and whispered back, 'Will you bust us out of here if I agree?'

Alicia's face flushed and her eyes glazed over a little. Whether she wanted to call it a misbehaving libido, passion, or lust, it was all the same damn thing in his opinion. This resistance was like a long, slow session of foreplay without the release – which only made him wonder how great it would be when she faced the fact they were inevitably going to end up in bed together.

It was only a matter of when. Shit, he could be patient. After all good things came to those who waited.

'We need to do an interview I scheduled then meet the last few guests.'

'Then we're free?' he checked.

Alicia nodded.

'So who's next?' he asked.

She pointed across the room to a woman he knew and loathed. The magazine had done a piece on his break-up and if he remembered correctly, she'd taken every word he'd said and made him look ten times worse. 'No way.'

Alicia sighed. 'Sebastian, she knows you're changing

and wants to be first to get the full scoop of what you have planned. She promised there'd be no funny business.'

She could make all the promises in the world, he still wouldn't trust her. But Alicia was staring at him with wide, pleading eyes and the blunt and final refusal died somewhere between his throat and his mouth. He groaned. 'You owe me for this.'

Alicia smirked. 'You'll owe me when you see the society pages tomorrow.'

He shook his head. 'That won't cut it.'

'Excuse me?'

Her frown told him she'd jumped to a conclusion that may involve burning off some of the chemistry between them. But that's not what he wanted. This time. 'Relax, Blondie. I'm not talking about your virtue.'

Her face flamed scarlet. 'I'm not –'

'Good to know,' he said, and meant it. At least now he could rule that out. 'I'll fill you in on what I want from you when we get out of here.'

Before she could protest, he took her hand and led her to the She-Bitch who'd been the first person to stick the knife in when his life fell into the shitter. If he looked closely, he could almost see the horns hidden beneath her hair.

Sebastian didn't release her as he led her through the crowds to meet the journalist from the *Independent* – which really didn't help with her concentration. He looked even hotter in the tux, with his hair combed back from his face. His golden tan seemed more pronounced against his white shirt.

And then there was the touching. Now he hand his hand on her hip. Innocent enough, but his heat seemed to scorch through her light silk gown and her pulse went crazy with the contact. She didn't think she'd get through the final meet and greets with his hands on her, but she didn't think she'd be able to stand if he let her go.

When they reached the journalist, Claire, Alicia introduced Sebastian and prayed he didn't say anything to screw up this meeting. The woman took her time giving him a once-over and Alicia didn't like the way her eyes glinted – though she didn't know whether it was because Claire was planning further sabotage or because she thought he was attractive. She offered a hand for Sebastian to shake, and when he brought it to his mouth for a kiss Alicia's green-eyed monster bubbled to the surface.

It was crazy – she didn't have a claim on him, and Sebastian didn't even like the journalist. Alicia didn't want a claim on him either, but when he unleashed his grin and Claire blushed, she couldn't take it a second more. 'You wanted to ask us a few questions.'

Claire continued to stare at him, ignoring her completely.

'Claire,' Alicia said in a harder tone. It wasn't polite, but neither was the way the woman was flirting with her eyes. With a guy who, as far as Claire knew, was taken.

'Yes, if that's OK, Mr Collins.' Now she fluttered her eyelashes.

Alicia's hand fisted around the stem of her champagne glass. Sebastian noticed, and turned that grin on her. She tried to take a deep breath, calm down a little, but it was hard when he knew exactly how she felt now. So much for the cool, confident new Alicia who was supposed to deal with situations like this with more poise and less … claws.

Sebastian directed that killer smile to a woman who not thirty seconds ago, he didn't want to speak with. Or had that been another lie? She couldn't tell anymore.

'Fine by me. I've been dying to tell the world about Alicia.'

Another lie delivered so convincingly that Alicia

almost believed him. She had to remember that in the future, especially when he got her so hot she wanted to forget her rules and let him take her back to his place.

'You do make a lovely couple,' Claire said, but didn't sound like she was convinced.

Sebastian said, 'She's perfect.'

If the room wasn't full of people looking for the next scandal to take the attention away from their own, Alicia would have pulled away when he lowered his head. Instead she froze, her lungs cramped, and maybe even her heart skipped a beat. He dropped a light kiss on her lips, which was over in less than a second, but the connection hummed through her until she was starved for more.

The jealously twisted inside along with her hormones and it took every shred of restraint she had not to ditch the glass, thread her fingers through his hair, and kiss him again – the way she'd kissed him last night.

'Let's get on with the interview,' Claire said in a dry tone, and pulled a small recording device from her handbag. 'Where did you two meet?'

She shoved the thing right in Alicia's face, but she couldn't call the official plan. She could barely call up her own name. How on earth could one chaste kiss scramble her mind like this?

Sebastian had to answer for her. 'We met through a mutual friend. I asked her out for coffee, and here we are.'

Alicia was glad he didn't mention dates. She couldn't face what her father would say if she was the focus of more gossip than necessary. And the media would definitely have tied-in the beginning of her relationship with the latest kiss-and-tell.

'Was this before or after Melbourne?' Claire asked.

'A couple of weeks after,' Alicia said. Heat crept up her neck. 'Sebastian has made mistakes – don't we all at some point? He wanted to take some time off to think about where he wanted to go from there.'

He didn't speak his agreement, just gave a tight nod. She got the feeling he didn't regret his behaviour, which could potentially make her job a nightmare, but at the same time, she was starting to see a different side of him despite not knowing when to believe him.

He still flirted when she'd asked him not to, he could drive her insane and turn her on at the same time, but he was focused on his career now. She reckoned the last few months must have been hard for him and she couldn't begin to imagine the pressure he was under. So many different stories from women had popped up in the media after his public affair when he was with Mai.

How many of those stories could be true? He was a professional tennis player who spent most of the time training. To have several lovers a night was bordering on the ridiculous. Or was she just so hot for him that she wanted to believe a lie to make what she wanted to do with him acceptable? Stifling a groan, she decided this was not the time or place to be thinking about things like that.

'Can we get a photo of the happy couple?' Claire said, waving her photographer over.

Sebastian nodded, then tucked Alicia more securely to his side. This was what they needed, to prove they were an item and her standing there like a statue wouldn't convince anyone. She set her champagne glass down and slid both arms around his waist. Though he must have been surprised, he didn't show it. Instead, he dropped a kiss on her forehead before turning so they faced the photographer – which reminded her to call Sam, the guy Sarah had suggested.

Of course, there was no need to invite him to a function like this when the media were out in full force. But with her whole body humming and her libido roaring to life, she decided spending less time together one-on-one was definitely the safest way to get through this contract.

The camera flashed and she hoped her expression was more besotted than flushed and frustrated. With his hard abs and the muscles in his back beneath her arms, it took all her effort just to paste a smile on and act like hugging him was the most natural thing in the world. She was just glad there wasn't a sign above her forehead to let them know what was running through her mind.

When they stopped taking pictures, she released him, but Sebastian took her hand and threaded his fingers through hers. Her pulse thrummed as he rubbed his thumb over her wrist and his grin indicated he knew exactly how he affected her.

Chapter Eight

The front door opened and a gust of wind blew through the house. Jack muted the TV and decided to keep his mouth shut about the draft. After all, he was still shaken from what he did to Mai last night – no way was he going to give her a hard time when this morning she'd been walking like she was still in agony.

'Hi,' she said when she reached the sitting room.

She didn't meet his eyes and he hoped it wasn't because she was frightened of him. Fuck, what had he been thinking last night? He'd gone out for a few drinks with mates, which should have worked for them both. Sloshed was the only state he could have sex with her in and not have to fantasise it was someone else – after all, she was a bag of skin and bones with bleached hair. Not even a notch on the sexy brunette he'd been head-over-heels for, who'd crushed his heart and dropped him when Collins came along.

But he hadn't meant to cause her pain. He wasn't a complete bastard – he just wanted her heart as broken as his had been when she'd left him for that arsehole.

'Hey. Do you want to go out for dinner? I thought we could go to that Italian you used to love.' He didn't fancy a stroll down memory lane with her. It would make taking everything she had and leaving her that much harder. But he'd been a shit and had a lot of making up to do.

'No, I'm off carbs this month.' Mai lowered herself into the farthest chair from him, wincing as she did.

A stab of guilt slammed into him, so much so he couldn't even get pissed off about her starving herself.

Hell, she was so thin that naked, she looked like a twelve-year-old girl with abnormally large boobs.

Instead, he changed the subject. 'How did today go?'

'OK, I think. I gave them enough to print a month-long feature on the deterioration of our engagement.' She scowled, like something had pissed her off.

Jack didn't ask what. He didn't particularly want to know if her conscience was kicking in or whether she still loved Collins. He had enough reason to hate them both. Himself too, after last night.

'I'm going to have a bath.' She winced again as she got up and he couldn't ignore the elephant in the room any longer.

It was hardly progressive to his plan if she started to loathe him. But not a conversation he'd wanted since, for the first time in over a year, he'd fallen asleep with Mai in his arms. That, coupled with what he did to her, was fucking with his head.

'Mai, I'm sorry for last night. I shouldn't have done it and I didn't mean to hurt you.' Not physically, anyway. That had never been his intention.

Tears made her eyes shiny before spilling down her cheeks. 'I know, it's OK. I'm just tired. Rehashing the past and being creative with the truth has taken it out of me.'

Great, so it was Collins she was crying for. Mai must have seen his mood change, because she came over to the sofa and reached out to him. He closed his eyes as she ran her fingers through his hair, remembering how much he used to love it when she did that after they'd fucked. Now it was like he'd been ripped in two, one half of him craving the softness and comfort of her and the other revolting from any contact at all.

'I love you, Jack. Just you,' she said.

The opposing sides tugged at each other until he thought he'd rip in half. He patted her hand, then pulled away. 'You too, babe. Enjoy your bath.'

She waited a second, probably to see if he'd join her, but he turned back to the TV and switched it on. Her footsteps drifted down the hall. When he heard the bathroom door close, he slammed his head into the back of the sofa and groaned.

Who knew how much longer he could live this fucked-up lie. The only question left was should he take what she had now and run, or wait it out a bit longer, hoping for some serious cash to come? Surely this feature would kick off a media frenzy with enough interviews to keep him going until he'd finished his script.

He'd just have to keep the intimacy between them to a minimum.

Despite Alicia's protests, Sebastian wouldn't take no for an answer.

Stuck in a party with him by her side was bad enough – at least there had been people around and she *had* to make sure things didn't go any farther between them. Now, in his sleek sports car, there was only temptation. Temptation that was getting harder and harder to resist.

'The tube will be faster,' she said as he pulled out of his parking space. She wished he'd drop her at the station.

Sebastian shook his head. 'If there are creepy guys lurking in shadows in Mayfair I don't want you out by yourself at night. How would I find another half-decent publicist at such short notice?'

'Half-decent!' He was lucky he could find *anyone* to put up with him.

He laughed. 'You're touchy tonight, Blondie.'

Touchy was one word for it. Since she left the office with Sarah, it had felt like her stomach was infested with a swarm of bees. After their kiss last night, the argument, and his lack of reply to her email, she was hours past nervous. And then throughout the party he'd flirted, held her close, and even kissed her, which had set off a barrage of different nerves. Though maybe a lot of those had been lust.

After tonight, she didn't think she had the willpower to say no to him, but she had to. Spending an evening with people like her parents had reminded her how not thinking about her actions had horrible consequences. Especially for a Simpson.

But she should make the effort to be polite, since he seemed to be showing concern for her safety. Despite the fact he'd followed it with an insult.

'I'm sorry, I don't mean to be cranky. It's been a long day,' she said.

'Don't worry about it.'

She relaxed into the seat and let silence wash over them. It wasn't uncomfortable despite the thrumming attraction in the air. She looked out at the brightly lit city she called home. London was so different from the Cumbrian estate she grew up in – which had always been so quiet, the grounds so perfect.

Too quiet. Creepily perfect.

Here there were thousands of different people, all going about their lives seemingly without a care in the world. Alicia bet none of them had to think through every word and outfit and decision before they acted. Being her father's daughter wasn't easy – not when she had to live up to her sisters and make up for the shame she'd caused him in the past.

And now she was dating the Casanova of the sporting world, it was one more black mark against her character. And her family's reputation.

She sighed and thought back to a time before she felt this pressure to succeed, this drive to please everyone. Back then, she was just a girl with dreams of growing older, marrying the boy she loved, and having her father walk her down the aisle with pride lighting up his smile.

It had happened so differently, though. Her father hadn't been proud, he'd been livid. Her hopes and dreams had been ripped away, leaving her crushed, broken, and ashamed of who she was.

'What's wrong?' Sebastian asked.

Alicia shook her head, more to clear the awful memories than answer him. She scrambled for something to distract him with. Her past was not a conversation she was willing to have. The wound was still too raw.

'You said I owed you.' After the interview with the flirty bitch from the *Independent*, she'd almost forgotten.

'True,' he said. He stopped the car at a set of traffic lights and turned to face her. 'Did you ever learn how to play tennis?'

She frowned. 'Of course.' Her mother had loved to play and her father had built a court in the grounds of the estate. During the summers of her childhood, playing each other was the only time they'd spent together as a proper family. 'Why are you asking me that?'

He pulled over at her street, then tugged up the handbrake. She blinked and looked around, seeing the building she stayed in. How did they get there so fast, or had she been so lost in thought she'd missed the whole journey?

'I'm asking because my trainer, James, hurt his knee today and I need someone to play with tomorrow. It'll be good to have an opponent with different moves than I'm used to.'

Her jaw went slack. He couldn't be serious. A leisurely game was all she was good for. 'I can't play *that* well.'

'Deal's a deal, Blondie. I did what you asked, now you return the favour. That's how these things work.' He didn't laugh or smile or do anything to hint he was joking.

'Sebastian –'

'I'll pick you up at eight so you don't have to get up too early. Relax, Alicia. You never know, you might have fun.'

Before she could protest again, he leaned closer. Her heart was in her throat and his lips were an inch from hers. She held her breath as want and need and fear tore through her until her muscles bunched so tight she was sure she would shatter.

He tugged the handle and pushed the door open with a smile playing around the corners of his mouth. 'Sweet dreams, Blondie.'

Sebastian leaned forward and for a second she thought he was going to kiss her the way he had the night before. All she could hear was her own heartbeat.

Just before his lips touched hers, he moved and planted a soft, lingering kiss on her cheek instead. She wanted nothing more than to grab the strands of hair that had fallen loose from his swept-back style and move him to her mouth, but he pulled away too quickly.

'I'll see you tomorrow.'

She blinked a few times, unable to believe what she'd heard. His voice had been so steady when she was almost gasping for the oxygen his proximity had stolen. Her face burned so hot she had no doubt it would be scarlet and Sebastian smiled at her, then put the car into gear.

The anger that followed gave her the strength to unbuckle her seatbelt and step out of the car. She could have done it more gracefully, with less stumbling, but she was getting madder by the second until reason drowned out. Slamming his door, she sucked in a breath to steady the rage, then stormed to the entrance of her building without a backward glance.

She'd barely made it into the foyer when she heard him speeding away. It didn't occur to her until then that she couldn't meet him tomorrow. She had to limit their time together, now more than ever if she couldn't even be that close to him and not want to throw caution to the wind.

Alicia ran through the meadow until she reached the spot where Darrell had laid down an old, tattered blanket on the grass. She threw her arms around him and greeted him with a kiss. Tingles danced down her spine as his fingers dug into her hips, pulling her closer to the hard muscles of his chest.

For the first time since they'd started dating, she broke away, unable to hold in the news she'd discovered the day before. But Darrell didn't look at her, instead, he took a step back. Her stomach gave a nervous flip. It had been doing that a lot today, but this was different. He was acting different.

'I missed you,' she said, but this time he didn't say the words back. Her heartbeat spiked and she stepped forward, reaching out to him. He dodged her and shook his head. 'Darrell, what's wrong?'

All he did was cover his beautiful face with his hands. For the first time, she saw the red bruises over his knuckles. Surely he hadn't gotten into another fight with his team mates? Her heart sliced in two for him, his pain becoming her own. He was a good rugby player but his family didn't have the money the others did, and they hadn't taken to him when he got asked to play.

'Are you hurt?' she asked, taking one of his hands.

He flinched away and shoved his hands in his pockets. 'I'm fine. Look, I didn't want to do it like this, Licia, but I can't keep leading you on.'

Her heart started to fissure, she knew because of the agony that ripped through her chest. He couldn't break up with her, not after everything they'd shared. Not after what she'd just found out. He ... No, she wouldn't believe it.

Ignoring the stinging in her eyes, she asked, 'Do what?'

'I'm leaving. My dad got a job in Wales and I've asked for a transfer to one of the teams there. It was approved yesterday. We're moving in a few days.'

The words didn't make sense in that second, she didn't want them to. Nor did she want to see the pain in his eyes. 'You're sixteen now. You can stay here with me.'

Darrell shook his head. 'No, I can't. I'm sorry. I should... go.'

He'd made it ten steps before it hit her that this was real. He was really leaving and she was just going to let him walk away? Alicia ran faster than she ever had and when she caught up to him, she grabbed his arm. 'This can't be the end. It can't be! What happened to us? We were supposed to get married. Have kids! Grow old together! You promised.'

There were tears on his cheeks and she reached up to wipe them away, her anger draining a little seeing this was killing him as much as it was killing her. 'I don't understand why this has to be the end.'

'We can't have any of it, Licia. Your father won't allow it.'

She was shaking her head before he finished. 'He's my father, it's his job to want me to be happy. You make me happy!'

His voice softened. 'You make me happy too, but I'm the son of a carpenter and he won't have me as a son-in-law. Now that Jonathan's gone, he needs someone he can be proud of to take over when he retires. That's not me.'

The mention of her older brother only made the pain in her chest all that sharper. 'How can we know until we tell him we're together?'

Darrell blew out a breath, then ran a hand through his hair. 'I don't know how he found out, but he knows. Who do you think put my dad forward for the job? He made it clear he wants me to leave too, or the deal's off.'

Her mouth gaped. There was no way her father would do that! She was his daughter and now she was ...

'I don't believe you.'

His expression crumpled. 'I would never lie to you.'

Blinking against the burn in her eyes, she tried to wrap her head around what he'd said. She knew her father had thrown Jonathan out, could he be so cruel as to do something that horrible to her too? Jonathan had gambled away most of the trust fund he'd gotten on his eighteenth birthday and her mother had told her he turned to drugs and was stealing from them. She could understand why her father hadn't wanted him in the house.

But what had she *done to deserve this?*

'Licia, listen to me.'

Darrell pulled her into a hug and she let him, even cried into his shoulder. She'd been like this for weeks, the littlest things setting her off, and now she knew why.

'I can come with you,' she said between sobs. After all, he'd promised they'd be together forever and he wouldn't lie to her.

He kissed her hair, then pulled back to cup her cheeks. With his thumbs he rubbed the tears away. 'You're only fifteen, your father will never let you.'

'Only for a few more months. If you have to go, we can write to each other and on my birthday –'

He pressed his fingers to his lips. 'I'm sorry, we can't.'

More tears fell, and she tried to breathe through her nose to stop them – really tried to pull it together, but her heart was being crushed beneath her ribs and the pain was too much to bear.

'You said you'd never lie to me. You told me we'd be together always.'

'I meant it then, Licia. I wish it could have been true.'

She tried to swallow against the lump in her throat. She still couldn't understand any of it – Darrell couldn't leave. Not now. Not ever.

The news she'd been so excited about telling him earlier felt like the last shred of hope in this nightmare – the one thing that might have a chance of keeping him.

'I'm pregnant.'

The blood drained from his face as he staggered away from her. Rolls of nausea washed over her as she watched the shock turn to fear. She'd been so sure this was what he wanted, for them to get married, have babies, and live in a little cottage in one of the villages surrounding her father's estate.

Now she could see the truth. He had been lying. All those things meant nothing to him.

'Are you sure?' he asked, the hope in his voice worse than if he'd slapped her in the face.

Alicia nodded.

'Shit. He's going to kill me this time. Fuck!' Darrell started pacing back and forth.

'Who? What do you mean "this time"?'

'Your father!' he shouted.

Now she was the one stepping back. 'Don't be ridiculous.'

He laughed once. 'Ridiculous? Do you call this *ridiculous?'*

He jerked up his T-shirt and bared his stomach. She didn't understand until he turned to the side and she saw it. Deep red marks – or the start of what looked like nasty bruises – covered his torso from his hips round to his back. She gasped and reached out to him, but he dropped his shirt and glared at her.

'That's why I'm leaving. Your precious father came to my house with a message. My dad has to take the job he was offered and I have to go with him. I fought for you, Licia, but he said a scumbag like me didn't have the class to date you. I hit him and he fought back harder.'

'When?' was all that would come out of her mouth, she was too horrified at what he'd revealed.

'An hour ago.'

Alicia glanced in the direction of the estate. Darrell was huge and tough, and her father wasn't. She wanted to run to him, make sure he was OK, but if he did tell Darrell and his family to leave, how could she even bring herself to care?

But none of it made sense. She bit her lip so hard she could taste blood. 'My father isn't a thug, he would never –'

'Wake up and look at the evidence!' Darrell shook her by the shoulders so hard her teeth clattered together. 'Your father will do anything to protect his precious family name without giving a shit who it hurts. You can't tell him about the baby, he'll come after me and kill me! You're going to have to take care of it.'

Pushing out of his hold, she frowned at him. 'What are you saying?'

'I'm saying you need to have an abortion. Fast.'

Chapter Nine

Sebastian rang Alicia's doorbell for what must have been the third time that morning. He'd arrived early but now she was ten minutes late.

He tapped out another text to her.

If this is payback for last night, Blondie, that's fine. Point made. Now come on!

The second he hit send, he regretted it. Technically, she hadn't agreed to come – and it wasn't like he'd given her a choice.

Yeah, he should have maybe *asked* instead of bribing. But she'd looked so sad when he was driving her home and he'd had a weird urge to find out what had upset her and make her smile again. For that, they had to spend time together, so instead of saying she owed him a fun day out he'd insisted she play a few games with him.

Scrolling down to her number, he walked back to his car at the side of the street and hit call. There was a dial tone, so at least she hadn't switched her mobile off. But she didn't pick up and he went through to voicemail. He didn't leave a message, just shoved the phone in his jacket pocket and reconsidered using the machine today. He hated the thing though, it was always too predictable.

It had nothing to do with the fact he'd been looking forward to seeing Blondie's eyes flare up when he teased her.

With a sigh, he opened the car door. It was probably best they didn't train together. He could think of better ways to make her sweaty and breathless – considering she ever let herself have what she wanted.

The front door to the building opened and he turned

around. At first, all he could focus on was her little white shorts and the miles of thigh and calf on display. But he soon noticed how the vest beneath her fleece hugged her stomach and he couldn't wait to get the full effect when they hit the gym.

'Bit cold for shorts, isn't it?' he asked. It was better than telling her how fuckable she looked without the frumpy suit. That might earn him another lecture on controlling wild libidos.

Alicia didn't say anything, just shrugged. She kept her head down as she came closer to the car and handed him her racket. He shoved it in the backseat while she climbed into the front with not so much as a smart comment or greeting.

When he got behind the wheel he turned to her, but Alicia was looking out of the passenger side window. Her shoulders were stooped and that urge to make her forget everything bad in her life came back stronger than ever.

She was shivering. He turned on the engine so the heater would warm her before he asked, 'Are you OK?'

'Yes, I just didn't sleep very well.'

The distant tone made him push when he probably should have dropped it. 'Nightmares?'

Her eyes slid shut. 'Something like that.'

'Tell me. You never know, it might make you feel better.' But she faced him then and he caught a glimpse of how red and puffy her eyes were. 'Jesus, Alicia. What happened?'

'Nothing, I'm fine. Can we just get this over with? I have a job to do afterwards.'

He took the hint and put the car in gear. But that didn't stop him from wanting to ask what the hell had happened to upset her. But she was right not to tell him. It was none of his business and if things were to progress between them, going down the road of telling each other everything would only confuse what kind of relationship they'd have. He could do flings, he could do fun, but he just wasn't made for steady or long-term. All his life he'd moved from one country to another, leaving behind people he cared about. Permanent didn't suit the career he'd chosen, no matter how much he craved stability, and it was time he accepted that.

Alicia pulled her fleece off and left it on the bench, barely registering the chilly temperature of the gym. She was too numb inside for that.

After he'd taken her home the night before, she'd gone straight to bed, hoping her emotional overload at the party and the almost-kiss in the car would mean she'd fall into a dreamless sleep within seconds.

If only she'd been that lucky.

Instead, she'd relived the day everything in her life had gone so horribly wrong. If she was honest it had crashed down before that, when she'd let things with Darrell progress to the next level. A shudder ran through her and she hugged her elbows to hide it.

But Sebastian frowned at her. There was no fooling him, it seemed.

He wore a long-sleeved polo shirt, probably because the whole of London was covered in a sheet of frost. Still, she hadn't shivered because she was cold. On the outside, anyway.

Before she could register what he was doing, Sebastian tugged his shirt off. Slicked with his sweat or dry, she'd never seen a body that impressive before. Not in real life, anyway.

'What are you doing?' she asked. Surely he wasn't going to play half-naked?

'Put this on,' he said, tossing the material to her.

She caught it and watched him rummage around in his bag. He pulled out another top, then two bottles of water. The smell of him clung to the shirt in her hands and she knew when her heartbeat increased that she should give it back. But it was warm from his body and her arms seemed to make the decision for her. Pulling it on, she bit her lip to stop a moan from escaping.

The shirt was far too big – she had to roll the sleeves up and it was so long it hid her shorts. But it was warm, smelled like his aftershave, and those complaints became pathetic in comparison to how she felt wearing it.

Sebastian winked. 'See, all better.'

She turned away, not wanting him to see how true his statement was. The numbness was fading slowly, giving her senses back. Now, adrenaline rocked through her veins while heat pulsed at her core. The way she felt near him never seemed to dull, not even a little.

Alicia was beginning to think it never would.

'You should serve, I'm rusty.' She took her phone out of her pocket, switched it to silent, and left it on top of her fleece. When she grabbed her racket and walked over to the court she didn't see it light up with a call. All she could see was his flexing muscles as he put on the other shirt.

Sebastian then pulled off his tracksuit bottoms, making her swallow. He had shorts on beneath but it didn't stop her getting a glimpse of his muscled rear. Or thighs more suited to a football player. As her core temperature scorched she wondered if accepting his top was a good idea. She was already close to sweating, was well on her way to panting, and they hadn't even started yet!

He grabbed a ball and his racket, then jogged over to the court. She stayed in the far box, trying to think through the fluster that hit her seeing him without a shirt. He moved to the box at the opposite side, then tossed the ball in the air.

Alicia grabbed the racket with both hands, remembering the power of his swings the other day when she'd walked in on him training. But Sebastian just caught the ball, then threw it in the air and caught it again.

'I thought we were going to play,' she said.

His eyes darkened – she could see it all the way across the court and too late she realised what the words could be construed as.

'We can play if you like, Blondie, but I thought you were the one who always insisted on work, work, and more work?'

His grin was of someone who knew he was pushing her buttons and it took every ounce of willpower to act like a lady instead of letting her annoyance have its way with her tongue. 'Have you forgotten how to serve?'

The smile that followed made her heart stutter.

'And to think I was worried I'd miss out on my daily dose of smack talk.'

This time he got into position for an underhand serve, the easiest shot there was. It would make setting up her next move as simple as a stroll down the street. At first it made her more annoyed, but then it occurred to her that if he was going to underestimate her this early, it could be fun proving him wrong. After all, how many people had ever gotten the chance to get a few points past Collins at the top of his game?

'I'm no stranger to smack talk,' she said. Hardly true, not when her parents had forbidden it at their games, but she'd watched her brother play with his friends when she'd been little, and heard language that should never be spoken in front of a lady.

He tossed the ball then went straight for the underarm swing. She could predict where it would touch down, a foot or so in front of her. All she had to do was step forward and volley it back, but she didn't want to let him know how insultingly easy he was making it for her.

Instead, she staggered back a few steps, watched the ball bounce off the floor a meter away, then bolted to the side for what should have looked like a last-minute lucky swing.

With the set-up, it didn't make much of an impact on his side and he returned the swing easily. After a few more sets she'd lost two, built up a light sweat, and was ready to rub his nose in his assumptions so they could really start to play – though that might mean he buried her, at least he'd have to admit she wasn't an uncoordinated idiot.

On her serve she went for an overhead, ignoring his raised eyebrows and 'Careful you don't pull something, Blondie.'

Aiming for a spot just before the line at the far end of his box, she tossed the ball and swung with all the strength she had. To see his eyes widen a little before he tore across the court made her grin like an idiot. The backhanded swing he was forced into didn't have the same kind of power, which made getting into position easy, and then she put everything she had into the return.

Sebastian was fast, and watching those thick muscles on his legs move him like the wind was all she could concentrate on. He missed the shot, as she knew he would, but he didn't say anything at first – just stared at the spot where the ball hand landed as if he couldn't believe what had happened.

Alicia couldn't hold back any longer. 'Next time you patronise me by playing like a five-year-old, I'll make the bitch slap sting twice as hard.'

'You'd think I'd have learned by now not to underestimate you,' he mumbled, then went after the ball.

Her mood lifted even higher, completely freeing her from the remnants of her dream. She darted over to the benches, removed his shirt, and took a long drink from one of the water bottles. This time she didn't think he would go easy on her, not if it meant risking his ego.

She needed to be ready.

'Do you need a time out, Blondie?' he asked, and she guessed it was supposed to be a way to tease her into action. But his voice was too deep and his gaze was riveted to her torso.

She looked down, wondering what was wrong with a white vest. It wasn't see-through and her nipples were well hidden behind the light padding of her bra. But from this angle she caught a glimpse of her cleavage and realised it wasn't actually her torso he was staring at, but her breasts.

The knowledge should have annoyed her, but she couldn't collect the appropriate ire. She liked his gaze on her – which was exactly why she should put the shirt back on. But she knew she'd have to work harder for the next game, and she was already sweating.

'Pig,' she called, making her way back to the far box.

'We're onto insults now?' he asked with a grin that she was beginning to dread.

'Felt like the moment called for it. How about you focus on the game?' She smirked when he met her eyes.

'It's hard to when you decide to wear that top, it barely hides anything. Or was that part of your ploy?' he said, raising one eyebrow.

'My ploy?'

He nodded. 'Get a point past me so I up my game, then distract me with your little flimsy top.'

After the almost-kiss last night, Alicia doubted anything she did would distract him too much – he'd barely even flushed while she'd been panting hard, like he was touching her. Of course, admitting that would be like admitting how he affected her.

Instead she said, 'Not everyone uses sexuality as a weapon and if you must know, this is what I wear to the gym.'

'Treadmill?' he asked.

Her brows pulled together but then she got what he meant. Breasts jiggling. Not very mature, but still, she had to smother a giggle. 'And you wondered why I called you a pig?'

The only reaction she got was a small smile, like something had secretly pleased him. She couldn't imagine the insult had done it, but didn't have time to think about it because Sebastian's serve was a doozy. She kept up through three games despite losing a few more points, but with the endorphins spreading through her from the workout and the adrenaline pumping from the challenge, she didn't care much about keeping score.

Sebastian did, rubbing it in her face every time he won another point. When she got another sneaky shot by him, she said, 'I thought you were supposed to be a pro.'

That's when he really started playing. Alicia didn't have half the endurance or a fraction of the skill he did, and called for a time out ten minutes in. She was panting, shaking, and her tongue was drier than the Sahara.

This time he'd built up a bit of a sweat and as they went for a drink, he pulled his shirt off. If she thought her tongue had been dry before, it was nothing compared to now. Her throat seemed to have closed and her already fast heartbeat seemed to go double time. She grabbed a drink and the towel he offered her, then took a seat on the bench.

The muscles in her legs were throbbing like she'd just broken her personal distance record on the treadmill and kept going, and her arms throbbed with the effort it had taken to hit the ball back as hard and fast as she could.

Sebastian, on the other hand, was barely out of breath.

'I don't think I can keep up with you.'

His grin was wicked. 'I'm sure you could if the motivation was different.'

She couldn't believe he was flirting with her when every inch of her skin was damp with perspiration. Maybe that was just him. He was a 'see women, flirt with women' kind of man. That, more than anything, reminded her she should steer clear. Not like her dream hadn't been warning enough. Guys didn't stick around for the real stuff. When the going got tough, they left her.

Not that she'd wanted to blame Darrell at first. They were young and he had her convinced her father was a monster. Until she got home and found her father in bed more beaten than her ex had been, a doctor tending to the cuts and bruises on his face. That had been the wake-up call she needed to start mending her broken heart. Darrell had made her fall hard and left her to deal with the pain alone, but more than anything she could never forgive him for what he did to her father – she couldn't even forgive herself.

And then when she started to show and her father found out about the rest …

'Are you ever going to tell me what that dream was about?' Sebastian asked.

She snapped out of her thoughts and realised she was hugging the towel to her chest. After swiping her face, she tried to find the light, carefree feeling she'd had on the court but it was no use. The endorphins were fading fast, and the drop in adrenaline was making her shake.

'Alicia, what's wrong?'

He stood, then came so close she could smell his musky scent. She could feel his body heat, see all those fabulous muscles, and for once she welcomed the slow burning in her core. He wrapped his arms around her and held her so close she didn't know where her sweat ended and his began, but it didn't matter. She buried her nose in his neck and let him whisper comforting words in her ear, all the while rubbing his hands up and down her spine.

For a silly moment she pretended that he did care, really care about her. Not just as his publicist. If he did, she'd be able to press her palms flat against his abs, feel the definition and warmth, and slide them over his chest. He'd bend his head, brush his lips against hers once, then devour her mouth like he'd been starved for it.

Heat flooded between her legs until she throbbed to have more of the fantasy. But sex was all he was offering, he'd never promised more. And didn't that make him different from Darrell? Safer, even. Or was she still looking for excuses to give into a part of her she should have destroyed long ago?

Sebastian was learning a lot about himself today. Like how he should never assume anything about Alicia. It would only end in an arse-kicking – verbal or on the court.

He also learned that he didn't listen to reason, not even his own. So much for drawing boundaries between them. He couldn't help it when he saw her mood shift and turn sad, couldn't help pulling her into her arms and offering comfort he had no business giving.

Which should have led to another problem, because having Alicia in his arms, all sweaty, soft, and willing, was *not* helping the sexual frustration that built whenever she was close. But he learned that sending a mental warning to his cock that if it misbehaved in any way he'd make sure it lost its two best friends actually worked.

She stiffened in his arms, then pulled away. The confusion and fear in her eyes made him wonder what was going on in that pretty head of hers. Though he wanted to pull her close again, her stance was so rigid he thought he might break her. What the hell had happened between last night and this morning to freak her out this much?

'I should go. I need to get ready for work.' She picked up her fleece and her phone clattered to the floor.

He bent down to pick it up. 'We've barely started.'

'It's almost noon, Sebastian.' She took her phone from him and checked the screen.

Her frown made his heart beat a little faster.

'What is it?'

'Missed calls from Maine. Lots of them.' She pressed a few buttons then put the phone to her ear.

He watched her expression and wished she'd put the thing on loudspeaker. This couldn't be good. 'You did tell them you were coming here today?'

'I'm on flexi-time so it shouldn't be a problem,' she whispered, then louder she said, 'Sarah, what's going on?'

The flush colouring her cheeks seemed to drain away until she was whiter than she'd been when he'd picked her up earlier. Now the skin around her eyes was grey, underlined with dark circles and he wished again she'd tell him what had happened. It couldn't have been the way he'd almost kissed her in the car. If anything, he should get a gold medal for his restraint and the acting skills it took to pretend pulling away wasn't the hardest thing in the world at that moment.

But an almost-kiss wouldn't make her this miserable, would it?

Sebastian wondered if her father had called again – maybe even laid down a few ultimatums. At first he didn't think anyone could be so reserved. But that was before the party last night. To think he envied people like her growing up for having a home, stability, and a family who were always around. It seemed both he and Alicia got the raw end of both deals.

'What?' she said, then after a pause, 'Which magazine?'

Great. Just fucking fantastic. The missed calls were about some other woman doing a tell-all story. As anger pounded into him he fisted his hands at his side, wishing there was something hard and concrete within punching distance. When would it all stop?

'OK, yes, I'll tell him.' She ended the call and seemed to morph into the woman he'd met on day one. The publicist who was all business and hadn't been shaking in his arms a few seconds ago.

'Tell me.' He wasn't in the mood for candy-coated bullshit.

Alicia didn't hesitate. '*Taylor Made* magazine have just started a feature called "The Beginning of the End". Mai's story is kicking it off.'

No surprise there. He'd let her keep their house, the car he'd bought her, and even what was left in their joint account. Still, it was never going to be enough for her. She was going to keep picking away at him until she'd bled every penny she could.

Sebastian sat down on the bench, then wiped himself down with the towel. Now the dampness was starting to dry, the cool air was working goosebumps onto his skin.

'Sebastian, did you hear what I said?' she asked.

He stared at her for a moment, seeing she'd pulled together that prim reserve that he hated right now more than ever.

'Crystal clear.' And he wasn't just talking about Mai's story. Play time was obviously over and that stung more than the thought of whatever Mai had dreamt up.

After slipping her phone into her pocket she said, 'I need to get back to the office and come up with something to discredit this.'

She didn't look at him before she headed for the door. He was about to tell her not to bother before she left, that Mai wasn't worth the effort but his ex's latest story could be what pushed his sponsors over the edge, and where would he be then? Plus, he had hired Alicia to do the job. He should let her.

'Keep me updated,' he called.

At the exit she turned to nod once, then she was gone.

Chapter Ten

'Is he here?' Alicia asked Sarah when she arrived at Maine.

Sarah shook her head. 'He has a meeting in the West End all afternoon.'

She closed her eyes for a second, grateful that she didn't have to put up with her boss on top of everything else. 'Thank God. Why didn't we know about this? I thought we had contacts at the magazine?'

'I just got off the phone with them – it went straight to the editor. No one wanted the idea to leak in case someone else picked it up. They have an exclusive with Mai for the next month.'

'Do you have a copy?' she asked.

Sarah handed her the magazine. She squished down whatever feelings she had for Collins and read the piece like someone who didn't know him would. It was harder than she'd thought, reading about his romantic proposal after months of Mai barely getting to see him and then the kiss with his partner at the mixed doubles at Wimbledon. Once she'd pushed aside the sting of jealousy, all she felt was compassion.

For Mai.

This was worse than she'd feared.

Alicia rapped her fingers against the reception desk and tried to think of a way to counter this. He was going to be hated by the public by the end of the series, and why would anyone want to back him then?

'I need to leak something to the press, something to give people another perspective on Sebastian. Do you think Sam could do something like that?' she asked, the idea cementing in her mind.

'I don't see why not. Do you want me to call him now?'

'I need to get some things together. Ask him to come here in an hour.' She started towards the corridor, mentally going over the papers she had here. Most were at home, but she could whip up an article for him to give to one of the bigger papers. It would mean there would be more interest in them and she'd have to be careful about being seen at the office, but she could work from home for a while.

'Will do. But, Alicia?'

She glanced back at Sarah.

Her friend had that look that said she could smell gossip a mile off. 'When did you stop calling him Collins?'

She almost said just before the first time he kissed her, but that would only open her up to questions she didn't want to answer. Instead she shrugged. 'Sebastian's his name.'

Sarah smirked. 'And the flush you're sporting is from playing tennis with him, not … well, you know?'

Her cheeks burned and she turned away. She called over her shoulder, 'Of course it is!' Then bolted down the hall to her office before Sarah jumped to any more conclusions.

One hour of happiness was all Mai got after she opened the magazine, saw her picture and payback against her ex. She'd woken Jack and insisted he read the whole thing, expecting him to be happy for her. Instead, she'd seen for the first time how angry he could be. After reading the article, he'd told her to get out while he calmed down.

Two days on and he hadn't spoken much to her, other than one-word answers every time she was brave enough to ask him a question. But she forgot about Jack and his mood the second she picked up the paper this morning.

There was a picture with Sebastian and the frumpy blonde kissing outside the restaurant, and a story saying there was evidence to suggest Sebastian and his new woman were working on their own charity to give children who couldn't afford it training from professionals to progress into a career in tennis.

It would ruin everything! How could the media even entertain this desperate attempt at cleaning up his reputation? It was ludicrous. He was a liar and a cheat who deserved every bad thing that happened to him.

And she deserved her vengeance.

She wished she hadn't called that reporter when she saw him and his new girlfriend going to lunch together – then maybe the stories printed wouldn't contradict everything she said.

Glancing at the closed door of their bedroom, she wanted to go in and find comfort in Jack's arms, but she'd pissed him off enough and he hated being interrupted when he was working on a story.

She had to find another, more solid way to discredit Sebastian. Something that would make the public believe her and keep the media attention coming.

Then the perfect solution occurred to her and she had to laugh at herself for not thinking of it sooner. It might piss off Jack a little, but he was already mad at her so what could it hurt?

Anyway, he'd soon forgive her when she finally made enough money that they could get married and finally have their happy ever after!

Still, she had to be careful. Her contract with *Taylor Made* meant she could only give them an exclusive – but the press followed Sebastian like bloodhounds, so it wouldn't be too difficult to pull her plan off.

To: Sebastian
From: Alicia

Sebastian,
The final draft of the press release for the charity is attached and everything is set up for the launch. We still need to think of a title. The Collins Campaign/Foundation/Trust? Let my secretary know your thoughts.

Kind regards,
Alicia Simpson
Publicist, Maine PR

Sebastian scowled at his smartphone. He hadn't spoken to her in days. All communication had been via emails.

Alicia had issued a schedule for the upcoming week now they'd leaked the news about the charity and given his fans something to consider other than Mai's stories.

It was a pity he couldn't think about much else. God, she'd bared her soul in those articles and his perception had shifted so much that his dreams were laced with guilt.

Now he'd been slotted in for two hours with Alicia at a press release to launch his new charity, then they would spend a few hours at the club opening. He would work the first day himself, with a retired pro who was friends with his dad taking over for the next few weeks for a small fee. Pennies in comparison to the way it would boost his likeability and hopefully make his sponsors renew their contracts.

He was impressed with what she'd managed to put together so quickly, but the attempt at professional distancing was getting on his nerves. He'd tried calling her and it went to voicemail or her secretary had taken messages. He'd visited her flat a few times but she'd either ignored the door or wasn't home – though where she could be when the media were hounding them night and day was a mystery.

Today, driven by the frustration to end this crap, he'd shaken off the press and walked through the open doors of her office. It was risky for her to be there but it would be the last place the media would look and he was certain he hadn't been followed.

The receptionist's jaw went slack and he forced a smile he hoped looked easy, but didn't stop to say hello. Marching through the corridors, he found her office. The door was open a crack and he heard her voice. His frustration melted under the current of adrenaline flaring beneath his skin. The swirl in his chest made him realise how much he'd missed teasing her, seeing her eyes flare with irritation and arousal.

'Sylvia, *please*. I need you to do this for me. Sebastian is busy training but Father wants him at the party and he won't listen to me.'

Gently, he pushed the door open further. She was resting her face in her palm, holding the phone to her ear, and he couldn't help wonder what party they were talking about. The whole point of this charade was to prove they were together and one evening wasn't going to knock him off his game.

'Because it's intense. He can't miss two days this close to a tournament and I don't think Father's tennis courts are suitable, since none of us can play very well.'

Her father had tennis courts? This he had to see. Sebastian cleared his throat and her head snapped up.

'I can miss a day or two, honey,' he said, loud enough for the person on the other end of the line to hear. 'I want to meet your family.'

The flare of irritation lit her eyes as she glared at him. 'Yes, that's him ... You're right, we'll see you next weekend then.' Alicia slammed the phone down. 'What are you doing?'

'I could ask you the same thing.' He closed the door,

shutting them in the office. 'Firing digital instructions to me and having a photographer follow me around is not what I had in mind when I hired Maine PR.'

'It's the only way this can work. Being together is a bad idea and this way we won't be tempted.'

He forced his teeth apart. 'It's ridiculous for you to think we can just be colleagues when we've got chemistry most people would kill for.'

'I hardly think any civilised human would kill to have a great spark. Sex isn't that life-altering.' She crossed her arms, daring him to argue with her skewed ideals.

He dared. 'Oh, Blondie. It is when it's done right.' Throwing in a suggestive smile for good measure, he made his way to her desk. 'Are all those aristocrats your family have thrown at you been selfish lovers?'

Her chin dropped, but she composed herself quickly. 'This conversation is inappropriate!'

She rose, hands on the desk like she needed the support. He could see her chest rise and fall beneath the boxy shirt which he really shouldn't have found sexy, but the image of her curves and her long legs from that day he trained with her was imprinted in his brain. As her anger flared, so did his, along with something hotter and more exciting. It was like having his ass whipped on the court, but also like winning at Wimbledon.

'I don't think it is. We're together in front of the camera, why not enjoy that arrangement behind the scenes too?'

Obviously training would be gruelling, but he was at the stage where instead of falling into bed exhausted, he had all this restless energy. So much so he'd been playing a friendly game or two at nights with a mate. Surely she felt the same? Her expression was easy to read and every time they'd been close he saw how much she wanted him.

'We could take advantage of the chemistry until –'

'No,' she said, though he could see the flare of

arousal in her eyes.

'OK, give me one good, solid reason.' He relaxed back into a chair. This would take a while, there wasn't one and she knew it.

'One? I have hundreds. Take your pick!' She retrieved a beige file bursting with papers from the side of her desk and flicked it open. '"My cheating ex gave me chlamydia", "Collins harassed me for months", "Golden boy of tennis broke my new boyfriend's nose", "Collins scores 15 women in under a month". Tell me when you've had enough.'

His heart hammered and his jaw hurt from clenching his teeth, but the pain didn't dull the anger. Nor did the way his fingers dug into his thighs hard enough to leave bruises. He'd been right that first day. Alicia believed every poisonous word that came out his ex's mouth.

And he knew most women believed it, but they were seduced by his 'bad boy' image or what they could make from telling the world about the night they bedded him. Who he was as a person never crossed their minds and until now, he had accepted that was what his life would be like. He had needs like any other red-blooded male, and after the trainwreck that was his relationship with Mai, he knew his dream of having a home and someone who'd always be there for him would never happen.

With Alicia, she'd wanted him because of her attraction to *him* despite whatever ridiculous excuse she had. Not his money or fame or the kiss-and-tell she'd get out of it.

Now he knew why she'd been fighting it so hard. She thought he was the lowest of the low. A scumbag who cheat, beat, and stalked. The adrenaline took on a different edge now, a dangerous one. Worse than the day his fist connected with that bastard Jack's nose. Except the spin had been he wouldn't let Mai move on and be happy. Nothing could have been further from the truth.

He had to get out of there before he hit something. At

the door he paused, then turned around. She clutched an article in one hand. For the most part, she had the prim, cool exterior back, looking too poised and calm. It was the ruffled paper in her fist that gave her away.

He hesitated, wondering if he should tell her the truth, but she wouldn't believe him – she'd already accused him of lying. There was no point. She only cared about what everyone else thought. 'God forbid you ever fall off that pedestal of yours and have to slum it down here in the real world.'

'Excuse me?' Her knuckles whitened, the only visible chink in her aloof stance.

'It's not all manners and missionary position at Christmas and birthdays. Life's there to be lived, however the hell you want, no holds barred. Don't wait until you're forty and married to a man who bores you to tears to open your eyes.'

The mask she wore slipped, but he didn't wait to hear how pissed off she was. He left the building on a jog, not stopping until he was well on his way to building up a sweat. His phone vibrated in his jeans and his heart leapt into his throat. By the time he'd fished it out of his front pocket, a few rings had passed. Not wanting to let her go to voicemail, he answered without checking the screen.

'Look, I'm sorry –'

'Kid, this isn't one of your women.'

Tony's resigned tone froze him to the spot. People must have had to skirt around him on the street but he didn't care. If his manager was angry it would mean something happened that could be fixed by throwing the F bomb at it. Resignation? Sebastian swallowed hard. 'What happened?'

'I've just got off the phone with the sports company. They've pulled the plug, Sebastian. There was nothing I could do.'

The buzz in his head that had stalked him for months before Christmas returned and a cold sweat broke out over his skin. 'They're my biggest sponsor.'

Which meant the bar job could be a possibility if anyone else walked. Just when he thought his day couldn't get any worse.

'I'm sorry, kid. I really am. Whatever Maine have planned, you need to push it harder and faster. You can't afford to lose the others.'

He scrubbed a shaking hand down his face, willing himself to relax, but the pressure in his head only got worse.

'I'll tell them.' Ending the call, he glanced around the street filled with people going about their everyday lives. Numbness settled like a chill deep inside. This was it. The beginning of the end.

'Hey, handsome. It's been too long.'

Sebastian didn't need to turn around to know who was behind him. Just when he thought nothing worse could happen, fate waited till he was on the ground then kicked him full force in the balls.

Chapter Eleven

She was an awful person.

No, she was much worse. She was a class-A snob. Possibly worse than her father. The guilt twisting her insides was proof of that. She'd poured a glass of wine the second she got home and slumped onto the sofa, wondering if she was the one with the drinking problem, and not Sebastian as all those articles had pointed out.

Didn't she think that the man who'd gone shopping with her couldn't be the man his ex had made him out to be? She'd believed him when he told her he hadn't slept with the twins in Melbourne and was even starting to believe he really hadn't thought about the kiss-and-tell when they were working on the press release. After all, he hadn't landed her in it during his interview with Claire.

In fact, if he told her the truth behind what the papers had reported in the headlines she'd reeled off, she'd probably believe him then too. But he didn't, and Alicia suspected that was because she'd hurt him by giving them as reasons why she couldn't enjoy some beneath the sheets time with him, when that wasn't the case at all.

It was her past that was holding her back. The person she so desperately tried to be was not who she really was, which terrified her. She couldn't cope if her father cut her off from her sisters, her mother. That would be too cruel. But her father believed she was with Sebastian now. The risk of that happening if she consummated their fake relationship wouldn't change a thing with her family.

But it could risk so much more.

Her mobile chimed and when she saw Sarah's number she was tempted to let it go to voicemail. She didn't want anyone else to know how horrible she'd been today. With a sigh, she changed her mind. It could be work.

'Hi, Sarah.'

'Alicia, have you heard? I've just taken a message from Collins' manager. His biggest sponsor pulled.'

Oh God. Before or after she'd castrated him? Her skin broke out in a cold sweat and her hands shook. Guilt? She never knew the meaning of the word until now. This was her fault for not moving forward quick enough, refusing to spend more time with him than necessary and now he was suffering.

'You there?' Sarah asked.

'Do you know what happened?' She did. His sponsors believed Mai's story and assumed some of his fans had too.

She hadn't pushed her plan hard enough, fast enough. She rubbed her eyes.

'Not about the sponsors, but I called David's brother and he's on Collins' tail. Apparently your tennis player is dressed for a night on the town.'

She gasped. 'Is he *insane*? A bender is the last thing he needs!'

Putting the call on speaker, she darted to her bedroom and lay her mobile face up on the bed, tugging off her clothes like they were doused in acid.

'He must be stressed. I can't imagine what he's going through.' Sarah's voice was so soft she barely heard her, but was rewarded with a fresh stab of guilt anyway.

'I need to know where he is, and what kind of shoes go with a green silk and black lace prom dress.' She tugged out the material and remembered the way Sebastian's eyes had darkened when she'd walked out of the dressing room. He'd teased her about scrubbing up

OK, but his voice had been too rough. She'd never dreamed back then he'd wanted her as much as she was starting to want him.

'Um, how about black stilettos? Though it's cold out. Ooo, do you have any of those shoe boots with the spiky heels?'

Alicia didn't feel the excitement that was in Sarah's voice at the prospect of shoes. She pulled out a box with a pair Sebastian had picked for her. 'The ones that are high at the front with a buckle at the heel? Oh, wait, these are peep toes.'

'Perfect! Yes, that's them. I'll text you when I know where he is. Go put those peep toes to use and give Collins a kick up the arse.'

Alicia bit her lip. She had a bit of grovelling to do before any arse kicking. 'Thanks.'

'No problem. And Alicia? Smoky eyes with nude, shiny lips.'

'Got it.'

She ended the call, slipped on her shoes, then upended her make-up bag. All she had was light pink lip gloss and a grey eyeshadow, which would have to do. After plugging in her curling wand, she used it on the ends of her hair and by the time she was done, Sarah had texted her Sebastian's location.

Alicia walked into the classy wine bar in Soho and was glad she'd made the effort to dress up. It oozed class, and everyone she passed looked like they'd jumped straight off the runway. She didn't pay much attention to them as she anxiously scanned the bar for Collins. He was with a dark-haired siren in a red dress perched on a stool next to him.

His back was to Alicia, but even she could see he was focused straight ahead instead of listening to whatever the scarlet flirt was saying. She approached, spying her photographer, Sam, a few chairs down with a frown on his face. He was clearly struggling with his morals. Getting a picture worth selling was why she'd given him access to her and Sebastian, but whatever picture he snapped now would end that deal. Unless …

A plan started to form as she crossed the room. She pulled on her best smile and made her way to the side of Sebastian which was scarlet-free. Both hands cupped a glass, and while the woman prattled on, his gaze was fixed on the bottled spirits lining the wall behind the bar.

Alicia reached out with fake confidence to touch his forearm. He turned to her with a frown, then his lips parted in shock.

'Sorry I'm late, sweetie. Do you want another drink?' she asked.

'Who are you?' The brunette peered around Sebastian with a look that said Alicia was not welcome.

A twinge of jealousy made her want to forget her manners, but she refrained. Instead, she slid an arm behind Sebastian's back, hoping he wasn't still so mad he'd call her out, and moved so she was flush against his side.

She smiled at Sebastian and tried to force an apology into her eyes. 'Introduce us?'

His gaze dipped down to her chest, then he swallowed. This dress was the most revealing she had, flashing more than a hint of cleavage. Heat swirled through her veins at his brief appraisal, and when he met her eyes again, his were melting. No doubt hers were too. In his dark, silver shirt and his hair all mussed-up, he looked better than chocolate to her eyes.

'This is Alicia, my girlfriend,' he said to the brunette, barely sparing her a glance. Instead, his gaze returned to Alicia's lips. 'I'm sorry, *sweetie*, I didn't catch her name.'

His breath brushed her face and Alicia sagged a little when all she could smell was a hint of mint toothpaste. But it fanned the fire low in her stomach, so much so the visions of him and her, wild and sweaty, came back. But this time, she had control.

She'd already offended him enough today, accusing him of things she knew deep down couldn't be one hundred per cent true. Kissing him now would be like slapping him in the face since she said she didn't want to get involved with him. Pity she couldn't believe the lie herself.

'Do you want to get a booth?' She'd spied a few near the back when she arrived.

He nodded, his eyes narrowing slightly. 'What would you like to drink?'

Lowering her voice so the rejected brunette wouldn't hear, she said, 'A bit of Dutch courage would be nice about now.'

That got a little smile from him, but it was short-lived. He ordered her a glass of white wine, then led her to a booth at the back. Sebastian didn't say anything when she slid in next to him, just turned so he could study her face.

Her cheeks flushed a little at the scrutiny and she wasn't sure if he was still mad at her, or curious as to why she was there, though the photographer's presence made the latter obvious. She thought he'd gone off the rails and he knew it. Now she had to apologise since what he'd ordered was mineral water with a slice of lime.

'Sebastian, I'm so sorry. About what I said in my office, and for tonight.'

He frowned. 'Why tonight?' Alicia reached for her wine, but he caught her wrist and shook his head. 'This time we're dealing without drink. We both know that leads to bad things.'

'Then why buy me wine?' she asked to dodge his other question.

His smirk wasn't like his other smiles; it too mocking to settle her nerves. 'You first.'

Licking her lips and swallowing against the lump in her throat, she wondered what she should tell him. But if they were going to move on and help him keep the rest of the sponsors, they had to be honest with each other.

'Before, when I pitched to you, I thought I could do this and not care whether any of the stories were true. Some I believed, but others were a bit far-fetched. After spending time with you I doubted them even more. Today was me trying to deflect your, um, suggestion. I didn't mean to hurt you.'

He ran a hand through his hair and blew out a breath. 'That's not what I asked.'

She shrugged. 'You have to know all the whys to get the full picture, wasn't it you who told me that?'

His smile returned. It was easier this time, and relaxed her. 'I did.'

'So that was deflection. I'd still like to know what happened the day you were filmed kissing that woman when you were engaged to Mai, and if there's anything else about you that might come out now. It will help me catch things before they go public, or at least come up with a counter story. And tonight, Sarah called to say you'd lost a sponsor and that Sam saw you dressed for a night out. I was worried.'

His knuckles whitened as he squeezed the glass. 'You're worried I'll embarrass you.'

It wasn't a question, and he turned away from her. The flare of hope that he'd forgiven her was snuffed out.

'That never crossed my mind.' She waited until she was sure she had his attention. 'I was worried about *you*. You've come so far, you've been working hard every day, and I didn't want that to go to waste because you were looking for a way to deal with stress. Me? When I'm down or have too much on my plate, I reach for wine to help me forget. I'm not judging, I just want to help. It's what you're paying me to do. But more than that, *I want to*.'

His brows furrowed. 'I don't need your help, Alicia. Really, I'm fine. See,' he lifted his glass and shoved it under her nose. 'Water.'

But there was an edge to him, one that hadn't been there when he'd walked into her office earlier. His eyes looked strained at the corners. 'You're not OK, though. Are you?'

Sebastian shrugged. 'I knew this was coming, just didn't expect it so fast, you know?'

She took his hand, entwined her fingers with his, and ignored the way he frowned down at the connection. She wanted to offer comfort, wanted to fix this and not just because it was her job, but because part of her knew he didn't deserve *all* the bad hype – he'd made mistakes but that didn't mean he had to lose everything.

And he wasn't as bad as she'd originally labelled him. He helped her with Mr Maine when he could have walked, he'd cared enough to give her a lift home when she saw someone snooping outside the party. He'd tried to cheer her up that day she trained with him when he had no reason to. He could have just flirted with the aim of getting her into bed, but she got the feeling it went deeper than that.

Not many people would have done any of it, never mind a guy with his reputation.

'I have a plan,' she said.

His smile made her heart stutter. 'I'm listening.'

Sebastian watched as Alicia dragged the photographer over and gave him a story to sell as well as the promise of pictures of the two of them together. He had to admit, hiring Blondie was the best decision he'd made for a while.

The guy got the lowdown on how Sebastian had taken his new girlfriend out for a few hours – while, of course, he stuck to mineral water – as a surprise after a week of intense training.

She also worked in an angle that he turned down several come-ons, telling those women he was spoken for and apologising before sending them on. Sam was almost positive he could get the story into one of the national papers by the end of the night, kicking off more good press about Sebastian. He just hoped the news of his sponsor pulling the plug didn't hit the headlines first.

Or that the very public argument he'd had with Mai on the street outside Maine PR earlier wouldn't get uncovered. He'd been so frazzled he hadn't checked they were alone, and when she'd tried to touch him … Sebastian fisted his hand around the glass so hard he was surprised it didn't crack.

Alicia glanced at him, a concerned line appearing between her eyebrows. The rage seemed to seep out of him just as quickly as it had bubbled. He squeezed her hand to let her know he was fine, and she went back to instructing Sam.

When they were alone again, he tugged her closer and lifted her wine. 'I think you've earned this.'

The smile she rewarded him with hit him straight in the chest.

'I don't know, I like having a clear head.'

'Of course.'

He shifted away, giving her more room. Maybe she wasn't fighting her attraction because she believed the rumours, but she still didn't want anything to really happen between them. It looked like he was going to have to relive the nightmare of the last few months and dissect the lies from the truth of every word before she'd trust him – considering she even believed him.

After a day like today, confession was a headache he could do without.

'That's not what I mean. Come on, it's starting soon.' She weaved her fingers through his and tugged. He raised a brow and she grinned. 'Wait for it.'

He was confused for a second, until the music

changed and a modern version of 'The Way You Look Tonight' started playing. He raised both his eyebrows.

'Care to dance, Collins? I'm sure this is the kind of music where you should twirl the daughter of an earl around the dance floor.'

The teasing glint in her eyes worked to clear his head of everything except her. As the buzz faded, he reckoned Miss Prim and Proper turning fun was the best form of painkiller.

'After you,' he said and slid out of the booth behind her.

He took one of her hands and laid it over his heart, before sliding an arm around her waist and clasping her other hand. This close, with her light, citrus fragrance and honey-smeared lips within licking distance, keeping a respectable space between them was mandatory.

Alicia didn't seem to agree. She pressed herself closer so her breasts skimmed his chest, and slid her free hand up to cup his nape. His body reacted in the most visceral way, and he closed his eyes on a curse.

'You OK?' she whispered, her breath brushing his neck and not at all helping with how his trousers were tightening.

'Just thinking about football.' Sweaty men in shorts would cool him off – if his mind didn't keep registering her scent and how the dip in the neck of her dress showed a teasing hint of what lay beneath.

She laughed. 'Football?'

He twirled her around, trying to focus on the more abhorrent image of sweaty men than the lush, sexy curves in his arms. 'It helps when dealing with misbehaving libidos.'

'Oh.'

That one word sounded breathy, and when he opened his eyes he saw why. Alicia trapped lower lip between her teeth and there was a flush scoring high across her cheekbones. He wasn't the only one feeling the spark, but after the fallout today and his meeting with the media whore from his own personal hell, he was in no rush to act on it.

So he shrugged it away, like he wasn't holding off the burning need to taste her with everything he had. 'Like you said, just a blip. I'm sure it will pass.'

'I lied. Well, not lied really. I just repeated what my father said to me once.'

His mouth opened and closed a couple of times, not sure whether he should be pissed on her behalf or horrified. Either way, it helped the issue with his libido. 'What?'

Her skin grew a few shades darker. 'I didn't mean anything … seedy. When I was fifteen I had a boyfriend and …'

She focused on his shoulder as her spine stiffened. He heated up again all right, but had a feeling that the acrid flare in his throat was pure rage. Fifteen? She wasn't even a consenting adult – he couldn't dislike her father for looking out for his daughter.

'Tell me what happened,' he said, but he didn't want the details. Didn't really want to hear it. If some bastard had forced her into something she didn't want to do …

Alicia snuggled closer like she needed the support. He placed her other hand on his shoulder and hugged both arms around her waist, which meant they could only sway a little from side to side, reminding him of school discos where he'd ask girls he barely knew to dance. This was different though, it meant so much more. He just wished she clung to him because she needed him, not just his support.

He shook off the thought. It was crazy, she shouldn't need him. That would just make everything so much harder for her when he left. He didn't want to hurt her. It seemed she'd been hurt enough for one lifetime.

Alicia pressed her cheek into his collarbone, so her breath whispered through the open collar of his shirt, sending a stab of desire through him. Sebastian couldn't help it, he pulled her closer.

'Can we not talk about him? I'm having fun.'

'Whatever you want,' he said, a little relieved even though he wanted to push. Whatever happened must have been bad if it meant she was so desperate to stifle who she was and be the woman her family probably wanted her to be.

She lifted her head to look at him and he could see the fire there, but not the angry kind. This was the girl she hid behind the frumpy suits and prissy tone. This was the Alicia he wanted to get to know better. What made her tick, what that passion was like when it was unleashed – preferably while she was all hot and sweaty and panting beneath him.

But he had to get his mind off that subject. She could have been hurt badly, maybe even abused. The thought brought the rage back and he wanted to hunt down her bastard of an ex and show him what pain really was.

Tilting her face up, she asked, 'Anything?'

The question threw him until he remembered promising she could have anything. She didn't look like a woman who'd been forced to do something she didn't want to by a boy. She looked like a woman full of passion and fire.

His attention zeroed in on her lips and he forgot for a second that she was waiting for an answer. Of course he would give her anything she asked for – as long as she didn't want anything more than he could offer. And especially if she demanded it in that Lady of the Manor voice. Sebastian nodded.

'I want you to kiss me properly. No holds barred.'

He blinked, snapping his focus back to her eyes. They were clear, without a hint that she was joking.

'You're sure? Because if I kiss you like I want to, I don't think I'll be able to stop this time.'

Chapter Twelve

Alicia could see the dark promise in his eyes, and her oversensitive body became more aware of every inch pressed against him. She could feel his solid chest against her breasts, the hard length of him against her lower stomach, and his thick thighs pressed against hers.

She'd been about to tell him what had happened before and the consequences she'd faced for acting, as her father had put it, like a common trollop. But here, being with him, she could see exactly how wrong her father had been.

A woman should be able to sleep with a man because she found him attractive, especially one she trusted and who wanted the same thing as her – a way to enjoy a little of the chemistry buzz for the now. They were both adults, she was on the pill and he could use a condom so the risk of the same thing happening again was moot.

Plus there were no empty promises this time. She knew Sebastian would be focused on his career, which meant he'd be travelling all over the world. Mr Maine would surely take her more seriously and give her more big clients if she salvaged Sebastian's reputation. She'd move up the corporate ladder in Maine PR, proving to her family she wasn't a complete failure.

They only had now, and she wasn't willing to let this opportunity pass her by. Sex with Sebastian would be anything but boring and considerate. She could feel it in the power of the body pressed against her. It would be wild, sweaty, and break the fear she had of her hormones once and for all.

'I've never been surer of anything in my life.' To

prove her point, she fisted her hands in his hair, rose on her tiptoes, and closed the distance between their lips.

The contact was electric, thrumming through every inch of her until her nipples speared his chest. When she opened to him, he kissed her deeply, skilfully, with a raw edge of desperation. His taste was sinful, incomparable with anything she'd ever experienced.

The space between her thighs burned, and Alicia pushed up higher on her toes, rocking her hips into him to find some kind of friction, but he was too tall and it frustrated her so much she groaned.

Sebastian jerked back, his eyes dark, and she went in for more. She needed more.

'Wait.' His breaths came too fast, like her own.

'Why?' she asked. He was enjoying it too. His fingers dug into her hips, holding her so close there wasn't so much as air between them.

Sebastian lowered his head and whispered in his ear. 'I've no idea why you've changed your mind, but that's irrelevant considering we're dry humping in public when you've given that photographer free rein to snap us.'

'You know, I'm a little insulted you can think at all at the moment, never mind worry.' She pouted and he laughed.

'Come on before I change my mind, drag you into the bathroom, and give the photographer something really juicy to snap.'

He took her hand and led her to the exit. All the while, her insides were melting at his dark promise. She'd never done anything naughty in a public place, even as a teenager when she let herself fall head over heels for Darrell.

And right now, Alicia didn't care if they did get caught.

'You'd really have dragged me into the bathroom?' she asked, breathless.

The disbelieving look he threw her was almost funny.

'That turns you on? Who are you and what have you done with Blondie?'

She did laugh then. 'I just realised the new and improved Alicia was a bit of a bore, so I'm working on a better version. This one likes the idea of being dragged off and ravished. Maybe not in a public loo, though.'

He shook his head, any trace of amusement gone. 'You don't have to pretend to be anyone. You're pretty amazing when you're just being you.'

She was glad when he turned away and started walking down the street, because there was no way to hide the well of emotion lighting her up from the inside at what he'd said. No one had ever called her amazing, or said she didn't have to change. It was ironic that the man who did think that was the one she'd been pushing away since she'd met him.

Whatever this was between them couldn't last, but that didn't matter. For the first time in ages she looked sexy, she *felt* sexy, and around Sebastian that was OK because he thought she was sexy.

There were no judgements on how her actions would lower her reputation, nothing but a mutual attraction with a man most women – she had to admit – would kill to have with him. And Alicia wasn't going to throw that away again.

Arthur Simpson didn't believe drinking solved anything, or tempered anyone's emotions. But when he ended the call to the private investigator he'd hired to follow Collins, he headed straight for the cabinet and poured himself a double brandy.

He hoped the smooth liquid would quench the rage burning through him, but had little hope. When it came to his family he knew what was best for them. Daria had listened and she'd ended up with a man who was more than fit to marry a daughter of his. After the engagement party, Sylvia would be matched with a man whose father he respected and had an iron-clad business relationship with.

Alicia, like before, was putting a black mark against his family's name. If he'd cut her out when she was fifteen instead of listening to Juliette he wouldn't have to face the public spectacle she was making of herself now.

And a spectacle was exactly how it was going to turn out if what was discovered today continued.

He swallowed the remainder of his brandy, but it didn't take the edge off his rage. If anything, it made it that much worse. First Collins dared to get close to his whore of an ex in public before he led her away from the street to God only knew where, and now he was embarrassing Alicia – and by extension, Arthur himself – by feeling up his daughter in a club?

His first instinct was to tell Juliette he was going to London to put an end to this, but it was late and she would have retired for the night. Plus, he didn't have long to wait until Alicia brought Collins to the house. Then he would have his chance to rid them of the disrespectful nuisance once and for all.

He would just have to be patient – and it would give him more time to gather enough evidence to convince Alicia to give him up. She may have done as he wished in the past, but he knew she'd grown more headstrong over the years. That she dared to argue with him when he told her to end the relationship was proof enough.

And at this point, Arthur wasn't above fabricating evidence if he had to. After all, he'd done worse to ensure his family name remained untainted.

They didn't talk much as Sebastian led her to his building, a few streets from the club. The tension between them wasn't uncomfortable, but it was underscored with worry that he was pushing her too fast and too hard.

The woman next to him was different from the one

he'd met a few weeks ago, a far cry even from the woman kicking him to the kerb in her office today. As he reached the steps leading up to the door to his building, he dropped her hand and turned to face her.

'You know what happens if we go up there, and I need to know you're ready. Also, I want to be straight with you. This thing between us –'

She pressed a finger against his mouth, a smile on her lips. 'Is temporary. We're focused on different careers that will draw us apart, but you were right. We can't ignore what's between us and I don't want to anymore. I want tonight to happen.'

His throat constricted and a sense of urgency made him speak without thinking. 'We can have more than tonight.'

'Let's see if that ego of yours lives up to the hype before we make any more promises.' She took the key from his hand and climbed the stairs, swinging her hips provocatively. If he didn't know any better he'd swear this was Alicia's twin, not the reserved woman he'd met in Maine's boardroom.

Sebastian caught up to her quickly. 'Be prepared to eat your words, Blondie. My ego's understated, if anything.'

She rolled her eyes. He smirked, then bent to pick her up so his arms were beneath her knees and back. Alicia squeaked a protest, but he silenced her with a kiss. He didn't think he'd get used to her taste, as sweet as honey and more. The way she let down the walls of who she thought she should be when their lips met was almost as good as winning at the Opens.

'Care to do the honours?' he asked, jerking his head toward the door.

She put the key in the lock and twisted, then opened the door. He carried her through, kicking it closed behind him and taking the stairs two at a time with Alicia cradled to his chest.

'You can put me down if you want. I'm not exactly svelte.'

It was his turn to roll his eyes. 'I have more endurance than your average guy, Blondie. We're good for another few flights.'

Her grin was wicked. 'I don't want to tire you out before we get started.'

He rounded the corner and jogged up the next set of stairs, controlling his breathing to prove his point. 'Where you're concerned, I have unlimited reserves of energy. The question is, can *you* keep up with me?'

'Um …'

Her cheeks flushed and her lids dropped, reminding him that though she wanted him, whatever had been holding her back wasn't easy for her to shake. When they reached his floor, he slowed as he carried her down the hall to his front door. Setting her on her feet, he took the keys then tilted her chin.

'We go at your pace, OK? If I go too fast, tell me and I'll slow down.' It wasn't just reassurance for her, he needed to believe he would because he had a feeling the second he got his hands on her behind closed doors, slow would be impossible.

'I don't want to overthink this,' she said, and he could see the desperate plea in her eyes.

He opened the door and let her in, barely giving her a minute to look around. Instead, he pulled her close, pressed his lips back against hers, and groaned when she gripped his hair. Remembering to go slow wasn't easy, especially since Alicia ground her hips against him again and again, making the erection he'd been sporting for the best part of an hour swell back to full capacity.

He slid his hands over her backside and squeezed her closer, but there were too many clothes in the way. Finding the hem, he tugged the dress up and she got the hint, letting go of his hair and helping him pull the material over her head and fall to the floor.

The gym shorts and vest that drove him insane at training was nothing compared to Alicia in a skimpy bra and thong. He caught her hips, rubbing his thumb up and down the silky indentations above her underwear, but it wasn't her body that snagged his attention, it was the hunger in her eyes, the flare of her nostrils, and the flush on her cheeks.

Still, her arms were stiff by her sides, like she was fighting whatever that voice of virtue in her head was telling her, and he couldn't have that. Moving them so she was pressed against the wall, he said, 'Who needs alcohol? I know a better way to forget. Do you want me to show you?'

He was giving her the choice, and although her hormones were screaming yes, standing in front of him almost naked was so unlike how she'd told herself she needed to be that she was torn.

Leaning close to brush his lips against her collarbone was all it took for the fire to smoulder through her, blurring her thoughts until all she could see and feel and smell was Sebastian.

'Let me show you,' he whispered against her throat.

She couldn't speak. Nothing got past her throat except puffs of air. Instead, she nodded, wanting more of what he wanted to do. In a move she barely registered, he'd unclipped her bra and pushed it off her shoulders. The cups fell away and cold air hardened the tips of her breasts. His mouth made its way down her cleavage with little licks and kisses, fanning the flames and making her knees feel bendy.

As soon as his mouth fastened over her nipple, Alicia slumped against the wall. The spark that ignited from that hot, wet suction sent a current between her legs. Sebastian caressed her with his tongue and lips, sucking gently until moans of bliss escaped her throat, but it wasn't enough. The ache between her thighs only got more urgent, and she shuffled forward, trying to get friction where she desperately needed it.

He pinned her back against the wall, taking one of her hands in his. After a final flick of his tongue against her breast, he placed her hand on her stomach, right above her thong, and whispered, 'Show me what you want.'

Panic froze her until his mouth gave her other nipple similar attention. The ache throbbed harder now the cool air hit her other breast. The warmth and cold mixed a cocktail of pure lust and she slid her hand down over her pants, pressing her index finger into the damp fabric at the spot which begged for his touch the most.

A gasp escaped her throat as his finger pressed down on hers harder, swirling the pad of her digit around and around. He kept up the light suction on her nipple, his hair tickling her chest and collarbone as the cocktail mixed and swirled inside her. Their fingers kept up a quick pace that left her gasping, but it still wasn't enough and she pulled at the waistband of her thong.

Sebastian released her then dropped to his knees. She grabbed the table next to them for support as he pulled the material down her legs, never taking his gaze off hers. Her heart beat so hard she felt winded, but at the same time she wanted this more than she'd wanted anything.

His mouth found her clit and she swayed as he mimed the licking and sucking he'd been using on her breasts, right where she needed him to. Then his finger speared her, followed by another, and her hips jerked into his face. The shame that should have engulfed her was lost in a wave of pulsing heat that stole her breath, her voice, and her ability to control her muscles.

Before she could fall, Sebastian scooped her up with her legs around his waist and carried her through to his room. He sat her on the edge of the bed, whipped his shirt over his head, and the sight of his torso, there and hers for as long as she could stay awake, gave her a second wind.

Grabbing his belt buckle, she pulled him closer. With her hands and mouth she explored his chest, licking his flat nipples and suckling them when they grew. Scoring her nails down his abs all the way to his waistband, she heard his groans, revelled in the quick movements of his chest.

Hastily, she undid his belt and buttons and greedily stroked his erection, tracing the thick vein on the underside with her thumb. She shouldn't have fought this. They'd already lost weeks because she refused to give into what she wanted. No more. She was going to take and take until this thing between them had run its course.

'Alicia …' Sebastian groaned as her finger swirled around the tip.

'Shh.' She leaned forward, inhaling that fabulous scent that was all him; male, musky, and totally virile. Closing her lips around the cap of his erection, she fisted the length and swirled her tongue.

A second later she was pinned back on the bed, his hands securing her wrists above her head and his chest heaving against hers. 'You're driving me insane.'

She pursed her lips, feeling a little disappointed she didn't get a chance to knock him off-kilter like he had her, but with his hips nudging his erection very close to where she wanted him, she couldn't protest too much.

'I thought missionary was too boring for you,' she said.

He swooped down and licked her breast, sending a stab of pure need south. 'It has its advantages.'

She shook her head, hiding a smile. 'Come on, surely you can be more creative than that.'

Of course she was teasing. No man had ever stripped her naked in his hallway and had her on the verge of screaming like he did. Only now she was realising there was no shame in that and for the first time in a long time, she didn't feel like what she desired was wrong. This wouldn't end in a broken heart and her father forcing her hand. She'd be careful.

It was like a weight had been lifted and she wanted to do so much more than what she'd been forced to believe a woman shouldn't do with a man, and she wanted to do that with Sebastian.

He rose, dragging her to the edge of the bed, and turned her around. She panicked a little until her feet found purchase on the lush carpet, then she looked over her shoulder. Sebastian tugged his jeans and boxers over his hips, until he stood there, looking down at her rear. His body was all hard lines and sexy angles. Definite chocolate, champagne, and caviar for the eyeballs.

Something cooled the flames inside a few degrees, probably unease at how exposed he had her. She refused to give into it, not now she'd been freed from her past, and wiggled her hips.

Though his eyes darkened, he grinned at her then slapped her bum lightly. Thrill flushed through her veins, heating her erogenous zones and leaving her panting. Sebastian's knowing look as he studied her expression should have embarrassed her. After all, just three weeks ago she'd never consider lying over a bed with her bum in the air enjoying a light spanking, but now …

Now she could. Now she wanted it.

'More,' she demanded.

His lips parted and his eyebrows shot up like he'd never expected her to admit how much she liked what he was doing. Well, he better get used to it because she had years of living like a nun to make up for.

He massaged her flesh, sending tingles up her spine. She bit her lip as she watched him, waiting for his next move and his chocolate eyes melted until they smouldered black.

One hand had barely left her skin before it cracked

down on her flesh again. The shock and sound was worse than the light sting. More thrilling than anything she'd ever experienced. She was about to beg for more, but his fingers slid into her and Alicia buried her face in the covers, hiding a groan while she bucked back into him. She was deliciously full, but not nearly enough. She wanted *him* inside her.

The sound of a drawer sliding open and the tear of foil barely registered as he worked his fingers inside her. Her muscles contracted around his digits, trying to pull him in deeper. The next slap and sting on her flesh sent more tingles and jolts catapulting over her skin, then his fingers were gone.

She looked back in time to see him settle against her opening, and the question in his strained expression was more like a plea. He didn't just want this, he *needed* this, just like she did. Her smile was all it took for him to jerk his hips and fill her.

Alicia fisted her hands in the covers, so full and so close to the edge she couldn't think or breathe. Sebastian leaned forward, resting his elbows either side of her, his lips whispering over her shoulder blades as he rolled into her again and again.

The friction was building and her stomach contracted. She couldn't move, couldn't roll her hips to try and control the building orgasm. The pressure magnified too intensely and she was pinned down, helpless to slow it even if she tried.

Even if she wanted to.

'I'm close, Alicia. Too close. I need you there with me.' He lifted a knee on the bed, slightly altering the angle until he stroked against where she needed him to.

She couldn't speak, couldn't move, and when the pressure exploded it was a never-ending spasm that rocked her to the core. Sebastian shuddered above her, then for a second she felt his full weight and though it knocked the breath out of her, it was nice.

Warm. Real.

He pressed a sloppy kiss to her shoulder, then he rolled off and headed to the bathroom. She had enough energy to turn her head. She smiled as she did. The sight of his rear, high and tight, wasn't the worst view she'd seen. Then she remembered the perks of missionary position and wondered if she'd recover enough to have him that way, digging her nails into his firm flesh. The thought sent a fresh sizzle of heat through her.

Chapter Thirteen

Sebastian flushed the condom then sat on the ledge of the tub to catch his breath. Christ, his cock was still hard, showing no signs of deflating despite the fact he was pretty sure he was going into shock.

He'd never smacked a woman to arouse her, especially not one as refined as Alicia. Though the second that pearly flesh was propped up, he couldn't help himself. Seeing it turned her on was one thing, but hearing her admit it knocked something inside him into overdrive.

She wanted to let loose, discover how good sex could be, and despite his shady reputation or the fact he hadn't told her everything about himself, she trusted him to be the one to do it. And he wanted to. It was like she called to a deep-rooted part of him that took control and gave what was needed, only now things were out of sync.

Now he wasn't sure casual and fun could factor into the equation.

The orgasm had knocked him for six and hers had only intensified everything, so maybe that's why he was having such a strong emotional reaction. Made sense. Good sex, hell, mind-blowing sex, could do that to anyone. Alicia's former innocence was all he was reacting to. No need to make a huge deal out of it.

Convinced he wasn't going soft, he splashed his face with water and towelled it off, ignoring the gnawing feeling in his gut that he was missing something important. He wasn't, he was just high on endorphins, and he'd been in the bathroom way too long.

When he got back to the room, Alicia had slipped

under the covers and lay on his side with her eyes closed. Her chest rose and fell steadily under his sheet, and he debated whether a shower would help cool off the last of his arousal, but changed his mind. She looked so peaceful and sated and right now he could do with some sleep. Over the last few weeks he'd been too restless, missing so much sleep because he couldn't get her out of his head. Now she was here maybe he'd get eight hours for a change.

Sliding in beside her, he slipped his arm beneath her shoulders and tugged her closer. Alicia rolled over so her head rested on the crook of his arm, but her leg came over his like she was subconsciously staking a claim and the unease he'd beat down earlier roared back.

Closing his eyes, he prayed for unconsciousness, but her smooth skin against his didn't help calm him. Sebastian buried his face in her hair, inhaling deep lungfuls of her light, citrusy shampoo – even better than the strawberry. Her slow, steady heartbeat thrummed against his palm and eventually he drifted off into a light sleep.

A too-stuffy heat woke Alicia. She looked around the pitch-black room, her mind still foggy and disorientated, when she realised why she was sweating. She was sprawled across a very naked Sebastian. Though her body was sticky from sweat where it touched his, she didn't want to move away anymore.

Which was why she should. Chemistry and insatiable hormones or not, he needed sleep so he could train. Slowly, she moved off him and rolled to the edge of the bed. His arm caught her around the waist and he scooted closer. The part of him pressing against her rear didn't feel asleep at all.

'Where are you running off to?' he asked, his voice rough and deliciously tempting.

'I wanted to let you get some rest.'

His hand slid up from her stomach, tweaking a nipple, but again the slight sting sparked a flood of heat until she arched into his palm. He trailed his nose along her shoulder, barely skimming her skin but it didn't matter. The contact had her squirming and pressing her thighs together to ease the ache.

'I can rest when I'm old,' he whispered against her skin.

Sebastian leaned over and she heard the drawer open on his bedside table. He handed her something, and she pressed her thumbs into it, feeling the circular ridge beneath the foil package.

'Open it,' he said, trailing his fingers down her stomach then between her legs.

She was ready for him, had been since she woke on his chest, and he slid inside with ease, making her hips jerk as the heel of his hand pressed against her clit. Alicia tore the package in half, almost dropping the condom as he ground his erection into the crease of her rear. He suckled on her neck, thrusting his hand in time with his hips until they were both gasping.

'Condom,' he muttered against her shoulder.

But she couldn't twist the way she wanted to and even then, she didn't have enough experience to get it right. Regretfully, she tugged his wrist until he withdrew, then handed it to him.

It didn't take long, and he lifted her leg up to get better access. 'Arch your back, Alicia.'

She did, and then he was inside her. They both froze, savouring the feel of being joined, then Sebastian leaned back and turned on the lamp. She squeezed her eyes shut against the bright light, but he started thrusting slowly until he hit the spot that made her insides burn and her eyes flew open.

There, at the side of the bed lining the wall, was a mirrored wardrobe and she could see them both, her breasts and stomach in shadow, her hips covered with the sheet pulled down by the angle he held her leg.

And down to where they were joined. She could see the sparkle of her arousal coating him as he thrust in and out. The visual coupled with his skilful thrusts just made her wetter.

Her skin was flushed and so was his. Despite their wild hair, their heaving breaths, and the sweat beading on their skin, seeing their reflection just revved her up more. Each thrust pushed her closer and closer. As she started to convulse under the waves of pleasure, Sebastian met her eyes in the mirror with a look of raw lust. She'd never felt so sexy or desired before.

But she wanted to see what he looked like when he went over the edge. Needed to touch him, every part of him. 'Sebastian, I want you on top.'

Instead of cracking a joke like she'd expected, he rolled her onto her back and made his way between her legs. As soon as they were joined, she took advantage and explored the smooth flesh covering muscles on his back and down, all the way to his hard buttocks. She dug her nails in, rising to meet each thrust. He feathered her neck with kisses, nibbling her collarbone and her nipples.

Mindless with pleasure, she kicked the sheets off, needing to see them totally joined. The image of her pale skin against his all-over bronze, his hips thrusting so powerfully into her, hitting that place that made her melt over and over, was beyond beautiful.

Sebastian kissed her jaw and the image didn't matter. Not when she could see and feel him first-hand. She turned so she could feel his lips on hers as he drove her over the edge again, taking her mouth as thoroughly as he was taking her body. He trembled, saying her name on a gasp as his hips jerked with his own orgasm.

After he rolled onto his back, his chest rising in wild jerks, she couldn't stop smiling. She'd done this to him. *Her.* The girl who until last week had convinced herself there was something bad and seedy about wanting hot, slick sex with a man she didn't have to fall in love with and then marry.

He caught her smiling and tugged her close. 'What are you thinking?'

'How did you know?' she asked.

'Know what?' His lids dropped as she snuggled closer.

His scent was divine, and although it might be weird she was even attracted to the man's sweat. But there wasn't time to worry, not when his slowing heartbeat was lulling her into sleep. 'That I'd like all that. I was a bit of a prude.'

He chuckled sleepily. 'Not a prude. Just misinformed. I knew you'd be a vixen.'

'Funny.' She wasn't a vixen.

'Go to sleep, Blondie. I promise there will be more taming of your libido tomorrow.'

Snorts weren't sexy, but she was too tired to care. 'I think you might have made it worse.'

'How so?' he mumbled, his arms contracting around her.

Because even now, when I can't move, I still want you. I don't know if this will ever stop.

But she didn't speak the words, they were too heavy for a temporary fling and besides, they still had time. She could get her fix and keep her head in the process. The French Opens was ages away.

Sebastian's breathing deepened and his body relaxed, saving her from having to lie. Still, Alicia wondered if she was cut out for a sex-only relationship, and that worry fought off sleep despite the fact she was exhausted.

Was that French?

Alicia forced an eye open, though it was harder than lifting a 10kg weight after a session at the local gym. It felt ungodly early, and a glance at the window showed the sun still wasn't up.

Sebastian entered the room, looking hot in a white polo with a pair of loose shorts that would no way keep him warm in London in January. He held a sleek cordless phone to his ear as he combed his shower damp hair, nattering in fluent French with the other person.

She blinked the sleep away, wondering why she was surprised. His mother was French and his parents lived in the country. After he finished smoothing out his hair, which was pointless considering it always got wavy and wild when it dried, he held up a finger to say he'd be a minute, then parked down next to her on the bed.

His clean scent affected her, as did the arm he wrapped around her. He trailed his fingers up and down her arm, enticing more than a few shivers.

He soon ended the call. 'You're awake.'

'Just. What time is it?' She swore it looked like the middle of the night.

'Four thirty.' His tone suggested that was a perfectly normal time to be up and about.

'You're insane. Why couldn't you pick a career that let you stay in bed till, I don't know, daytime?'

The bed shook with his laughter and he lightly smacked the side of her thigh, reminding her of what he did to her last night. What she'd wanted him to do. Suddenly it didn't feel so early, and a spark of restless energy woke her all the way up.

'What would be the fun in that? I like the sportsmanship.' He tugged at the covers, exposing her breasts. 'And if I wasn't training as much as I have been, I wouldn't have lasted as long the second time. Though I have to say, you're more than enough incentive.'

He trailed his finger around her areola and she was almost lost in the need. But it wasn't fair to keep him, not when he had work to do. Plus her job was to make him look good, not slack off.

'You don't have an accent,' she pointed out, desperately trying to change the subject. 'I mean, you grew up in France, didn't you?'

He stopped torturing her to shift so he was lying on his side looking down at her. 'No, we moved around a lot. My dad liked to train in the country he was competing in and my mum liked to travel.'

She tried to imagine what that was like, flitting from country to country all his life. In a way, she'd been lucky with her father as she'd had the same friends through school with minimal upheaval. But she'd never travelled, never explored the world like Sylvia and Daria did every day. While a huge part of her needed to feel grounded and secure, the wistful part wanted to travel the world and do the things she'd been too afraid to. Which wasn't going to happen full-time. But she should holiday more. Maybe she should use her vacation time to catch up with her sisters.

'Was that your mum?'

He nodded. 'She wants me to spend the time leading up to the Opens in France with her and Dad.'

'Oh.' Alicia tried to hide the surge of disappointment, and obviously failed miserably because he grinned broadly.

'I told her I had some things to sort out here.' His gaze drifted down to her breasts suggestively before returning to her face. 'And anyway, James is the best trainer I've had. He'd kick my arse if I didn't give him a chance to get a win in.'

She grinned, feeling instantly better knowing he'd be around to enjoy for a while longer. There was no way she'd had her fill yet. 'I guess I should get dressed and let you go.'

His lips pressed against hers, hot, coaxing and way too briefly. 'Get some sleep first. There's not much appealing in the fridge, but you can help yourself. When you head home, take that with you.'

She glanced at the sports bag he pointed to, next to the chair with her dress draped over it. Her cheeks flushed remembering him taking it off her. 'What's in the bag?'

'Clothes. I'll come by after training and we can slot in a press release. Then I'm taking you out.'

'You know, bossy Sebastian is kind of sexy.' Well, very sexy, actually, but he didn't need his ego inflating. It was big enough to block out the sun as it was.

'Glad you think so,' he said, then kissed the tip of her nose. 'I'll see you later.'

'Bye.'

A few minutes later, she heard the door click closed behind him and she rolled onto her side, catching her reflection in the mirror. Her hair was mussed, but in a sexy bedhead kind of way. Her lips were red and puffy from the spine-tingling kisses and she swore her skin was glowing. Alicia grinned, thinking a little R&R with a notorious playboy had its advantages.

Her mood had only lightened since she saw the stories headlining the news. Sebastian was in the spotlight again, but for the right reasons this time. She'd collected every rag she could, took a long detour to the office to make sure no paparazzi followed, and spent the first half hour with her coffee going over all the spins on the 'reformed tennis *player*' articles.

Until Mr Maine arrived with a look that said she was in trouble. 'Miss Simpson, can I have a word?'

This couldn't be good, not when he was addressing her so formally. 'Sure, er, yes. Come in.'

Mr Maine did, closing the door behind him. She smiled politely though her hands dampened and her stomach was all swishy. When he took the chair across from her desk, he glanced down at the papers with a frown.

Alicia decided a bit of good news might make what

was coming easier to deal with. She turned a few of the newspapers around so he could read them. 'I heard one of Collins' sponsors dropped, so had a freelance photographer follow us to a club and leak these stories. The press seem to have bought it.'

He opened one of the nationals and flicked to a page she hadn't read yet, then turned the thing around. There was a picture of her and Sebastian wrapped around each other on the middle of the club's dance floor, lip locked like they were about to dry hump right there. Which, if the photographer had a video camera, would have been caught on tape.

Alicia waited for the blush to come, for some outward sign of her discomfort, then realised slightly trembling hands was all she had. Her mind fogged over remembering when she'd been in his arms, pressed against every delicious inch of him, and decided it was time to give up her father's idea of what was right for her. She was an adult and they were doing nothing seedy or offending, but Mr Maine wasn't worried about her virtue.

'We had to make the whole thing look convincing.' She shrugged, trying to look blasé over the most incredible night of her life. 'There aren't many pictures of us together, and we needed to get something out there before the launch of the charity later this week in case his sponsor pulling gets out first. And with the new feature Mai's doing, this seemed like the only option.'

The frown Mr Maine sported smoothed a little. 'These things should be run past me first. This could have gone either way.'

Sensing the storm had settled, she smiled. 'Of course, next time I will if I can. It was a time-sensitive decision and the photographer needed something newsworthy.'

He studied her expression and she pulled on the cool, polite mask that had saved her before.

Nodding, he said, 'It was a good idea, I just had to

check you were both doing this for publicity.'

She smiled, even though her neck beaded with sweat having to lie to her boss. 'Of course we are.'

Rising, he smiled back. 'I honestly didn't expect you to be able to do such a good job, but it seems you're full of surprises.'

She froze, though the urge to squirm was strong. She didn't deserve Mr Maine's praise, not when she was going behind his back and risking her job. 'Thank you.'

The second he left, she pulled her mobile out her handbag and sent a text to Sebastian.

Maine saw the picture of us dancing. Had to think fast. If Tony asks, we planned the whole night.

For the next hour, she organised everything, only stopping when her mobile rang. Seeing Sebastian's name sent a thrill through her. She frowned at the device before answering. No way should she be this excited to speak to him. She had to remember this wasn't a proper relationship, and that when he went to France she'd be single again.

Her good mood plummeted and she answered with less enthusiasm than she'd had calling her father after the news they were a couple broke. 'Hi.'

'What's happened?'

Great, now she couldn't even hide the glum from him. Forcing false enthusiasm into her voice, she lied. 'Hmm, nothing. Sorry, I space out when I'm idea-bouncing.'

'*OK.* I called to ask when we leave to visit your family. James is talking about slotting in extra hours before and after.'

Oh god, she'd almost forgotten he was coming. Rubbing her temples didn't ease the tension making her brain swell. 'Friday afternoon and the party's on Saturday. We should be back by dinner time Sunday, but you really don't have to go.'

'Is that what's bugging you? You don't want me

there?'

'Nothing's bugging me. I told you, I'm working.' Her stomach was uneasy, like she'd eaten something too acidic. Either that or all this lying had given her an ulcer, but how could she tell him she was down because they'd be over soon when they weren't really together? She couldn't. It would ruin what time they had or worse, end it sooner.

'You're forgetting I've heard you lie, Blondie. You suck at it. Now spill.'

'It's nothing, really, and I'd prefer it if you didn't meet my family. They're so ... stuffy and strict. We'd have to be on our best behaviour and I wouldn't be surprised if my father makes us sleep in separate wings.'

His laugh coaxed a smile out of her. 'There are ways of getting around that. And I'll be with you – my fresh air so I can breathe.'

Alicia snorted. 'That's cheesy.'

'But true.' She could picture his grin, mischievous and wicked while he feigned innocence.

She rolled her eyes. 'Goodbye, Sebastian. I'll see you later.'

'Wait. I'm putting in a few extra hours here just to make up the time I'll lose. We could have a quiet night instead.'

His tone suggested it wouldn't all be quiet, and her heart sped in anticipation. Enough to quell the slither of disappointment that they wouldn't be going out, but what did she expect? She was having a fling with someone who put as much time into his work as she did. 'Can't wait.'

Chapter Fourteen

Sebastian hadn't exactly lied to Alicia. He *had* put more hours into training and it was late afternoon when he called it a day. And even though he wanted nothing more than to go to Alicia's flat and fall into her warmth, he had to do something he should have done a long time ago.

It was harder than it should have been to open the gate of the white picket fence, and walk up the cobble stone path which, last year, had been lined with shrubs and brightly coloured flowers. Now that he'd taken away the funding for a gardener, weeds had grown out, but he wasn't surprised Mai had let them – she'd always cared more about manicures than getting her hands dirty.

This wasn't just his old home, it was his *dream*. Everything he'd thought he could never have, right there in brick and stone. A base for his life, a woman who would love him, and a future set out so differently from his past.

That dream had been shattered into a million sharp and pointy pieces months ago – but it was only now he realised Mai wasn't the reason. He could have done more to hold on to everything, could have given her more than he did, but he'd followed in the footsteps of his father and put his career before everything else.

But that was OK, the sport was his life now and he accepted that. He was good at what he did. Hell, he even loved it most of the time. Tennis was all he'd ever known. But leading Mai on with promises he didn't know how to keep hadn't been fair.

Despite the fact she'd almost ruined his career,

reading the first part of the feature made him realise she wasn't just angry, she was upset. Maybe even broken. He'd done that, and he had to make it right. Even if it meant facing the bastard she'd jumped into bed with the day after he lost her at Wimbledon.

A glance around the street showed there wasn't anyone around who looked suspicious. All the cars were in their garages apart from a red Chevy that pulled into the street, but the guy drove on to the end of the road and out of sight. Convinced he hadn't been followed, Sebastian knocked the door.

Heavy footsteps sounded from the house and he almost groaned when he guessed who they belonged to. His suspicions were confirmed when a dark-haired, scrawny guy opened the door and scowled at him.

'What the fuck do you want?' Jack asked, his hands curling into fists.

'Relax.' He held his hands up and tried his best to keep his tone civil, though it grated his throat on the way out. 'I just want to speak to Mai.'

Jack stepped outside and slammed the door behind him. 'You're not getting anywhere near her, so go back to your new girl and keep your hands off my woman!'

Did this waste of space actually think he'd take Mai back, or that she'd have anything to do with him? 'Trust me, my hands won't be anywhere near her. Is she here?'

Jack pulled back a fist, but before he took the swing Sebastian said, 'Remember what happened last time you tried that shit? I see the hospital fucked up the set on your nose. You're looking a little crooked.'

Though Jack lowered his arm, he shook all over with the rage that twisted his face. 'Get off my property or I'm calling the press.'

Sebastian wasn't surprised Jack was as much a media whore as his other half, and he couldn't resist reminding him, 'A property that I paid for. Now are you going to tell me where she is or do I have to hire someone to track her down?'

'Trust me when I say you're the last bastard she wants to speak to,' Jack said.

'She seemed happy enough to start an argument with me yesterday. Just text her, give her the choice.' He wasn't going to beg. If he had to he'd come back, but with training doubling up and with Alicia in his life he wanted to get this over with.

He would have said something yesterday if he hadn't just found out his biggest sponsor had been dropped, not to mention the row with Alicia. And Mai hadn't exactly been in the mood for civil conversation.

Jack's scowl didn't ease up as he tapped out a text to Mai, or so Sebastian assumed.

'You know, Collins, with your new blonde piece of arse, why do you even give a shit about her?'

Sebastian had to grit his teeth and stick his fists into his pocket in case he did something he might regret. Eventually. Alicia wasn't a piece of arse, never had been, but he didn't need to go there with Jack.

After a deep breath to calm himself, he said, 'I'm not going to fuck this relationship up. I told you, I only want to speak to Mai.'

A mocking laugh was all he got in reply.

He should turn around and walk away, but there was something he'd always wondered about and if he was ever going to get a chance to ask, this was it. 'I can't understand why you're sitting back and letting Mai sell all these stories. Why would you want the world thinking she still cares about how much I hurt her when you're with her?'

Jack's smirk made him think there was something he was missing. Before he could ask anything else, the other guy's phone beeped. 'Looks like you're in luck. She says she'll meet you at the boat hire shop in Hyde Park.'

Sebastian didn't say he'd rather cut off his own ear

than meet up with her at the place they'd had their first date, but it was tempting. Still, he had things he needed to discuss, and if Mai wanted to meet him there he could give her that. It was the least he could do. 'When?'

Jack told him and he headed back to his car. He wanted to get this over with as quickly as he could, knowing that made him a jerk. But Alicia would be waiting for him and he wanted nothing more than to hold her, make her hot and ready for him. Maybe even show her all the things she'd been missing out on trying to be someone she wasn't.

The perfect thing about Alicia was she didn't have Mai's expectations. She accepted their relationship for what it was, and more importantly, he wouldn't break her when their time together was over.

It was amazing what one could get done in an hour, Mai thought as she made her way through the park to Serpentine Boat Hire. Ever since she'd signed with *Taylor Made*, she'd had to keep her mouth shut. She wasn't allowed to give exclusives on her relationship with Sebastian to anyone else, which meant she should have to suffer through this mystery meeting with Collins without the monetary gain.

But she'd had an idea since getting Jack's text, and had sent out a few texts of her own. She didn't doubt Sebastian had called this meeting to tell her off for yesterday – that wasn't an opportunity for more work she could let pass.

And it was brilliant. She couldn't have thought of something better if she'd tried. When she'd bumped into him in the street after a horrible morning with a grouchy Jack, she couldn't help screaming at him. All the anger at her lover had boiled over until vengeance made her want to hurt Sebastian – after all, he was the reason Jack was distant. All these interviews and having to drag up the past just to get by couldn't be fun for him to watch.

Words were the only arsenal she had, and she'd used a few choice ones with Sebastian.

But for this meeting, she'd had time to think and an hour to form a plan that would screw him over so hard he might even lose his latest squeeze. Mai didn't care about the posh girl's feelings. She was too chubby for him anyway, and he'd no doubt get caught with his dick in another woman. She was just speeding up the inevitable.

She saw him on the bench where they'd shared a few steamy kisses on their first proper date. He'd then taken her out onto the lake and she could remember how happy she'd been – how much he'd made her laugh. The tales he'd told her from his travels had engrossed her, but when a sad wistfulness entered his tone when he talked about the people he'd left behind, she'd shed a few tears for him.

Mai dragged her mind back from the past. After all, she didn't ask him to come to the lake to revisit memories she was brutally trying to forget. He was here because what better place to get the best story than where they'd had their first date?

As she neared, Sebastian looked up at her. He was in a hoodie and a baseball cap, probably to avoid being seen with her, but it didn't make him look any less striking. He was still well-built, still had hair she could hold onto when he sunk into her over and over.

He still had the ability to steal her breath.

Mai realised she'd stopped walking, stopped breathing, and forced herself to resume both. It was ridiculous that she still felt this way around him. She thought lust was a feeling that fizzled out over time. More than likely it was this place, what she was remembering of the past, and not the man waiting for her on the bench.

Well, she wouldn't be ruled by it anymore. She had an argument to win – she just hoped the journalist from

Taylor Made arrived soon enough to hear it.

'Sebastian,' she said as she approached him. 'If you think I'm going to apologise for yesterday –'

'That's not why I'm here, Mai. Take a seat.' He gestured to the spot next to him.

She hesitated, but they were out in broad daylight with people walking by. He wouldn't try anything awful, would he? Mai sat at the edge of the bench and waited for him to say something. When he didn't, she wondered for a moment if this was his way of trying to bully her into admitting to the world she'd played with the truth when it came to her stories.

But that didn't make sense, especially when he just stared out over the lake. She glanced around, looking for signs the journalist had arrived. There was a blond-haired man a few benches down and he held a paper, but didn't look like he was paying much attention. He had more focus than the other people about, turning pages in a timely, methodical way. Maybe he was a guy from *Taylor Made*.

Deciding to get the show going, she asked, 'Then why did you insist on meeting?'

He turned to face her. Even with his eyes cast in the shadow thrown by his cap, they still snagged her attention like nothing else in the world could. They were wary now and full of something she'd never seen on him. Was it remorse?

No. Sebastian never had any regrets.

He sighed deep, then said, 'I don't know how to start other than to say I'm sorry. For the way things turned out, hell, for everything, really.'

Her suspicious nature at least made sure she wasn't a complete idiot, even though part of her wanted to believe he did feel shitty – he deserved to. 'I suppose this is the part where you tell me how hurt you are, that I've had enough payback, and I should retract all my statements?' She laughed a little. Like that would *ever* happen.

'No, I'm not going to ask for anything from you. I just want you to know that even though you don't believe me, I never cheated on you. I'm guilty of a lot of things – especially treating you like you weren't important to me, but I never betrayed you.'

Either he was the most talented liar in the world, or he really meant it. If it was the latter, then everything she'd done after that day at Wimbledon had hurt him just as much as she thought he hurt her.

Which meant, since she jumped straight into their bed with her ex-boyfriend, that *she* was the one who betrayed *him*. God, no wonder Sebastian had broken Jack's nose.

'She was all over you,' Mai said, refusing to believe it. There was too much evidence and stories about what happened.

Sebastian sighed. 'We'd just won the mixed doubles and it was her first big win. Mai, she was excited and took it too far. Her career began and ended that day. She was a winner, but also the woman who was supposedly having an affair with an engaged man. No one would sponsor her after that. She had to quit.'

Mai dipped her head, unable to look at him for a second longer. If he really was telling her the truth – and she couldn't find a sign he was lying – she'd overreacted to the extremes. Hell, she'd caused such a fuss that the woman lost her career.

But she couldn't believe it yet. There were too many things that didn't fit. 'You were so distant. After we got engaged I barely saw you. I didn't know what to think.'

Moisture pooled in her eyes and a tear slipped free, trailing down her cheek. She wiped it away, hoping the journalist was too far away to hear their hushed conversation or she'd be in serious trouble with the magazine – the whole world, if *this* story broke.

Sebastian took her hand and squeezed it. The tingles that danced through her veins at the connection iced her stomach with guilt. She'd had so much with him, but it always seemed too good to be true. When she thought he'd cheated, it made more sense than him wanting to be with her forever. She was an orphan who grew up passed from foster carer to foster carer, a burden to everyone who'd briefly taken her in.

Was it so wrong to want someone's undivided attention, to be adored for once?

Sebastian hadn't given her that. No one had, but she knew in her heart that Jack loved her and she was trying to accept the way he showed her love. But as Sebastian rubbed his thumb over her palm, her insides melted like they never had with Jack.

'I mean it, Mai. I want to make things right between us, and the only way I can think to do that is by apologising.'

She tugged her hand back, feeling like she was betraying her lover by touching him. 'I don't see the point of this conversation. Nothing's changed.'

He looked out across the lake again. 'I read the article in *Taylor Made*.'

There was no anger in his voice and he seemed relaxed, lounging back against the bench. She always assumed if they ever met in the future, when she'd got her revenge and he'd lost everything, that he'd hate her.

She'd been prepared for that. She even had a speech prepared that would rub his nose in it over and over.

To see that he wasn't upset or angry threw her off-kilter.

He took his cap off, then ran a hand through his hair. It had grown out and looked just as silky as she remembered. Mai folded her arms in case she had another moment of weakness and reached out to him.

Sebastian met her eyes when he said, 'I had no idea you felt the way you did. All I've thought about since I read the piece is how I could have done things differently. I just can't think of anything except maybe retiring, but I wasn't ready to back then.'

Her heart took off on a canter as hope and attraction pulsed through her. Not only was he thinking about her, regretting how he treated her, but he was willing to retire soon? That would mean he'd be free to give her everything she'd wanted from him last year – everything she'd ever wanted from anyone.

Mai shifted so her thigh was touching his. The sparks that sizzled in what little air was between them clouded her mind. When she placed her hand against his cheek, he didn't flinch away.

His brows pulled together, but she didn't want him thinking about all the reasons why this was a bad idea – *she* didn't want to think of all the reasons either. So she closed the distance and kissed him with everything she had.

He took hold of her shoulders and pushed her back. Her heart was going so fast she swayed a little and he pulled her closer until she could see properly. Mai cupped his face with both hands this time, but Sebastian pulled them away, then scooted over until he was at the edge of the bench.

She looked at him then, saw the shock in his widened eyes, the irritation in his clenched jaw, and the lust for him sizzled into anger until she was too livid to speak.

'Jesus, Mai. What the hell was that about?' He glanced around, then cursed when someone caught his eye. 'Did you have someone follow us?'

She looked across the grass to see a dark-haired man with a camera. He gave Mai the thumbs up. Sebastian stood and the man bolted in the opposite direction, scoring another few curses from Sebastian.

Mai smiled despite the fact he'd made her so angry by reeling her in only to reject her again. How silly she'd been to believe a bastard like him could change, could care. But she'd have her revenge for this. And it would be sweeter than an argument caught on camera.

This would be the beginning of his end.

'Mai!' Sebastian grabbed her shoulder and shook. 'Where's he from?'

She flashed her teeth and poured all her hatred for him into her scowl. 'You'll find out soon enough, you bastard. Now if you'll excuse me, I have somewhere to be.' She got up, shoved out of his hold but he followed her. 'I swear to God, Sebastian. You touch me again and I'll scream bloody murder.'

Chapter Fifteen

Efficient was her middle name today.

Alicia gathered the last of the papers scattered across the floor of her sitting room and shoved them into the file she had for the charity. Everything was set up and ready to go. She'd planned fundraising events for the next few years and set them in motion: she'd contacted all of the people Sebastian said may be interested, and even managed to get a few of the top names in sports out of them who'd also agreed.

Several teenage hostels and youth centres in London had promised to send kids their way once the centre opened, and she'd sorted out the lease for the building, a few volunteers to run the show, and the equipment was scheduled to arrive any day.

And to top it all off, she'd prepared a meal suited to his strict diet but would taste amazing.

All in all, she'd totally kicked the day's arse.

By the time the knock at the door came a little after seven, she'd even had a chance to run the vacuum around her flat. Skipping to the door, anticipation curled in her stomach and she wondered if he'd be too hungry to squeeze in some fun before dinner.

Alicia pulled the door open and was about to pounce on him, but Sebastian's jaw was taut and his stance was so rigid he might as well have worn a sign round his neck saying 'Stay away'.

'Are you alright?' she asked, opening the door wider and standing to the side to let him in.

He didn't get far before he pulled her into his arms and buried his face in her neck. Alicia wrapped her arms around his waist and squeezed. The fact that he was looking for comfort frightened her.

He was strong, he was self-assured, and a little egotistic. Whatever happened today must be bad.

She tried again. 'Sebastian, what happened?'

Still no answer, but after a second of holding her so hard she couldn't breathe, he pulled back, threw off his cap, then his mouth was on hers.

This wasn't the kind of kiss that made her want to put off dinner until, say, five in the morning – though the way her body reacted to him wasn't far off.

Sebastian kissed her with a tenderness laced with desperation, like he had something to prove. Or something to make up for?

Oh God, what had he done? Her blood ran cold as her mind pictured him with someone else. She pulled away. 'I need to know what happened.'

His chest rose and fell in quick succession and she waited for what felt like forever, dreading what he would say. Would he lie to her, make her feel like everything was fine, or would he tell her something she didn't want to hear?

Her stomach felt heavy as his silence stretched on. Alicia closed the door and locked it, though he might not be staying for long if he was going to admit what she dreaded the most.

He walked away from her and into the sitting room but she didn't follow. Her legs felt weak, just like her heart. Hadn't she known they were just working out the chemistry until he left for the French Opens? She did, and she believed it, so she had no idea why her heart stuttered like it was breaking.

'I fucked up,' he said.

Alicia squeezed her eyes shut to stop them from watering. This was ridiculous. She shouldn't be so upset, not when they'd never made any promises to each other. She had her rules, but she'd broken the first.

She told herself the reason her heart had splintered was because whatever he did would drag her into a shameful media frenzy that would bring scandal to her family. She almost believed it too.

'Don't freak out on me,' he said.

If anyone was freaking out it was him. He was raking his hands through his hair, taking out the kink left by his cap.

Alicia decided she had to treat the situation with professional calm – it was either that or she was going to freak out and then who knew? She made her way to the living room, grateful her legs were steady and didn't give away her anxiety.

She sat down on the end of the sofa and gave him the choice. He took the chair, which was when she knew this was going to be bad – he'd never allowed much space between them before.

'Do you want a coffee?' she asked, but what she really wanted to do was pick up the charity file and beat him over the head with it until he told her what was happening.

Sebastian frowned at her. 'Don't use that prim voice. We're not strangers.'

Right now it felt like they were, but she wasn't going to tell him that. Not if she wanted honesty. 'I'm sorry. What happened?'

He scrubbed a hand down his face. 'I went to see Mai.'

Relief crashed through her. She'd thought he'd been with someone else, to hear he hadn't made her want to laugh. But then he was going crazy on the chair and she knew there was more to this. So she waited.

Sebastian studied her expression for a long moment. 'When I read the latest article I was pissed off at her. But then I read it back and saw more than her trashing me. I'd hurt her, really hurt her, and I thought it was long past time I apologised.'

Alicia blinked, but was too shocked to say anything. She'd known when she started this he wasn't happy with the part of her plan to show the world he'd made a mistake. Let alone his ex.

'We met in Hyde Park, next to the boating place. I told her the truth – that I'd never cheated on her and I think she believed me.'

'That's good, isn't it?' she said. 'Maybe now she'll stop …'

But Sebastian was shaking his head.

'She kissed me.'

The words had her heart racing again, worse than before. Panic and pain interlaced until her lungs cramped with the effort it took to breathe. She knew what was coming next – it was written all over his expression.

'Mai called the press.'

He nodded.

Alicia bit her tongue against other questions – more pressing ones. Did he kiss her back? Was there still attraction there beneath the bitterness? But his publicist didn't need to know those things.

She tried to think through the pain, the hurt, and focus on the most important part – his reputation as a renowned cheat. And stopping this article from going to print and her father finding out.

She raked in the cupboard beside the sofa and pulled out the phone book, then flicked through the pages. If she was right, a magazine like *Taylor Made* would sign Mai exclusively for a feature, maybe every other story for a while yet. It was her last hope.

'Is Mai's number registered?'

'I think so. She'd want the press to be able to get in touch. Alicia –'

'One issue at a time, Sebastian.' She found the number and dialled it from her cell, blocking the number.

'What are you going to do?' he asked, but she didn't

answer.

A second later, Mai picked up. Alicia put on her best Cockney accent and said she was a freelancer for a gossip mag.

'You want me to tell you more about the split?' Mai said.

Alicia tsked. 'That's old news, sweets. I was thinking about doing a piece on how your life has improved when his is going down the lav.'

He made a face at her and she couldn't help but smile, despite the fact she had a trillion questions for him about that kiss.

'Oh, uh. Yes, that sounds good. But does it have to be now?' Mai asked.

'Now's the only chance. We need to fill a spot and I've managed to squeeze you into the next issue.' Alicia crossed her fingers and earned a puzzled look from him.

'Oh … I'm sorry, but I've given someone else the exclusives for the next month.'

She closed her eyes, thankful at least that she knew who would be splashing the kiss all over their pages, but getting them to reconsider printing the pictures would be the hard part.

'Maybe another time.' Alicia closed her cell. '*Taylor Made* have all the exclusives for the next month. That's probably where the … kiss will be printed.'

Sebastian crossed to the sofa and knelt in front of her. He took her phone, set it down on the table, then grabbed her hands. Looked her right in the eye. 'I pushed her away. Whatever I felt for Mai is gone. The only reason I went to see her was to apologise – now I wish I hadn't.'

She blinked again, but this time it was to stop her eyes from getting all watery.

'You didn't need to tell me that.' But she was glad he did.

'I'd say since we've seen each other naked that I should.' She narrowed her eyes and he grinned, but it was short-lived. 'And you're my publicist. Bet you've never had a client as hellish as me.'

She wanted to see the grin again, especially now he'd told her the truth – but it was hard to force herself to be light. There was still the potential article coming with God knew what spin Mai had put on it. But she had some time. The next issue of *Taylor Made* wasn't out for a fortnight.

She tried a joke. 'Before we met I thought working for you would be like trying to shove Hitler's skeletons into a closet.'

It worked, he laughed a little. 'I don't have skeletons. Just a scorned ex.'

'Maybe covering up after Hitler would be easier than facing off against what Mai keeps throwing at you.' Alicia wasn't kidding this time.

He tugged her off the sofa, then stood, holding her close. She let him pull her into a kiss that melted her to the core and made her heart pound in a much better way than before. Maybe dinner could wait, and so could dealing with this mess, especially since his hands were sliding beneath her shirt and up her spine. She shivered and he pulled away.

'I was going to get us takeout,' he said.

She frowned. 'That's what you were thinking about when you kissed me?'

He laughed. 'No, but I'm trying to take my mind off dragging you to bed. We should eat first, though. We'll need the energy.'

The shivers turned into a heat she couldn't shake off. 'Well, we don't have to wait. I cooked today.'

His eyes glinted. 'I'll thank you properly after.'

Juliette dialled the number of her first-born daughter, feeling more excited than she had in a long time. Her desk was covered in papers and she had been so busy this week she'd barely touched the liquor the gardener had brought her. It was times like now, when she saw her daughters happy, that her misery was overshadowed completely.

'Mother, I was just going to call. How are you?' Daria answered.

Juliette rolled her eyes – a bad habit she'd picked up from her children, but it fit with her daughter's fib. Daria sounded distant, which meant she was probably heavily into a new range of designs. She barely kept track of time when she started a project.

'I'm wonderful, dear.' At least, this time she was. She hated having to force out lies. There had been so many since she married Arthur that she'd lost count. 'Have you made a decision on who you want to cover the wedding?'

'Is it really necessary? Blair and I thought it would just be a quiet, family thing.' At least Daria sounded like she was paying attention now.

'You know your father.' Well, she knew enough of him to know events like this in their household were events he wanted the wold to witness. His filthy secrets and betrayals on the other hand …

'OK, I'll think about it,' Daria said, but it sounded more like a way to end the topic.

'Thank you. Have you spoken with the French designer about the dresses? We can't leave that much longer.' Then there were the caterers, the decorators, the flowers. So much to do in such a short time. The distraction from her life was heaven sent.

'Actually, would you mind taking a look at what I've drawn up? I've been working on dresses for Alicia, Sylvia, and myself.'

Juliette frowned. Arthur would not allow his eldest daughter to be in anything but the best – even though she'd be happy as long as Daria was. Something else she'd have to subtly fight for without overstepping her place as the dutiful wife. 'Email them to me and I'll run them past your father.'

'You know what he'll say,' Daria said, then sighed. 'Thanks for trying though.'

Juliette knew alright. She knew everything about that man – every scandalous detail. 'I can't promise he'll agree but I'll try.'

'You're the best,' she said.

Juliette smiled and her heart swelled. This was the kind of relationship she wished she could have had with her mother, one full of confidences and love. Her children's love was the only love she'd known.

'I'll call you tomorrow, dear,' she said.

Daria said her goodbyes. Juliette had just returned the phone to the cradle when Arthur stormed into her study. She jumped a little, but quickly regained composure. Had he been listening to her conversation?

But then he threw a file down on the table over her plans for the wedding. 'This is the last straw! If you won't let me do something about this then you should. She's your daughter too!'

Startled at his anger, she opened the file to reveal a dozen photographs. She didn't recognise the couple at first. Not until she noticed the man's dark hair beneath the cap. Though it was hard to make out his face in some, she recognised the woman attached to it.

Juliette gasped and dropped the pictures. 'Where did you get these?'

'Does it matter? He's playing Alicia for a fool. You have to talk to her, make her see sense. It's either that or the press get to them first.'

For once she couldn't hide her anger. 'Is that what you care about, Arthur? That your daughter's embarrassment will cause your own? Alicia will be heartbroken.'

The old fool sputtered. 'I saved her from that before and look how she thanked me! No, now I care about the things she doesn't. This family's reputation is much more important –'

'You forced her to kill her child,' Juliette snapped, unable to hide the hatred she had for him.

His scowl turned dangerous, like it did the day he kicked Jonathan out. Part of her wanted the same fate, but she'd be shamed. Just like Arthur's son. Still, it meant she would be freed from this life, wouldn't it?

'She was just a child herself. Imagine the hell she'd have gone through if I didn't! Do you think any respectable man would have had her, lumbered with a baby at sixteen?' he countered, but his voice had turned icy cool.

Juliette knew she couldn't push him further. Not that she wasn't tempted. But she wouldn't risk him turning her children against her. They were all she had.

He must have known he'd beaten her, because he smiled. 'Talk to her, make her see sense or I'll forbid her from ever setting foot in this house or associating with any of us again.'

She gritted her teeth. 'You can't fault her for falling in love – it's not a crime. And if anyone bothered to scratch the surface of the façade we all put on, they'll find more to bring us down with than a cheating boyfriend.'

'Maybe so, but nobody has reason to, and the past is buried deeply.' He walked away, but issued one final command. 'This weekend I want you to give Alicia these pictures. And if she doesn't believe them, there are plenty more.'

'You hired someone to dig up dirt on her boyfriend?' And she'd assumed there were no new ways her husband could shock her.

'Yes, and he's only just scratched the surface.'

Chapter Sixteen

'That was amazing,' Sebastian said, pulling her onto his lap and nibbling her collarbone.

It had the affect he was hoping for – Alicia shivered and a moan escaped her lips.

'Did you think that because we had a cook I'd never put a meal together before?' she asked, arching her neck to give him better access.

Sebastian pushed her hair out of the way, exposing her pale, smooth skin. He trailed his tongue down her artery and a flash of heat arrowed straight to his groin. 'Everything you put your mind to turns out brilliant.'

It was the truth. Over dinner she'd caught him up on what she'd done for the charity. In a few days she'd put everything together better than a professional probably could have. Not to mention the way she'd dealt with his confession. It made him feel like an idiot for going to see Mai and not expecting she had a ploy to make a mint off him. And he felt even worse for not telling Alicia what he'd been up to beforehand.

'Flattery will get you everywhere, Collins.' She twisted in his arms until she'd straddled his hips. 'Maybe it's time we moved this from the sofa?'

He traced the outline of her lips with his thumb, putting the way his heart swelled down to gratitude. Other women may not have heard him out before they jumped to conclusions but Alicia hadn't pushed for answers. She'd just tried to fix it, even though he'd seen the flash of hurt in her eyes. Sure, he was paying her to clean up his rep but they were also together for now. He owed her the truth.

'I'll make you a deal,' he said.

'OK,' she agreed, but it was more than curiosity in her eyes.

Sebastian tugged her so close their lips were almost touching. 'I'll do anything you want tonight, but you have to ask me for it.'

Her eyes widened. 'In detail?'

He couldn't be sure if she was turned on or terrified by what he was asking, but decided to push her that bit farther. He knew she was passionate with a lot more of herself to give. Something in her past was holding her back and he wanted her to be free of it almost as much as he wanted to wipe the floor with his opponents at Wimbledon.

'Yup. You don't ask, you don't get.' He grinned.

Red scored her cheekbones. 'I ... don't know.'

Sebastian kissed her – hoping to make her so hot her embarrassment would fade. It backfired when she met him full-on, opening to him and caressing his tongue with hers. When her centre pressed against his erection, causing a friction that made his blood boil and reason fade, he had to pull back.

They were both breathless as he waited, and finally she said, 'I want you to kiss me like that. In my bedroom.'

Any more kissing would mean he'd get way too impatient to wait for instructions, but he reckoned that was her plan. Still, he obliged because she asked and tried to pull himself back from the edge so he didn't give in too soon.

Her bed helped. It was all pink and fluffy with a few stuffed animals placed by her cushions. Alicia's face turned a darker shade of red and he couldn't hold in a chuckle. 'It's not the manliest place in the world.'

She pulled off the toys and placed them on her dressing table, like she was in a rush to get rid of the evidence. 'There're never any men in here, so it's not normally a problem.'

Her admission brought back the feelings he'd had last night, in his bathroom after the first time they'd been together. It felt a lot like an instinctual need to claim and devour, which helped clear his head. This wasn't about marking Alicia as his – she could never be. Their lives were too different and no matter how much he'd wanted a steady partner, a home, someone to love, that was never going to happen. He'd learned his lesson with Mai.

'I want you to undress,' she said.

All thoughts of the day and previous night got shoved aside. Alicia was asking for what she wanted and there wasn't a shred of embarrassment in her eyes now. He tugged off his T-shirt, then went to work on his jeans. She watched his hands as he undid the buttons and pushed them down his hips.

The carnal look in her eyes made waiting for her to ask feel like torture.

'Now I strip you?' he asked, too impatient to wait. He didn't see the sweater that hid her figure or the jeans that didn't do a thing to showcase her long, lean legs. All he could see was her soft curves, pale, smooth, and sexy as hell.

But Alicia wasn't listening. Her gaze roved over his exposed skin with parted lips, like she couldn't get enough. His plan to get her to ask for what she wanted and open up didn't seem as important as having his hands on her in that moment.

When he tugged her into his arms and kissed her, he knew this was a better idea. She pressed herself closer, and all he could think was that there were far too many clothes in the way. Going to work on her jean buttons he kept her close and kissed her deeper. Alicia got rid of her top and he shoved the trousers down to her knees with her pants.

'Sebastian, there's something I want.'

She didn't meet his eyes, instead focused on his

throat. The colour flushing her cheeks meant she was about to ask for something he probably wouldn't mind giving her.

'Name it.'

He nibbled her throat while he unclasped her bra. Alicia dug her nails into his biceps as a sigh escaped her lips. 'I want you to do what you did last night. I ... liked that.'

He did too. Just thinking about it made his cock harden.

Turning them both, he sat on the edge of the bed, tugged her close. Her breasts were taunting him and no matter how hard he tried he couldn't resist a taste. Alicia threaded her fingers through his hair and held him to her.

He ran his thumb between her legs, groaning when he felt the silky proof of how ready she was. She jerked her hips into him, urging him on, and he didn't tease her anymore. Sliding two fingers inside was all it took to push his patience to breaking point.

'Where's my bag?' he asked, but didn't let up on what he was doing.

She was panting so hard she didn't hear him and he wanted nothing more than to pull her down on him and bury himself as deep as his fingers.

But they needed protection and he didn't think that was something Alicia kept in her bedside cabinets.

'Sebastian, I'm ... I need ...'

He swirled her clit with his thumb, over and over until her nails bit into his shoulders so hard he thought she might draw blood. She convulsed around his digits, but he didn't stop – even though the need to feel her doing that around his cock made it impossible to think.

She swayed a little and he pulled her against him, bracketing her thighs with his for support. When the tremors stopped raking her body she slumped against his chest, panting against his neck. His throat felt too thick as he watched her face, bright with colour and wearing a satisfied smile.

'Wow,' she said.

He had to agree – she was spectacular. 'That was just the beginning.'

Tonight had been crazy – in more ways than one.

When she found out what he'd done with his day, Alicia's emotions had been all over the place, and then there was the minor miracle she'd have to pull off to keep what happened out of the press.

But Sebastian's husky promise made it easy to forget those worries for now.

'You asked for your bag,' she said, wondering if she had enough control over her leg muscles to make it to the sitting room.

He grinned. 'You heard that?'

A fiery flush scored her cheekbones. She'd heard him, but couldn't actually process the words. Not when he'd been driving her towards an epic orgasm. Alicia untangled herself, but he kept hold of her waist. His grin faded as he looked her over and those dark eyes got so hot she forgot why she'd stood up.

'We need condoms. I've got a packet in my bag.'

Right, the bag. But she didn't move. Instead, she wondered what it would be like to have him inside her without the flimsy barrier – nothing but skin on skin. An ache formed between her legs, but squeezing her thighs together didn't help much.

She'd been on the pill since her father found out what had happened – not that she'd ever had unprotected sex with Darrell. Accidents happened no matter how careful she'd been, so she'd kept taking them all these years.

Still, the thought of having Sebastian with nothing between them was tempting. 'We don't really need them, do we? I'm covered.'

He met her eyes then and she could see the want in them. That was the only answer she needed. She climbed onto his lap. His hand on her hips stopped her from positioning herself where she wanted to be.

'We'll talk about this later,' he said, though from the way every muscle in his arms tensed she guessed he was holding on by a thread.

That was probably a good idea. Even though there was no risk of pregnancy, there were other things to worry about. She shifted so she was sitting next to him instead. 'It's beside the chair in the living room.'

Alicia got treated to him walking away. She'd have melted into her mattress if she wasn't so revved up with adrenaline. He'd promised to give her what she wanted and she definitely wanted more spanking. Was even getting used to the fact it wasn't something she'd been brought up to do. Her mother had always stressed the importance of keeping her virtue, but she'd lost that a long time ago.

What was one more vice? Nothing in the grand scheme of things.

Sebastian was back in record time and ready to go. He threw the box down on her bedside cabinet, then he was on her. She lay back, curled her legs around his hips, and pulled him into position. The way he kissed her showed how desperate he was to have her, which only made her need for him grow – but he didn't thrust inside.

She squirmed, growing more impatient under his tingling kisses. Sebastian lifted her off the bed, then sat back down. This time when she tilted her hips to the right angle, he let her. The power running through her at the control he was offering was foreign, but didn't feel wrong – quite the opposite. It gave her the confidence she'd never had to take him in, at a pace that teased them both and gave just enough friction where it counted.

His fingers dug into the flesh on her rear, but he didn't rush her. When she took his erection fully into her, one of his hands left her bum, then crashed down hard enough to sting a little. The thrill of it made her jerk, and he studied her with concern creasing his forehead. Alicia smiled to reassure him this was what she wanted, and wriggled on his lap, gasping when he swelled even more inside her.

His jaw tightened and he rested his forehead against hers. She could feel in his tense muscles the effort it was taking to let her go at her own pace, to let her get used to this new position and sensations.

Something suspiciously close to emotion wrapped around her heart and she had to remind herself again that falling in love with men like him only ended in heartache. Instead of going to that dark place, she pushed up on her knees, then sunk back down, earning another slap from him. Every nerve ending felt raw and exposed, so much so that when she changed to grind against him, the tension coiled faster than ever.

He kept slapping her skin, alternating sides, and each time it pushed her closer, nearer the edge until her head got light and her skin felt like a current was pulsing over it, throbbing in erogenous zones she didn't know existed.

Picking up her pace, she revelled in the way he thrust his hips – like he couldn't help himself. He pulled her down so every dip dragged the head of his erection over the spot inside that created the tension. The smacks kept coming, harder each time until she was shaking with the orgasm waiting to break free. But she held on a little longer, wanting him to fall over the edge with her.

His breaths came faster and his thighs tensed like rocks. She kept up the pace, knowing he was close, and then let go of the flimsy hold she had on control. The coil snapped, allowing the heady warmth of pleasure to pulse around her whole body. She kept moving, unsteady now she couldn't feel her legs. He gasped out her name while he jerked his hips into her a few times.

When he sagged back onto the bed, she followed, nestling her head above his collarbone. Sebastian cupped the nape of her neck, holding her in place while their chests rose and fell. The tingling sensation flowing through her was better than having a glass of wine after a hard day in the office. It was better than the buzz she got from pushing herself past her limits at the gym.

She suspected it was a feeling she'd easily get addicted to.

Alicia snapped out of the afterglow and jumped off him too quickly. Scrambling around for a something to cover herself with couldn't have been her sexiest moment, but she had to get away. If she let him see her now, who knew what he'd see in her eyes? The emotions she'd felt before were back and no doubt written over her face.

Finding a pair of flannel pyjamas, she left for the bathroom and got changed. She avoided the mirror, which wasn't easy when she brushed her teeth, but she managed it. Then after splashing her face with cold water and towelling off, she was almost sure she had it under control so headed back to the bedroom.

The lights were out, which meant he must have got up. Glad he couldn't see her, she crossed the room to the bed. His breathing was slow, steady. If he was asleep it meant she could claw back some much-needed distance. Slipping into the edge of the bed, she pulled what covers were left over her.

Sebastian tugged her into the centre of the bed and held her against his chest. His warmth seeped through her skin and melted the protest on the tip of her tongue. No matter how scary these feelings were, lying with him like this was bliss and though she knew she shouldn't, she relaxed into him.

'G'dnight, Blondie,' he said.

'Goodnight, Sebastian.'

Alicia woke up alone. The sheets were cool behind her and something like panic gripped her throat. It was still dark in her room, but her curtains were thick. Surely he hadn't left her in the middle of the night?

But when she checked her alarm, it was nine. If yesterday was anything to go by he'd have left hours ago. Without saying goodbye?

Her eyes stung and she squeezed them shut. 'Stop it right now.'

This was getting too much. Just remembering how easily Darrell had walked away when she needed him wasn't enough to keep her heart safe from Sebastian. Then again, Sebastian wasn't promising her more than a few weeks, months at most. She had him in her life until his reputation was squeaky clean – though after last night she doubted it would be for a while.

Which reminded her. She had calls to make and favours to beg.

Throwing the quilt back exposed her to the chilly air, but it didn't stop her getting out of bed and darting to the living room. Her heart launched into her throat when she saw he'd taken his holdall. Still, there wasn't time to dwell on that. She snatched her mobile off the coffee table and made her way to the kitchen.

And froze. Sebastian had tidied up. The dishes she'd left to air dry the night before were gone, and there was a pot of coffee brewing in the machine. He'd even cleaned the burner on the cooker and taken the bin out. Was this his way of saying 'thanks for a great night but I've had enough'?

Again, not something she wanted to dwell on – there was too much to fix already. She poured a mug of steamy coffee then scrolled through her phone until she found the number she wanted.

Daria sounded groggy when she answered, 'Hi, sis.'

Alicia was about to ask her question, but it would be rude to blurt it out and Daria didn't know the full story. 'How are wedding plans going?'

Her sister sighed. 'Father vetoed the dresses I designed. He wants some French designer who was

191

clearly born in the sixteen hundreds to do them.'

That made her smile. 'Old-fashioned?'

'An understatement. Be prepared for a shapeless, cleavageless monstrosity. Mother did try to change his mind, but he obviously doesn't want his daughters to look like women on the day.'

If they were anything like their mother's wedding dress, they were all going to look like throwbacks from the Victorian era. She knew how much that would hurt Daria, but since it was their father paying for everything, she couldn't really argue. 'I'm sorry.'

'I'm tempted not to invite him and wear what I want.' She sighed again. 'It's a nice thought but I'm not that brave.'

Alicia laughed. 'You're braver than me. I wouldn't have asked in the first place.'

Hadn't that been her problem all her life? She'd kept her mouth shut, not stood up for what she wanted, and had to suffer the consequences. She envied Daria and Sylvia. They spoke up when they felt passionate about something even if it meant rejection.

'You've always been the wimp.' Daria chuckled. 'So what can I do for you, little sister? Or did you wake me up to find out about the wedding of the century?'

Now for the hard part. Alicia took a sip of coffee, wishing it wasn't too early for wine. How was she going to explain? Tell the truth first, or just come out with it? She didn't want to lie to her family, but who knew what would leak if she told the truth? Daria wouldn't drop her in it though she might mention it to Blair and …

'Getting old here, Alicia,' Daria said.

'I need a favour.' She cleared her throat. 'Have you picked a magazine to cover the wedding yet?'

There was a long pause, then, 'No, I don't really want one there. I was hoping to leave it so late that no one will be available, but Mother's putting pressure on me to choose.'

Guilt froze the request in her throat. Of course her sister would want a quiet, intimate wedding. Wouldn't *she* when the time came? She couldn't ask, she should be helping Daria get her way.

But how else was she going to stop those pictures from coming out? If they did, she wouldn't be allowed at the wedding. She probably wouldn't be allowed to speak with her sisters.

Her hand fisted around the mug until the heat got too much. 'Do you want me to speak with Mother?'

'No, it's no use. Father wants coverage and you know what he's like. What were you going to ask?'

Alicia bit her lip.

'Come on, Alicia. You can ask me anything.'

She took a deep breath then said, 'Can you give the contract to *Taylor Made*?'

There was another long pause, no doubt while Daria thought through the request. 'Do you think they'll pull the story Sebastian's ex is running if they do?'

'It's too late for that,' she said. 'But … I want to make sure they don't print anything else.'

'Licia, the press print what they want, you know that. What makes you think somewhere else won't take Mai on?'

Her sister's voice was soft, just like it had been that night when she got back from the hospital. Alicia knew then that her sister believed the stories as much as anyone else – though why she'd encouraged the fake relationship was a mystery. Still, she pushed those thoughts aside and thought of a way to explain that wouldn't give away her secret.

'There's more. Mai fixed him up yesterday. *Taylor Made* have a contract with her that means she can't talk to anyone else while the feature's running. He's really trying to be better and is training all the time. Another scandal isn't something he needs right now. He's already lost his biggest sponsor.'

'Tell me something. Are you working for him?' she asked.

Alicia hesitated. Had Daria figured it out? She didn't want to lie, so skirted around the truth a little. 'How can I not help him? I'm a publicist and he needs a PR clean up.'

'You can talk to me, Licia. You know that, don't you?'

She took a bigger gulp of coffee this time, trying to rid the lump in her throat. 'I know, and I will. It's just …'

'You can't now.' Daria didn't sound cross, which was a relief.

'No, not now.'

'OK, hire *Taylor Made* for my wedding on whatever condition you want. Blair and I don't want any money for it.'

'Thank you, Daria,' she said, with her throat all choked up.

'Anytime. Just promise me one thing. Take care of yourself.'

'I will, I promise.' Another reminder that she shouldn't get close to Sebastian – like she needed it.

'See you on Friday!' Daria said, a little cheerier than before.

Alicia wasn't feeling as enthusiastic. How could she when she and Sebastian would be under her father's watch every second of every day they were there?

Chapter Seventeen

'Something on your mind, pretty boy?' James asked as Sebastian missed the ball.

Again.

He wasn't exhausted, but since he'd left the warmth of Alicia's bed the consequences of the day before had come back to haunt him. If this latest story got out, not only would his sponsors be even more likely to pull, but Alicia would be publicly humiliated.

So he'd made a decision. When the story came out he was going to deny it with everything he had and tell the world the truth – that he'd read the article Mai sold and wanted to apologise. At least then there would be two sides and people would see Alicia standing by him. Maybe they'd wonder if any of what Mai said was true.

But it wasn't part of Alicia's master plan to save his career, and wondering how she'd react to the news was making him lose focus today.

'How about we come back in a few hours?' he suggested.

After all, he still had to get home and get a change of clothes. He liked going back to her place after training and today he'd head straight there. No more stupid ideas for him.

'Fine, but get your head back in the game. The French Opens are coming up fast and you need to give it your all,' James said.

The reminder was timely. He shouldn't be worrying about what the press were saying or wondering if what little time he had with Alicia would be enough. He should be researching his opponents, finding out their handicaps, and getting ready to whip their arses on the court.

All good in theory, but practice was more difficult. 'I get it. See you in a few.'

After packing up his racket, he headed for his car. A red Chevy parked down the street caught his eye and he frowned. Wasn't that the car he saw yesterday outside Mai's? He ditched his bag on the backseat and crossed the road. Before he got close enough to make out the driver the thing pulled away. As the car turned, the early afternoon sun shone through the window and he saw a glint of gold hair.

He remembered Alicia saying she had seen a blond-haired man outside the party just as he had arrived. If it was any other time in his life it would be crazy to put the coincidences together. After what had happened the day before, Sebastian wasn't so sure.

When he was back in his car he pulled out his mobile and called Alicia.

'Hi,' she answered cautiously.

Distracted, he asked, 'Is everything OK?'

'I was about to ask you the same thing.'

His first thought was that the story was out already. But then *Taylor Made* didn't release daily. Still, they could have sold the story to someone else. 'Are the pictures out?'

'No, I meant … you left.'

The last part was said so quietly he wasn't sure if he heard her properly. But he grinned. 'You were snoring so hard you didn't pause when I tried to wake you up.'

'I don't snore!' Her voice was stronger now, filled with annoyance and it made him chuckle.

'It's a cute snore. Girlie.'

'Sebastian!'

'Chill, Blondie. I think it's adorable. Anyway, teasing aside there's something I wanted to ask you. That man you saw at the party, did he have wavy blond hair?'

'I think so. Why are you asking?'

He sat back in the seat, thudding his skull against the headrest. Shit. 'I think he's following me. Unless the photographer you hired has a partner?'

She didn't answer for so long he knew the answer. 'No. I told Sam I'd get in touch when we had something worth printing.'

Shit, shit, shit. '*Taylor Made* or someone else?'

The guy in the park yesterday was dark-haired, which meant it had to be someone else. Christ, could he not go five fucking minutes without someone wanting enough scandal to destroy him?

'Definitely not *Taylor Made*. I just got off the phone with them. They've agreed to give me all the photographs taken yesterday,' she said.

'How did you pull that off?' he asked, and if there was awe in his voice he didn't care. She'd done the impossible, and he thought Dynamo was good.

'My sister. She agreed to let me make the deal. *Taylor Made* get full coverage of Daria's wedding if I get the photographs and a promise from them they won't print anything bad about you again. Well, after the month feature, anyway.'

She didn't sound happy, which meant there was a catch. 'Did you tell her the truth?'

Alicia sighed. 'I didn't lie, but I wasn't completely honest either.'

He realised then why she wasn't thrilled. Alicia was honest and sweet. She'd probably never had to keep secrets from her family before. Just one more tick in her favour. If he'd met Alicia before Mai …

Sebastian stopped that thought dead. He'd have hurt her, like he hurt every woman who got close to him.

Changing gears, he asked, 'Why did they agree? I mean, your father is newsworthy but scandal versus a squeaky clean wedding?'

'Squeaky clean, yes. But Daria's marrying Blair

Roberts. His father is retiring this year, which makes Blair the sole director of Roberts Industries.'

OK, now he got it. The company had a hand in everything from alcohol to sponsoring up-and-coming sports brands and designers. A Simpson daughter marrying into a multi-billion pound family would definitely rank higher than a kiss between exes.

It also meant Alicia had to rely more on the family connection she'd been so freaked out about using in the beginning. All to save his arse. He didn't have words to express how grateful he was. 'I don't know what to say.'

She laughed a little. 'You don't have to say anything. I'm just doing my job.'

Was she, though? Part of him was beginning to wonder, and playing on her emotions to save his career wasn't fair. 'I really appreciate it, I do. But I don't want you to have to bring your family into this.'

'I'm not going to. You can thank me by behaving yourself from now on.'

He smiled at the bossy, prissy tone. 'Yes, ma'am.'

He relaxed back against the seat and all the tension drained from his muscles as he listened to her breathing on the other end of the line. He should say goodbye, hang up, but he couldn't force the words out.

'So, are you … er …?' She didn't say anything else.

'Am I …?' he asked.

She whispered, 'Coming over later?'

Closing his eyes, he wondered if she was wary about saying it because she'd rather he didn't. He didn't want to look too closely at why her rejection hurt like a bitch.

'Not if you don't want me to.'

'I do,' she said too quickly.

He sighed with relief. 'Then I will. I'm going home to get a change of clothes first.'

'You can bring a few if you want to stay until we leave for Cumbria,' she said.

His smile got wider. 'Better shift all those vibrators to

make room for my shoes.'

Alicia laughed and it was the loveliest sound he'd heard all day. 'I've a feeling I won't need any.'

'Nope, not one.' Well, maybe *one*. But he didn't think now was the time to bring that up. 'See you later, Blondie.'

'Not if I see you first, Collins.'

He ended the call, grin still in place and feeling a lot lighter than he had earlier. Now there was no chance of taking her down with him, his stress levels could return to normal. Tonight he'd make it up to her, but now he could give it his all on the court. Which, he reminded himself, was what he should be focusing on instead of all the ways he'd thank Alicia later.

The week had gone by too quickly for Sebastian and the buzz he'd been running on after practice every day had almost fizzled out. Even the cameras flashing in his face and the constant fire of questions the media reps kept up didn't stop him yawning.

Alicia stood next to him and his arm around her shoulders was practically holding him up. A late-night press conference on a Thursday drew swarms of those responsible for stressing him out the last few months. But that wasn't why exhaustion was creeping in.

Training was getting intense and though he was shattered by the time he got to her flat each night, he couldn't keep his hands off her. Not that there were any more twice in one night performances, and he'd yet to make things up to her properly after the deal she'd struck with *Taylor Made*, but he tried to make up for it in other ways and hid his fatigue as best he could.

One of the reporters from a national newspaper asked him something about the charity, but he couldn't quite make it out. Literally dead on his feet was not the best side of him to bring to a press conference, but if he hadn't insisted on going with her tomorrow to her family home, he'd have finished training earlier and wouldn't be so exhausted.

Alicia answered, saving him again. 'Sebastian was really keen to set this up. As you know, his grandfather worked two jobs to keep a home for his grandmother and father. They didn't have much and his dedication to his family meant Sebastian's father could do what he loved, and it paid off. If it wasn't for a kind older man's help, he'd never have got that far. The Collins Trust means kids who can't afford it will get professional help and support for free.'

That set off another round of questions and Sebastian wondered how she found out about his grandfather. It was long before he came along and his father didn't talk much about his upbringing.

Alicia amazed him every day, and feeling crappy about the lack of attention he'd been paying her after his promises of unlimited endurance, he wanted to give her something for her. Credit was a good place to start.

'Actually, if it wasn't for Alicia, the Collins Trust wouldn't be here. With me training morning, noon, and evening, she's been a lifesaver.' He pressed a kiss against her temple, only then registering how rigid she was.

Her trademark calm expression was back, but there was tension in her body. 'What did I say?' he whispered low enough so only she heard.

She smiled at him, but he caught a flash of fear in her eyes. 'Later,' she breathed.

His mind shot to high alert like he'd been injected with caffeine, even though the rest of the conference dragged. On the ride home he waited for her to say something, but she kept quiet and he had the crazy sensation that she'd shoved something invisible between them. A line he couldn't cross, which only made him more determined.

'What went on back there?' he asked, glancing at her

briefly before returning his concentration to the road. She stared out the passenger side window. Her spine was too straight and her expression was fixed in that mask he hated.

'You shouldn't have said I was involved. Remember rule three? Don't talk to the press unless you run it by me first.'

What the …? 'Alicia, are you pissed because I broke one of your rules? For Christ's sake, we've already tossed the first two. What's one more?'

He felt her glare, but kept his attention on the road in front of them.

'I think the rules are moot. What I'm talking about is telling the world I'm pretty much running the charity for you. What happens when we officially split? It's just going to make you look worse because I helped you set everything up.'

He turned into her street, conceding she had a point. 'We can figure something out, make it look amicable and we stayed friends. Tony's going to scout around for new sponsors and when the money rolls in for that I'll hire someone to take care of the charity.'

The silence stretched out as he parked and left the car. She didn't wait for him to open the door for her like he wanted to, but it was raining. They jogged to her building and as soon as the door opened they went inside. The routine of coming back after a long day of hard work and having her there had kept him mellow and on an even keel. Now, with her barely saying a word as they climbed the stairs, he had time to reflect on the conversation.

When they got in she headed straight for the kitchen. A curse sounded and he followed her. She was holding one end of a corkscrew but the metal had snapped and stuck out tauntingly from the bottle of red he'd bought yesterday.

Sebastian put his hands on her shoulders to rub the

tension away, but she shrugged out of his hold. Solid proof he wasn't imagining the wedge she'd put between them. He took the bottle from her. 'You talk, I'll open this.'

'There's nothing to say that hasn't been said.'

'Alicia, just spit it out,' he said.

'Fine! I don't know what makes you the expert on good ways to publicise a break-up, so don't patronise me for being annoyed.'

The fission of anger coursing through him made opening the bottle easier than it should have been. When the cork popped, he placed the wine down none too gently on the counter.

With a forced grin, he said, 'That's what makes me the expert. I'll do the opposite of what I did last time. Enjoy your wine.'

What really niggled was that she knew what happened but threw the press version in his face just because she was mad at him. For trying to give credit where credit was due!

Still, her words ate at him as he cleared out of the kitchen and left her to it. He thought she'd gotten over his past when she made the decision to start seeing him. Looked like he was wrong, though he shouldn't be surprised. He wasn't good with relationships, never would be. This was just more proof that he shouldn't get any closer to her. What started a fling was moving into dangerous waters.

For a few minutes, he debated going home and coming by to pick her up tomorrow for their journey to Cumbria, but then vetoed the idea as another yawn escaped. Instead, he lay down on the sofa and shut his eyes.

Mai wanted to scream and scream until her throat hurt and her voice gave out. But she hadn't. Not when the editor had told her they wouldn't be printing the story of

Sebastian in the park. Not even when the editor had said they'd traded the pictures – her pictures! – for coverage of a poncy wedding!

No, she'd kept calm despite the fact her left eye had twitched all through the meeting, right until she reached her front door. When she got inside, she was tempted to let the shriek out, but a groan coming from somewhere in the house caught her attention. It was Jack. Ice laced her veins as she imagined him with someone else. Fucking some dirty skank – after everything they'd been through!

The pain twisted alongside her anger and turned into rage. It propelled her down the hall to their bedroom and she heard the woman's scream of ecstasy. Mai shoved the door open so hard it slammed against the wall, crumbling the plaster, but she didn't care.

What she saw froze her to the spot. Jack's hand was a blur on his erection and his laptop was on the pillow next to him. She heard the woman's scream again and realised exactly what was going on. He was … watching porn. In *her* house on *her* bed – a bed she hadn't been able to get him to touch her in for over a week!

He glanced at her, a look of bliss and extreme pleasure on his face that she'd never seen before. Just then, he released all over his hands, his shirt, the sheets.

Her sheets!

Mai didn't think. She launched herself at him, crossing the room in what felt like no time at all. The rage, the anger, the jealousy tore through her like a wrecking ball and even the sting on her palm as it connected with his jaw didn't snap her out of the madness. She hit him again and again until she was thumping at his chest.

The look of pleasure drained from his expression as his face twisted with something nasty – exactly how she was feeling.

Mai pulled back her arm, fisted her hand, and

shouted, 'You bastard!'

His arm shot out quicker than she could move and he backhanded her so hard she fell back and landed in a heap on the floor. Something sticky and warm pooled from her nose, over her lips and chin. She was bleeding. The thought brought her back from her rage and his feet on the floor next to her face shot a dash of fear through her. She covered her face with her hands, wincing as agony broke through the adrenaline.

'If you fucking hit me again, it will be the last thing you do,' Jack said, a growl in his voice.

Her mind couldn't put Jack, the man who took her back in and who'd loved her so much, with one who could say these things to her. One who could hurt her like he had. Self-defence or not, this wasn't the man she adored.

'Jack. *Jack*, don't hurt me. I'm sorry.' She was shaking now, practically vibrating with fear.

He didn't speak, just stepped over her and left the room. A few minutes later she heard the shower come on. She sat up, then took off her cardigan and pressed it to her face to soak up the blood, stunned that he'd left her when she'd been hurt.

Shocked speechless that *he'd* been the one to hurt her.

The pain didn't ebb, not for a second, and with horror she realised he'd broken her nose. Maybe even her jaw. Someone who loved her couldn't do that, could they?

No. Jack wasn't any better than Sebastian. He might not be cheating on her with another woman but he was getting his sexual kicks from watching them fuck. She picked up his laptop, seeing the site he used to get himself off. The video that starred an ugly, fat brunette who made Mai's eyes hurt to look at. She was about to throw the thing across the room, but that wouldn't do.

She wanted him out. Gone. Then he'd be free to google whatever fat sluts he wanted.

After a quick clean-up on her face, she grabbed an ice pack from the freezer and left her house with one destination in mind – the police station. Jack was going to pay for what he'd done, she'd make sure of it!

Alicia sipped her coffee and nibbled pieces of fruit she'd chopped for their breakfast, watching Sebastian sprawled across her sofa. His massive frame dwarfed the biggest piece of furniture she had. Again, she wondered if she should have woken him last night.

She couldn't believe how quickly he'd drifted off. A glass of wine was all it took to cool her off and for guilt to kick in. She hadn't meant the dig about his track record with break-ups and felt awful about it. But as she sat alone enjoying the wine he'd bought her, it wasn't just the comment she felt a pang of remorse over. She'd kept him up for hours most nights, even when he'd been training vigorously for days. It hadn't been until she draped a quilt over him that she noticed the dark circles under his eyes, the strain lines on his face.

Mostly because every night he made sure to give her his A-game in bed, even when she'd be happy with Sebastian's mediocre. It wasn't fair to him, but every day when he left to go to the gym and she thought about ending what it is they had, her chest hurt and her eyes stung like she was grieving a loss. She knew then she was in too deep, and that had caused her outburst last night. It was herself she was really mad at for starting to care too much, not Sebastian.

He stirred, rolling onto his side and almost toppling onto the floor. Catching himself on the coffee table, he grunted. She wanted to help, but didn't know what kind of mood he'd be in or if he was still mad at her.

Alicia decided to test the waters. 'Morning. I made breakfast.'

Blinking the last of the sleep away he sat up, rolled his shoulders, and stretched out his chest and back. Her coffee tasted acrid as guilt laced her throat. She shouldn't have left him on the sofa. It was barely big enough for her and he looked far from well-rested. This weekend would be perfect for him; he'd be able to recharge his batteries and sleep as long as he liked.

'I'm not hungry. Think I'll grab a shower and we can get going.' Sebastian didn't spare her a glance as he disappeared into her bedroom, making her feel even worse.

Referring to his past last night had been a low blow, and it had obviously hurt him. The creaky pipes echoed through her flat as he switched the water on. Well, if he wasn't willing to talk to her, she had another idea how to make it up to him.

Luckily, Sebastian never closed the bathroom door, never mind locked it. She glanced at his clothes lying crumpled on her bedroom floor and couldn't help but smile. Other woman would be irked by that. Sarah was forever moaning about David's untidiness, but Sebastian's clothes in her flat meant he was there. Where they were didn't matter to her.

He was in the shower, his back facing her. The glass had fogged so much she could barely make out that fantastic backside. It was almost the first thing she'd noticed about him in the boardroom and now she'd seen it in the flesh. Again and again and again.

But she wasn't there to perv on his bum.

She opened the cubical door and he turned, taking the spray of the water against his back. Some escaped over his shoulders, falling in rivulets down his chiselled muscles. He was semi-hard and from the last few days waking up next to him, she knew he must be really pissed at her to not have a full erection.

Before he could speak, she said, 'I came to apologise.' Then stepped into the shower, still wearing her sleep shorts and vest.

The steam clung to her and she was sprayed a little as

he stepped back, a frown marring his brow. But he took the bait and his gaze dropped to her chest. The white top had gone completely translucent.

Sebastian swallowed. 'What are you doing?'

'I told you, I've come to apologise. I was horrible to you last night and I'm sorry.'

She dropped to her knees. The hard floor wasn't the most comfortable place in the world, but she had a lot of making up to do. She grabbed the length of him and felt his pulse quicken.

Sebastian gasped. 'Alicia …'

She took that as invitation and licked him slowly from the root to the tip. Again and again. He slammed a hand into the tiles while he balled the other into a fist.

Capturing the tip between her lips, she used her tongue to drive a low groan from him, then his hands were in her damp hair, grabbing at the roots but not pulling her closer. The sting made her shiver with her own pleasure, and she sucked him in as far as he could go.

It wasn't the first time she'd given him pleasure like this, but it was the first time she'd see it through till the end. The more she worked him with her mouth, tongue, and hands, the more she wanted to finish with him in her mouth, her throat. The spot between her legs pulsed out a protest, but she ignored it.

'Alicia, I'm going to …'

He released her, giving her the chance to pull away. She grabbed his buttocks. She wasn't going anywhere. His hips jerked forward with his orgasm and she swallowed everything he gave her. So sweet, with a little bite, and all him. Pure, virile, and delicious.

Sebastian tugged her to her feet and the twinge in her knees was lost in the heat flaring through her. The feel of the water spraying her oversensitive skin revved her up more. She needed him to … she shook off the thought. This was about him.

Panting, he pulled her close and held her until his breathing slowed enough to speak. 'You're more than forgiven.'

She grinned at him then kissed his jaw. 'Hurry up, you're hogging the shower and we have somewhere to be.'

'I believe you started it, Blondie.' He tugged her wet vest off. 'But we can always share. You know, save time.' Her shorts were next.

'Good point.' She reached for the shower gel but he beat her to it.

'Turn around.'

Biting her lip, she did what he asked but looked back over her shoulder. 'I thought we were in a hurry.'

'Hmm.' He soaped up his hands then moved them over her back, under her arms, grazing the sides her breasts. 'I think we have time.'

He continued to wash her back thoroughly, leaving no inch neglected. As he reached around to wash her breasts, she sighed and relaxed back into him, feeling how almost ready he was again. Wiggling her bottom against him, she tried to speed up the process. He squeezed her nipples and sucked her earlobe.

The current that ran through her body, scalding hot and delicious, made her moan. When he slipped his fingers into her, she was ready to take him. All of him, and his digits weren't enough.

She leaned forward, bracing her hands on the tile, and let the water pelt her back.

'I need you in me. Now.' Asking was getting easier as the days past and her need for him got stronger.

As always, he gave her what she asked for, filling her completely. She could feel his rapid heartbeat, or maybe that was hers. When they were together the lines seemed to blur until it was them, not individual people, and that became more addictive than the way he worked her into a frenzy.

Sebastian cursed. 'We need a condom.'

Squeezing her muscles, she tried to keep him inside. 'It's OK, I'm on the pill.'

His hands tightened on her hips. 'Alicia –'

'I trust you, Sebastian. Please.' She knew he worried.

The articles about him giving his ex a disease had to be one of the false ones. He was usually so meticulous about protection, but they'd never had the conversation since.

He retreated anyway. She turned, about to offer more reassurances. Instead, her lips were caught by his. Her feet left the floor as he lifted her and she wrapped her legs around his waist, welcoming him in. Pressing her back against the tiles, he kissed her manically, like he was beyond desperate for her, as the movement of his hips drover her closer to release.

Another swivel was all it took to send her over the edge. Pleasure pulsed through her as she clung to his trembling arms, drawing out the last of his orgasm. He didn't set her down and kept kissing her, slowly, like he was thanking her, and she kissed him back with the same gratitude.

Finally, he set her down and stared straight into her eyes. 'Thank you for trusting me.'

His expression was serious, his eyes holding an intensity and wonder she'd never seen and her heart lurched. She did trust him, hated that he'd had to go through this public grilling. Loved that he came out the other end and was still Sebastian, still with her.

'You're a good man, Sebastian. How could I not?'

Chapter Eighteen

The drive to her family home was a long one, but Alicia gave him the scoop on what he should expect. If he hadn't known her before, the prim and proper version, then he'd have accused her of exaggerating.

He expected a grilling, maybe some rules. But the routine of breakfast, brunch, lunch, and dinner seemed over the top – especially when she told him all would be served in different dining rooms and he was expected to dress up each night. He doubted her father would approve of the jogging bottoms he'd brought with him to chill out in.

But what niggled at him more was what happened in the shower. Not the sex or the prelude, that was always amazing. In fact, it got even better every time. Though when she told him he was a good man, that's when it had hit him like a kick to the chest. He cared about her far too much. Leaving her next month was going to be the hardest thing he'd have to do.

Despite the fact he knew she cared, that she believed him, Alicia wasn't his mother. She was focused on her career, had admitted that to him when they'd decided to get involved. Asking her to give that up for a life of travelling, a life he'd hated growing up, wouldn't be fair.

Leaving her in London while he was gone would be worse. He trusted her enough to know he wouldn't come home to find a guy in her bed, but at the same time the worry would always be at the back of his mind. Plus, he had a lot of traveling to do, coupled with training as intense and exhausting as last week if he wanted to be at the top of his game. He couldn't expect her to stick around when for weeks at a time he'd be as lively as a zombie.

'It's the next left.'

She pointed to a dirt road in front of them, snapping his focus back to the present. Besides, this was stuff he could worry about when the time came. No point in stressing himself out now.

'Simpson Manor,' he read the sign aloud as they drove in.

'It gets worse from here.'

As he pulled into the courtyard in front of the biggest house he'd ever seen, he conceded Alicia was right. He'd thought she'd been kidding about the wings and that maybe the tennis court had been an over-exaggeration, but there was no fence to mark off a garden in the surrounding countryside. Which only pissed him off. How could someone with this obvious wealth let their daughter stay in a tiny London flat with dodgy plumbing? Or was that Alicia's choice?

There were several sports cars and a Bentley parked to the right, so he pulled into a space. Messing up the earl's pristine courtyard with his two-year-old Porsche Cayman wouldn't be a wise move considering he got the feeling the guy already didn't like him.

After collecting the bags, he walked side by side with her. The entrance was huge, and Alicia pushed the door all the way open. An older woman with the same bone structure as Alicia stood in the foyer next to a man who looked like the eighteenth century had thrown up on him. He guessed they were her parents.

'Mother, Father, this is Sebastian.' Alicia's voice was prim again, with a snooty edge he'd never heard her use.

He waited, expecting the two to embrace their daughter. Maybe shake his hand. They didn't move an inch, just studied him with blank expressions. He felt like a smear of dirt on their pristine floor.

'Pleased to meet you, Mr and Mrs Simpson.' He'd do

polite, but no way was he pretending to be a snob in front of these emotionless drones. Now he had a bit more of an insight as to why Alicia had been fighting against her attraction. She'd been brought up with parents as warm as a snowstorm.

'Is Daria here?' she asked.

Her father answered, his expression softening a little. 'Not yet, she and Blair arrive tonight.'

She nodded. 'Where is Sebastian sleeping? I'll show him to his room.'

Mrs Simpson looked at her husband, who didn't acknowledge her. He just stared at Sebastian. Maybe even through him. There was a volatility about him that made Sebastian antsy. Hell, he should have taken Alicia's advice and stayed away this weekend.

'Henry will show him.' Mr Simpson clicked his fingers and a butler appeared from the doorway at the right. 'We need to talk.'

He frowned at his daughter and Alicia almost wilted. He was about to step in front of her and offer protection from the heavy disapproval radiating from her father, but that wouldn't be a smart move. He was already on the guy's shit list and the Alicia he'd spent the last week with could take care of herself.

Instead, he followed the butler up the stairs, throwing her a look he hoped showed his support. Her wild eyes didn't sit right in her pale, smooth face and he hesitated, his gut twisting as he left her to the sharks. But that was ridiculous, wasn't it? She'd grown up in this house, with these people. Still, he couldn't make his feet take him any further.

Her father clicked his fingers at her and walked into the other room with her mother, a clear instruction for her to follow that had him grinding his molars. She swallowed, then offered him a smile before mouthing, 'I'll be fine.'

'Hurry back. This house gives me the creeps.'

She laughed silently, then rolled her eyes. 'Warm the bed up.'

Sebastian blinked, not sure he'd made that out right, but she had already turned and made her way into another room. As he climbed the stairs, the paintings of all the previous titled Simpsons followed him. By the time he'd reached the top, the eyes seemed to mock him. Even they knew he shouldn't be there.

'I want to report an assault,' Mai told the policeman at the front desk. She didn't have to fake the tears or the hitch in her voice. As well as the pain in her nose and jaw, those things came from her heart being ripped in two.

'I'll have someone take your statement shortly. Do you need medical assistance?'

'Probably,' she said.

'I'll have someone take you to the hospital later. Please, take a seat.'

He gestured to the empty chairs lining the wall. The station was quiet, but it was barely midday. She expected night would be busier – especially at the weekend. To pass the time she pulled out her mobile and set up the camera for a selfie. She'd not had time to check for damage earlier and photographic evidence could never be a bad thing.

After snapping the picture she winced when it flashed up on her screen. Between the swelling and dried blood, she looked horrific. Just then, her phone chimed with a text and she opened it.

Babe, I'm so sorry. Please come home and we'll talk. I didn't mean to hurt you, I love you.

Jack's message just made her eyes water more. He didn't love her – he wasn't even attracted to her! She replied, *Porn? PORN, Jack? Fuck you!*

She tried to switch it off, but he was faster with his reply.

I know, I can't help it. I've been watching since you left me. It's an addiction, babe. Help me, don't leave me.

Her finger froze over the off button as she stared at the words. Guilt twisted her lungs until it got hard to breathe. If he had a problem, that was on her. After all, she'd cheated on him with Sebastian, hadn't she? She'd also tore into him this morning, taking out her anger on him when she should have probably stayed calm and listened. Maybe then she wouldn't be sitting in a police station with a swollen face.

I'm not leaving you. Just going to the hospital.

Collins. It all came down to him, didn't it? If he hadn't struck a deal for his new slut's family wedding, none of this would have happened. The fury came back, but now she was aiming it at the right person.

Jack's reply distracted her.

I'm so sorry, Mai. I can't believe I did that.

She frowned, wishing he wouldn't torture himself. She'd put him through enough.

Water under the bridge, babe. I love you and will see you soon xoxo

'Miss, you wanted to make a statement?'

Her head snapped up as a man in uniform stepped closer. Mai nodded. 'Yes, I want to press charges against the man who did this to my face.'

'Let's go to one of the interview rooms.'

She switched off her mobile this time and followed the man through the station, smiling a little as a plan formed for the perfect payback. When she was seated and had refused the policeman's offer of a hot drink, he switched on the tape and recorded the time, date, and their names.

'Now, tell me what happened,' the man said.

'This morning, my ex punched me.'

'I need a name, Miss.'

She squeezed out a few tears for effect – which wasn't hard given the pain she was still in. 'Collins.

Sebastian Collins. I want him arrested for assaulting me.'

Alicia followed her parents into her father's study. Unease prickled the back of her neck. It had been years since she'd been called to this room, but her mother hadn't been there. As far as she knew, her mother had never been allowed. Until now.

Her mother took the chair her father gestured to at the side of the desk, then he rounded it and stared Alicia down. She straightened her shoulders and tried to keep her fear from showing, just like her mother had taught her, but one glance at the woman and she could see emotion had cracked through the mask she always wore.

That's when she lost the ability to hold her tongue. 'What's going on?'

Her father winced – no doubt at her choice of words. 'Juliette?'

Oh God. Why was he letting her mother lead the conversation? Alicia sat down in the chair before her legs gave out. This must be something that required more tact than he was capable of.

Her mother rose and crossed to the desk. She picked up a folder, then handed it to Alicia. Her eyes were too shiny and Alicia didn't want to open the file. She guessed the contents were bad – maybe even copies of the photographs from the park the other day. How could she explain that?

'I'm so sorry, sweetheart.' Juliette sat next to her and squeezed her thigh. 'We thought you should see these.'

Alicia opened the folder and her worst fear slapped her in the face. They were of Mai and Sebastian in Hyde Park. First them talking, then Mai with tears in her eyes, then a picture that made her sick to her stomach – the kiss.

But something was different. She couldn't see Sebastian's face in any of these pictures. The ones she'd bargained for from *Taylor Made* were side on and caught everything. This only showed Mai's hands in his hair when she kissed him, like there had been someone else taking pictures behind him.

Someone who was blackmailing them? She met her mother's concerned gaze with rising panic. 'Where did you get these? They don't want money, do they?'

'No, they don't want money, Alicia.'

'Good,' Alicia put the photos on the desk with shaking hands, but the relief of finding out her family wasn't being blackmailed relaxed her enough to think straight. 'How did you get these?' Her mother didn't meet her eyes, which raised her suspicions. She turned to her father. 'Who took the pictures?'

'That hardly matters, not when you're missing the obvious. Your *boyfriend* is having an affair!' He said the word 'boyfriend' with his expression twisted with disgust.

'I know about this,' she said, staring him down for the first time. 'Mai kissed him. What I want to know is where these pictures came from.'

'Irrelevant! You can't believe him. He's taking you and this family for fools. I will not allow it.'

'Arthur,' her mother cautioned but he barrelled on.

'No, Juliette. Do you want to see your daughter humiliated in those gossip rags? Be known as another one of the man's trollops?'

The reminder that he didn't think more of her than a common slut cut deep, but she didn't feel sorry for herself this time. Now anger boiled through her veins and she rose, literally standing up to a man she'd spent so long trying to please.

'You don't know anything about me and Sebastian, Father. Now tell me where these pictures came from!'

His face turned a deep shade of puce, but he didn't speak unless she could count the angry sputter that escaped his lips.

'He hired a private investigator,' her mother said.

'Juliette, leave us. Now!' he shouted.

Alicia grabbed her arm. The fear in her mother's expression reminded her that her father was still powerful. He could still do awful things and there wasn't anything any of them could do, not even her brave mother, who'd stood up for Alicia so many times before.

It was time for her to grow a backbone and deal with her father as an adult instead of looking at him like a giant who could crush her at will.

She turned to face him, releasing her mother's arm so she could leave. 'You've invaded my privacy and Sebastian's.'

Her father planted both hands on the wooden desk and leaned forward. 'If I hadn't you'd never have known what kind of a man he is!'

'Like I said, I knew already. If your private investigator had been paying enough attention, he'd have heard Sebastian apologise for what happened and see that Mai took it the wrong way. He might have even noticed the journalist who caught the kiss on camera.'

He threw his hands in the air. 'See? I knew something like this would happen. Scandal is what comes when you associate yourself with –'

'There's no scandal, Father. Who do you think got the pictures off the press? I'm a good publicist, and I know how to stop things like this leaking or getting blown out of proportion.'

He sputtered again, but she saw something in his eyes she'd never seen before. Respect? However grudgingly, it was there and she felt like she'd grown five inches because of it. He may be mad at her, he might even be livid at Sebastian, but he couldn't deny anymore that she wasn't capable of dealing with things in her own life. Her own way.

She wondered if telling him the truth – that Sebastian was just a client – would calm him down. But if he was being followed, no doubt by the blond-haired man, then her father would already know Sebastian was spending the night at her flat. She didn't want to have to explain their casual relationship – that would be information overload.

'You need to accept that Sebastian is trying. If you've been keeping tabs on him, you'll know how hard he's been working, right through to the evening. Father, please give him a chance.'

The colour slowly drained from his face and soon his breathing returned to normal, but his expression was still one of a man who was not happy things weren't going his way. Eventually he said, 'One last chance.'

She was so relieved she had the brief urge to hug him, but of course that would earn her scorn for her idiocy. In his eyes, showing emotions was almost as bad as what she'd done when she was a teenager. 'Thank you.'

She turned to leave but stopped when he said.

'This is the final chance. For him and you.'

Swallowing, she forced her feet to move on a floor that seemed like it was covered with drying superglue. One more chance, then she'd suffer the same fate as Jonathan. Not that it would make much of a financial difference – he'd already told her she wouldn't get her trust fund until she proved she was worthy of it. But it would emotionally, especially if her mother and sisters obeyed his wishes.

Chapter Nineteen

A knock on the glass jolted Sebastian awake. Cursing, he tried to push the last of the dream away and got up. He headed for the door but the next knock came from behind him. Still half asleep and achy from an all-nighter on the sofa, he turned. Alicia clung to the rail outside the French doors, mouthing, 'Let me in.'

He rushed across the room, stumbling over one of his bags. Seeing her laugh only pissed him off. Pulling open the doors, he almost growled at her. 'What the hell are you doing? You could have been hurt.'

Or worse. Dread lined his stomach at the thought of her falling …

'Relax.' She hiked a leg over the rail and he caught her waist, lifting her the rest of the way over. 'It's not hard.'

'You've done this before?' He didn't know whether to be shocked or impressed.

Her grin made his heart beat a little easier. He hugged her closer, more than glad she was here, regardless of the stupid way came.

'Once. Maybe twice.' At his frown she hurried on to explain. 'Well, a lot. We had an eight o'clock curfew, even at the weekend when our parents would entertain. Daria, Sylvia, and I all used to sneak into each other's rooms.'

'Why not use the hall?' he asked, baffled they'd go to such extremes.

Alicia wrinkled her nose. 'Henry snoops around at night and he'd tell our father.'

Spiderman moves to scale the wall, a strict curfew,

and a nosy butler. What else was he going to find out about this crazy family? 'How old were you?'

'Fourteen.' She kissed him, but his mind was reeling.

Sebastian pulled away while he tried to get his head around it. 'And your older sister would be, what, sixteen? Shouldn't you have been sneaking out instead? To meet boyfriends or something?'

It seemed like a lot of hassle just to see each other. He couldn't imagine ever being given a curfew. His parents took him to events and hadn't put much limitations on him at all. Alicia paled and pulled out of his hold.

'We weren't allowed boyfriends.'

He sat on the edge of the bed while she paced in front of him. 'Ever?'

She shook her head. 'Mother told us early on we had to save ourselves for a suitable husband, and that Father would be cross if we didn't. She was wrong. He didn't get cross, he was …'

Her eyes widened as she stared at him and he figured she was thinking to the time her dad had told her to ignore her misbehaving libido. His hands curled into fists. He'd have liked Mr Simpson to be right there so he could plant one in his face for making her ashamed for being passionate. He couldn't call himself a father.

'You can tell me. I won't judge you.' She should know that.

She settled into one of the antique armchairs in the room and stared out at the sprawling gardens. He'd been surprised to see not only a tennis court, but also a cricket field and a small lake in the distance that seemed to be part of the manor grounds.

'I met a boy when I was fifteen. His father was a carpenter and they lived outside town in a small cottage. Nothing like here. I snuck out a lot, to go and see him because I couldn't tell my father I was dating him – we were supposed to save ourselves for someone he deemed suitable. I thought he was. I thought I was in love.'

His lungs cramped at her admission of loving someone else, but she was talking and that's what he should focus on. Not the fact Alicia had been with other men. Hell, he knew she wasn't a virgin but she'd only been fifteen. The thought turned his stomach as his mind jumped to all kinds of conclusions.

He forced himself to concentrate and settled on the footstool next to her, taking her hands in his. 'He found out, your father?'

He'd found out alright, about everything. For a while, Alicia wished her father had discovered her relationship earlier and put an end to it before anything worse happened. She had been naïve, uninformed. The mess that followed giving into her hormones was ugly. A time in her life she didn't particularly want to relive or share. Especially with Sebastian.

Instead she nodded, letting him think that was the worst part.

'He was mad?'

His dark, melting eyes were focused on her and filled with sympathy. She knew he wouldn't judge her, wouldn't think she was a trollop. People made mistakes and he'd made his fair share. Why not let him know? She opened her mouth, but couldn't force the words out.

'There was more?'

She pressed her lips together hard, nodding again.

A knock sounded at the door and Henry's voice rang through. 'Dinner will be served at seven, Mr Collins.'

'Fine,' he called loud enough to be heard, his eyes never leaving hers. Quietly, he said, 'Tell me.'

'Master Simpson asks that you join him for drinks at six thirty,' the butler continued.

'Not a problem,' he said, though his shoulders stiffened.

Alicia knew then she couldn't tell him what her father

did when he found out, or about the private investigator he'd hired. Not now, when Sebastian was going to spend alone time with him. It was already clear he didn't like her father, and she couldn't blame him. The man wasn't the most welcoming, and worse, he'd had Sebastian followed for weeks!

When the sound of footsteps in the hall trailed away, she smiled. 'None of that matters anymore. I've spent every day since trying to make him proud of me again, thinking it will make him love me like he does Daria and Sylvia. Now I'm not so sure I want that.'

'What do you mean?' His thumbs trailed gentle, soothing circles across the veins at her wrists.

'Daria's marrying a man who she never sees, because she believes he's perfect for her. He's perfect in our father's eyes and Daria thinks that's enough.'

His incredulous expression was more proof that her one-eighty was the right decision. Normal people married for love, for passion, because they wanted to be with that person for the rest of their lives and grow old together – as friends and lovers. Not because their parents deemed the man suitable, which her father had made perfectly clear that Sebastian probably would never be.

His warning about last chances rang in her head again, but she didn't dwell on it. She'd known what could happen when all this started, what she hadn't expected was how much she would want Sebastian after she had him. It made thinking of their time being over too painful to worry about.

'Your family are crazy.' He shook his head. 'It must have been like living with emotionless humanoids.'

She forced out a laugh. 'You're not far wrong.'

But she didn't want to talk more about her family, or worry about the time when they were over for good. Instead, she scooted closer so she could kiss him. How he pulled her into his arms made her feel cherished and the way she fit against him was easy and right, heating her all over and making her tingle. As Sebastian slid his hands up her spine, taking her shirt with them, she thought this was exactly how relationships were supposed to be.

Warm, exciting, and fuelled by passion.

Dinner was stuffy, refined, and over the top. The brandy shared with Mr Simpson before hadn't been much better. The conversation painted a colourful picture of why Alicia had been so worried to have him there. As far as the old earl was concerned, Sebastian wasn't a suitable addition to his precious family.

Alicia's sister arrived, and the greeting was less formal. Daria hugged her and had even thrown a smirk his way with a wink that reassured him the Simpsons weren't all soulless creatures.

Still, the respectable distance between the happy couple made him wonder if Alicia's sister had stuck with her mother's advice. He doubted the guy would be scaling a wall on questionable ladders to have some time with his girl – like Sebastian was doing now.

Alicia opened her bedroom window and he climbed in, praying the rickety wooden steps would stay in place or he'd be forced to go back via the hall and risk getting busted by the nosy butler.

'I was about to send out a search party,' she teased.

He was about to quip back but her room caught him off-guard. It was all pinks and silvers with an antique dressing table, mirror, and those fancy things he'd expect the queen to have. Her bed was a mountain of pillows and quilts, looking like something fresh out of a fairy tale. Not that different from her smaller, less fussy bed at her flat.

'This is enough to emasculate any man,' he muttered as he looked around.

'I'm sure you're more than masculine enough to deal

with it.' In one swift move, she pulled the black dinner dress over her head, revealing lacy red underwear that left nothing to his imagination.

Instantly, his focus was glued on her, the girlie room forgotten. He also remembered what he'd brought with him, though after last night he wasn't sure it was a good move to bring it here. Still, if Alicia was serious about this new outlook of hers, she'd enjoy it. He knew he would.

'Tonight, I'm in charge,' he said, raking his gaze over her bare curves. 'Strip.'

Her eyes flared and her skin took on a pink glow, a sure sign she liked where this was going. Slowly, she unclipped her bra and let it slide off her arms. A flare of heat arrowed south and his hands itched to touch her, but he couldn't yet.

She hooked her thumbs under the material at her sides, then wiggled her hips as she pushed, letting her knickers fall to the floor. Her arms hung limp at her sides and she looked at him, half curious, half nervous for what came next.

Sebastian stepped closer and it took everything he had to not touch her. Instead, he dug his hands into his pocket, one fisting around the little metal bullet he'd bought. He cleared his throat. 'Get comfy on the bed, any way you like.'

She moved backward until her thighs hit the edge. Crawling in reverse, she gave him a mouth-wateringly intimate view. He hardened, his arousal digging painfully into his trousers and his heart beating too fast. Sweat slicked his brow with the effort it took to hold back.

'This is the hottest thing you've done and you haven't even touched me.'

Her voice was ragged and dripped with the same need he felt. A need he worried would never go away. She'd move on and after tonight, be able to enjoy all the things she'd been too afraid to do before. Back where it all started for her, he'd free her completely from the stuffy, reserved life she'd been brought up to believe she should have. It was the only way he could think to repay her for everything she'd done for him.

'I'm not going to touch you, but you're going to enjoy it. Then I'll give you what you really want.'

Her brows furrowed in confusion as she settled against the jumble of pillows, her blonde hair splayed out around her shoulders, making her look like an angel. 'I don't get what you … oh.' Her eyes widened. 'Sebastian, I can't.'

'You can, Alicia. You can do anything you want. This might help.' He tossed her the vibrator and she caught it, the shock parting her lips a sign this wouldn't be as easy as he'd hoped. 'Do you know how hot it will make me?'

Her gaze dipped down his body and her cheeks flushed. 'You too. I'm not doing this solo.'

He grinned, more than on board with that plan. He undid his button, pulled down the zip, and freed himself. 'You're on.'

Alicia twisted the device and the buzz hummed through the room. Her cheeks turned a deep pink, betraying her bravado. As she trailed the little silver bullet over her nipples, he had to clamp down on the pressure building in him and slowed his strokes.

Then she went south and circled her clit with the vibrator. She moaned, her head falling back and her eyes closing as she worked it around herself. His erection thickened in his hand and he had to let go or he was going to fall over the edge with her like he hadn't had an orgasm for a week, not a few bloody hours.

She undiluted on the sheets and her hips jerked as she worked her arm. Cold, irrational jealousy of the device cut through the desire, but that was ridiculous. It was a machine, and she did the same beneath him when she

227

was close. Still, his gut clenched hard as she moaned and her thigh muscles tightened.

Unable to stick to his own plan, he stripped down, stalked to the bed, and tugged her to the edge by the ankles. Ignoring her gasp, he took the vibrator from her and tossed it across the room, not giving a damn where it landed.

'I thought you said I had to do it before I got what I wanted,' she protested, but wrapped her legs around his waist anyway.

'I changed my mind. From now on, when I'm around it's only me who gets to make you come.' He entered her in one long, slow thrust.

She clung to his wrists, pulling him down so she could take his mouth. He let her, tangling his fingers through her hair as he made love to her with everything he had, not caring that this time it wasn't just about the need and desire. This time it was about so much more. Right now, she was his and worse, he was hers.

A tight hold on her arm was all that kept her legs moving, one in front of the other, until they reached the steps to the clinic. Alicia was numb, inside and out. This was the right thing, her father had told her so. The proper thing.

Doing this would mean she'd no longer be tainted. A few hours and it would all be over, he'd said.

Sweat beaded on her brow and she started to shake. A nurse appeared with a smile for her father, but her expression morphed to disdain when she looked at Alicia. Dirty, that's how she felt. Dirty and alone.

But she wasn't, she reminded herself as she hugged the tiny bump at her waist. It was the reason she was there, to say goodbye to her child. The reminder had her breath coming too fast and shallow again. Her throat tightened and her eyes watered, but her heart hammered on, proving she was still alive, still a person.

'I can't, Father. Please don't make me!' The tears *poured from her eyes now, never stopping.*

'You have to, Alicia. Do you want to be alone forever? A disgrace to your family? Because we'll all suffer if you don't do this.'

Sobs racked through her chest, making it hard to speak. She didn't want to end up like Jonathan, but when the nurse led them into a room across the way, her feet dragged and she wanted nothing more than to run. 'Please ... no.'

'Alicia, wake up.'

She was shaken out of the awful dream, still sobbing and clinging to her waist while reality bled away the past.

'No,' she said, rubbing her empty stomach. 'No.'

The loss hit her as hard as it did the day she lost her child, and she couldn't break free from it. Not that she deserved to. She should suffer for what she'd done.

'Jesus, Alicia. Come here.' He pulled her onto his lap and held her tight.

She let his warmth seep through her chilled skin, crying into his shoulder like a child and feeling even worse for allowing herself this shred of comfort. She didn't do anything to deserve it. Suffering was the price she should pay.

'Don't ...' Her throat was too thick to tell him to leave her, so she tried to pull away.

He just held her closer, running his hands over her back and through her hair too quickly to be comforting. 'Tell me what happened. It might help.'

She shook her head against his chest while more sobs broke free.

'Shhh, you're OK, you're safe,' he whispered, rocking her back and forth for what seemed like hours.

She wasn't OK, but the tremors stilled eventually and she managed to breathe. 'I'm sorry.'

'Don't be.' He pulled back, wiped the last of her tears away and she saw the concern in his eyes in the moonlight. 'Nightmare or memory?'

When she didn't answer, his gaze dropped to her hands, protecting her empty stomach, and he cursed. 'There was more, wasn't there?'

She nodded, still trapped in the horror of the dream and the fact that now, he'd know what she did.

'He got you pregnant, that boy.' Sebastian's voice was soft, but his jaw was clenched like it was an effort to stay calm.

'He didn't mean to,' she said, not wanting him to jump to conclusions. 'When I found out, I was almost sixteen. I thought we'd get married soon anyway – it's what he promised. By the time I found out, it was too late. My father had discovered our relationship and managed to get his dad a job in Wales. Darrell was into rugby, which was more important than I was, and he saw the opportunity to go to another team, to further his career.'

He watched her with a frown, probably worried she'd burst into tears again but she'd wasted enough on Darrell. No more.

'You didn't tell him?' Sebastian asked.

'I told him. He left anyway.' That part was harder to say. Her own personal proof that life didn't have fairy tale endings. Not for her, anyway.

She felt his hands turn into fists behind her back and his frown morphed to anger. 'Those bastards.'

Alicia didn't speak, she didn't want to have to tell him what happened then. For Sebastian to look at her like the murderer she was. 'It's over now. I don't care about Darrell anymore.'

His eyebrows pulled together then his jaw dropped. 'Please don't make me – that's what you said in your dream. Alicia, did someone force you to have an abortion? Your father?'

'It was my choice,' she whispered. 'I didn't want to be outlawed like my brother.'

He tilted her chin and all the traces of anger had gone. Her heart tripped over itself with the compassion she saw in his eyes. The emotions she felt for him seemed reflected in his gaze. How could he walk away after a month when he cared for her like this?

'You were just a child, you shouldn't have been made to choose. He forced you to do something you didn't want to.'

Maybe, but …

'I could have said no. I could have fought harder and I didn't. I lost my baby because I was too ashamed and broken-hearted to fight.'

Tears welled in her eyes again and he pulled her closer, kissed her lips softly. 'You're strong now, Alicia. Don't let him make you choose again. He can't keep controlling you forever.'

'I'm trying.' She kissed him – the need to revel in his acceptance made it mandatory.

Sebastian didn't say anything else, just kissed her back tenderly, like she was someone worthy of being adored. She almost believed it too.

Chapter Twenty

Jack woke up with Mai in his arms. She was still sound asleep, probably from the painkillers the doctor had given her to ease the pain. Again, the shitty feeling in his stomach flared until he felt sick with it.

What the fuck had he done?

He'd been in a haze of lust, enjoying the afterglow of a great orgasm, and then she'd attacked him. The pain of what were pathetic slaps stung more than they should, and the anger that roared through him had been impossible to stop.

Even seeing her lying on the floor, her face covered in blood, hadn't calmed him down. He'd barely heard her apology through the rage, and it was all he could do to walk away before he'd caused serious damage.

The fact she'd forgiven him had been a miracle. That she wanted to help him get over his 'addiction' was unbelievable. How could she even look at him after what he'd done?

He swept a few stray hairs away from her face and her eyes fluttered open. He'd fallen into her blue depths once. Hard and sure. And now, even though he was horizontal, he had the oddest feeling of vertigo.

'Morning, babe,' she said, snuggling closer.

His arms constricted around her automatically, and his head was more messed-up than her face. She brushed a kiss on his jaw, making his eyes sting and his heart swell. Shit, this wasn't supposed to happen. Hurt or not, she was a slut who'd ripped his heart out, burst it with her pointy nails, and flattened it with her new Collins-bought stilettos.

The plan. He needed to focus on the plan.

'Marry me, Mai. I don't care about a big, white wedding. All I care about is you.'

The lie tasted bitter on his tongue – or was that the guilt from hitting her? Conning her shouldn't have made him feel bad. Hell, she'd done worse to him.

'Really? Now? But what about money, security?' She rose on her elbow and looked down at him.

He tried not to wince at the mess he'd made of her face. 'Do you really care about that stuff? We have a home that's paid up, I'm almost done with my script, and don't you have some cash saved. Or is it gone already?'

Her eyes glazed over, in that way they did when she was overwhelmed. 'I have some, but it's hard to save when I have to keep up with fashion.'

Wasn't that why he was still stuck there, waiting for a huge pay out that was a long time coming? 'I don't give a shit what you wear, and your hair was gorgeous without the fortnightly bleaching. We can do this, we can save. Haven't you always just wanted a family who loved you? I can give you that.'

Tears leaked from her eyes, coursing down her battered cheek. 'I do! Jack, that's all I want!'

He couldn't avoid the kiss, but it didn't matter. Not when he was a step closer to winning, so he put everything he had into it. Still, he was careful to keep away from her bruises.

Sliding her hand down his chest, she aimed for his groin but there was nothing going on below his navel. She pulled away when she realised he wasn't up for anything like that.

'I have an idea,' Mai said.

She darted out of the room. When she returned, it was with his laptop. He frowned. 'What's that for?'

'Fire it up! Whatever you like. We'll watch together.'

His chin dropped as she handed him the laptop, and

when he saw her waiting patiently for him to open it he realised she wasn't joking.

'Mai …' Shit, he didn't know what to say.

'I'm going to show you that you don't need to do this alone, and maybe one day you won't need it to get aroused around me.' Her gaze dropped when she said the last bit.

Telling her he'd be aroused if she'd never left him, never turned into a skinny, vengeance-seeking whore, would only fuck up everything he'd worked so hard for. Instead, he flicked on the computer and went to the site he visited most.

'You can pick,' he said, passing the thing to her.

He didn't know if it was jealousy of someone who looked like she thought she had to be or because it was the film that had been playing when he got busted, but Mai hit play on his favourite video, then proceeded to attend to his dick like the brunette on the screen was. Over and over until he was harder than steel and about ready to come.

He tugged her away, then returned the favour, all the while watching the actor go to work on the brunette in the same way. It was easier to enjoy it with the visual and the brunette's moans as he made his way between Mai's legs.

But as she writhed against him and moaned his name, something shifted inside him – something that nearly choked him. Climbing up her body, he kissed and lightly nipped her skin like she used to love, until she was begging him to take her and he couldn't speed it up to get it over with. Hell, he couldn't even concentrate on the pretty brunette.

When he slid into Mai slowly, savouring the feeling and the way her eyes glossed over with pleasure, he couldn't take his eyes off her. So he rocked into her in the same slow way, trailing kisses down her neck and across her collarbone until all he could hear and feel and touch was Mai.

When they both fell over the edge together, Jack couldn't keep his eyes open. As he drifted into sleep again with her in his arms, he knew he'd fucked up and done the one thing he promised himself he'd never do again – fall in love with Mai.

'Jack, that was amazing.' She snuggled closer. He was too far gone to reply. 'I have just over seventy thousand. I'll withdraw it today and you can keep it for us so I don't spend it. Sleep well, babe.'

His brain switched back on as she left the bed, but he didn't dare open his eyes. Seventy fucking grand? That was more than enough to tide him over for a while. Screw love, screw this feeling. He was going to get his revenge.

Alicia spent the next day at their in-house spa with her sisters, talking travel, shoes, and the upcoming nuptials. Though really, she listened and even then she didn't hear much. They were being pampered by a team her mother had brought in for the day, but her mind kept drifting to the night before.

Daria must have noticed, because she called her on it. 'Sis, you have it bad.'

Sylvia pulled cucumber slices from her eyes. 'The tennis player? I bet he packs stamina.'

Her mouth dropped open in shock.

Before she could process the words, Daria jumped in. 'Mmhmm. And he's smoking hot. How are you getting around the separate room thing? I climbed through Blair's window last night.'

She blinked, utterly gobsmacked that her reserved sisters were not as perfect as she'd thought. 'You snuck in through Blair's window?'

Sylvia laughed. 'What? You're not the only one who gets to have fun. You just need to be careful you don't get caught.'

'I thought …' Alicia trailed off. She didn't want to say she thought her sisters were virgins. 'You took Mother's advice.'

They both burst out laughing. Through the giggles, Sylvia said, 'That might have worked for Mother, but can you imagine marrying someone like Father?' She shuddered.

Alicia shook her head.

'Anyway, spill. We want all the details.' Daria said.

'When are you getting married? I figured with the publicity that you two must be getting serious,' Sylvia chimed in.

Alicia debated whether to tell them the media version, but her sisters were not as sheltered as she'd thought. And anyway, she was sick of secrets. Confessing her sins to Sebastian had made her realise that people were forgiving – everyone except her father, anyway. But he wasn't here and she trusted her sisters to keep her secrets.

She told them the truth, from scoring him as a client, the way their father had him followed (to which neither seemed as shocked as she'd been), to the watered-down version of what they did last night. She'd felt a shift in him after her confession, something more than casual emotion – had even seen it too. It had been impossible not to let him seep into her heart.

'I don't know how it can ever work. He'll have to travel around the world for tournaments and I'll be stuck in London,' she finished.

Sylvia squeezed her hand, but Daria pursed her lips like she was thinking things through. 'You say you love your job, but you're also saying you're "stuck" in London, which makes me think that's not where you want to be.'

Alicia shrugged. 'I wanted to be successful, like you two. Until recently I've been living my life trying to make Father proud of me again. Now … I don't know if that's any kind of a life – not if he's going to insist on running it for me.'

They wrapped their arms around her. 'Listen,' Daria said. 'You do what your heart tells you is right and don't worry about Father. All you have to do is play the game in front of him. He never visits, so how will he know what's true and what's fabricated for his benefit?'

Sylvia nodded seriously, then said, 'And we're not children anymore. We won't let him banish you from our lives. He'll have to get rid of the three of us!'

'That won't ever happen,' Daria agreed.

'Thank you,' she said, her eyes getting watery again and they hugged her tighter. 'What's this about playing the game?'

Sylvia smirked. 'Watch and learn, sis.'

Alicia's brows pulled together.

'Blair was flung at me when Father wanted to make a deal with his dad. Luckily, we were attracted to each other but of course we'd never show it in front of him.' Daria's sigh was blissful and made Alicia's cheeks heat. 'He's an animal in the bedroom.'

She didn't have time to recover from the shock before Sylvia said, 'Father is trying to set me up with the son of a stuffy man he does business with, but I'm going to make it work for me.' She was about to ask how, when Sylvia grinned. 'Gavin's gay, which is frowned upon by his father. We're going to announce our engagement after Daria's wedding.'

Alicia couldn't form words, she was so stumped. Daria glared at their younger sister. 'How on earth is that going to work for you?'

'Well, not only will I get my trust fund but Father will get off my back about settling down. Gavin will let me work and live my life the way I want.'

'Until he starts talking about grandchildren,' Alicia reminded her, still staggered that her little sister would marry just to get their father off her back. Or was that really the key to being in his good graces? If it was, she wasn't the one with the problem. It was her father.

'We'll think of an excuse to put it off. I'll still be working and traveling,' Sylvia said.

She envied her sisters, but they were right. She had to start living the life she wanted, not the one her father would approve of, and why couldn't she? God knew she'd worked her way up from the bottom at Maine – she knew everything there was about being a publicist.

Why couldn't she do that on her own, build a client base all over the world and maybe even get to keep Sebastian at the end of it? After all, things had changed between them, she was sure of it. If she left Maine she could work from anywhere she wished.

Sebastian stuck close to Blair when they got to the big room in Simpson Manor that acted as a ballroom. He still couldn't get his head around the size of the place. Earlier, during a friendly game of cricket, Blair had said that he just had to play up to Mr Simpson's expectations to make life simpler. Sebastian had wanted to call out the old bastard for putting his daughter through what he had, but he knew Alicia wouldn't appreciate any drama. In the end he'd done all he could do to make life easier for her and forced himself to be polite to her father. When the old earl suggested they play a quick game of tennis, Sebastian paired up with him and did his best to make him think they'd won because he had a hand in it.

Sebastian might have had to smother the urge to whack him with the racket more than once, but he'd managed to keep things friendly.

Since then, there'd been no more warnings from Alicia, and he was actually starting to be on better terms with her father, which – for some reason he couldn't understand – was what she seemed to want. Probably a waste of time considering they'd be over in a few weeks, but he was sick of losing all the time. Plus, she'd been through the ringer enough for one lifetime, she didn't need his animosity against her parent making life harder for her.

'There they are.'

Blair's voice took on a sissy-sounding purr whenever he spoke of his fiancée and at first, Sebastian had teased him. The fact that the guy didn't care at all who knew how he felt about his woman made Sebastian respect him more. He also had to admit he'd been wrong the day before about their relationship being reserved. Blair was just playing the game for Mr Simpson's benefit so he could be with his daughter.

Which begged the question whether that's what he was doing with Alicia. She was grounded, beautiful, and the chemistry between them only sizzled hotter as the weeks went on. Unlike other women he'd been with before and after his split, she didn't want him for whatever he could buy her. She wanted *him*, pure and simple. Without any of the fuss.

Pity that's not all he wanted from her. In another life, she'd have been the woman he could come home to. But he wasn't blessed with a nine-to-five and Alicia wasn't built for a life of traveling. She'd want to be independent, not live off of his winnings – not that he'd mind sharing.

He looked in the direction Blair did and his breath caught in his throat. Alicia and her sisters walked into the room together, Daria in a dazzling red gown, Sylvia in a short, icy blue dress, and Alicia wearing a bottle green silk gown that hugged every curve but still remained classy. Her hair hung in loose curls around her shoulders and though all three were blonde, she was the only one who made his heart beat faster just by being there.

Blair elbowed him. 'And you called me a sissy for going gaga over my girl. Might want to pick your chin up off the floor, Collins.'

A hard knot formed in his stomach as the three approached. She wasn't his girl, never could or would be. He'd known all along, but the reminder that he'd have to give her up in a few short weeks made his mood plummet.

'You scrub up well.' Alicia came in for a kiss, but he took her hand instead and brushed a kiss on the top, earning a frown from her.

He leaned close and whispered in his ear. 'We can save the rest for a private venue.'

She smiled. 'Look at you acting all chivalrous.'

He shrugged. 'I can pull it off when I want to. Plus, the society journalists are here tonight and I'm supposed to be a reformed gigolo, remember?'

Alicia rolled her eyes. 'They shouldn't believe everything they read in the newspapers.'

'You did,' he reminded her.

A blush highlighted her cheekbones. 'I regret that now.'

'Come on, let's dance. And not a repeat of last week. Your father might shoot me with his hunting gun if there aren't a good five inches between us.' He winked, trying to lighten the conversation and the glum mood he'd been in.

She took his hand and he led her across the dance floor where other couples had already gathered. He didn't know anyone and suspected they were all part of England's elite social circle – like the people he'd endured at that horrible party she'd dragged him to. The second he'd walked into the room he'd been faced with scornful looks and hushed voices gossiping. Didn't take a genius to figure out why.

'My father wouldn't shoot you. He may not like you too much, but he's not *that* bad.' She placed a hand on his shoulders, the other in his waiting palm.

Maybe, but he wasn't so sure. If the guy could force his sixteen year old daughter to kill her child, who knew what he was capable of. He judged the distance between their bodies and led her in a slow waltz, hoping he remembered some of the steps in the ten years since his mother had sent him to lessons.

'You never did tell me how your father found out about you and the boy,' he said, pretending to sound blasé about the whole thing but anger was just bubbling beneath the surface.

Alicia tensed and smoothed her expression. 'I've no idea. Can we just drop it for tonight? I don't want to relive that part of my life.'

He knew it was hard, and he didn't want to go into the details or make her relive any of it. If he could he'd take the awful memories from her, but if Alicia was being as careful as they'd been sneaking around behind her father's back, how could he have known?

'We don't have to go there. I just don't understand why you're not curious about how he found out. Isn't that part of your job – to find out how people get hold of information?'

She chewed on her lip.

'Alicia –'

'You're hardly forthcoming about everything. You keep your feelings, hopes, and dreams to yourself, so stop pushing me for information.'

He wanted to wipe away the sheen of moisture away from her eyes, but didn't want to draw attention to her. Manoeuvring her around the dance floor, he had to agree she was right. He hadn't told her much about him – not his past. Not his hopes for the future.

'I did break Mai's boyfriend's nose,' he admitted. 'But not for the reason they printed.'

Her eyes widened and her plum-coloured lips parted. She was too beautiful and he just wanted to enjoy her. But Alicia was right. Though she'd researched him, he'd never been forthcoming with anything personal.

'After Wimbledon, she threw me out. I went back a

week later to see if I could make things right and he was there. In my bed. With Mai.'

'Sebastian, I'm so sorry.'

He shrugged, trying to focus on the steps and not the pity shining from her eyes. 'Don't be, I'm over it and probably deserved it. She wasn't the person I was supposed to be with and I can see that now. It was just easier at the time. We both seemed to want the same things, but not many women could put up with a man who can't function for weeks on end because they have to train so hard. Nor should they have to.'

Chapter Twenty-one

Alicia could see now why he'd opted for variety over another relationship, and her hope that they could be more didn't seem as shiny as it did that afternoon. He had commitment issues, which she thought she understood, only now her perspective had shifted. It wasn't Sebastian who was incapable of staying in a relationship.

He couldn't see why a woman would want to stay.

'Sex shouldn't be all that's important, though,' she mumbled.

They may have started out as a sex-only deal, but they'd both grown closer this past week and would get closer still. She had to believe that.

'If it was I wouldn't have been living like a nun for the last few years.' She hoped the hint got through to him.

Sebastian shook his head. 'It's not just that. Some games are mentally draining. A few days this week I haven't been able to hold a conversation and the press conference,' he made a face, 'Well, it didn't go great, did it?'

She shook her head. An urgency to prove him wrong, to change his outlook, made her heart gallop. This felt like her chance to make him see not every woman was like his ex, but when she tried, the song changed. He took her hand and led her to the bar.

Alicia didn't get much alone time with him after that. It seemed everyone, even the journalists, wanted to speak to the 'it' couple and she felt bad for stealing Daria's thunder. From the conversation with her sisters earlier today, she knew Daria would probably be grateful. She'd been on the dance floor with Blair for hours, showing no sign of wanting to let her fiancé go. Alicia wished she could have that with the man next to her, not conversing with a magazine reporter. She zoned out of the conversation until the words 'wedding bells' snapped her focus back.

'What?' she asked.

Sebastian laughed and rubbed a reassuring thumb across the back of her hand.

'We've just started dating,' he answered, then looked down at Alicia and winked. 'But anything's possible.'

Her heart took off full speed while adrenaline fizzed through her veins. She was pretty sure her hands were shaking too and the butterflies in her stomach felt more like mutated insects. She needed to calm down. He was only playing to the press – his wink had said it all. But for a moment, underneath the shock, she'd wanted him to be telling the truth.

She managed to hold it together through the rest of the informal interview, sipping the champagne in her hand instead of swallowing the fizzy liquid in one go. What she really needed was something stronger, something with more bite, but her father wouldn't serve anything less than the good stuff.

As soon as they were out of earshot from the reporter, Alicia said, 'I need some air.'

Without waiting for him to reply, she tugged her hand free and made her way to the balcony overlooking the gardens. The water features were all lit up with white and the gold and ivory roses her mother had ordered in the thousands were placed in bouquets all over the place, making tonight feel like a wedding. She shuddered to think what they'd do on the big day.

She shuddered to think what she'd do, showing up single after the public humiliation she'd put her father's name through by dating Sebastian.

246

'There you are.'

He slid his arms around her waist and pulled her back so she was resting against his chest. She should move away, having Sebastian touch her and hold her was becoming too addictive and there were too many variables working against them. Not least his view on relationships. Her eyes pricked and she was glad she had her back to him.

'Wanna tell me why you ran away?' His breath stirred her hair.

No, she really didn't. But all this lying – to him, her boss, and parents – was going to give her an ulcer if it hadn't already. It was time to be honest, with him at least. She couldn't go through weeks of this if he was just going to walk away at the end of it. Could she?

She swallowed and kept her back to him. It was easier when he couldn't see her face, when she couldn't see the pity in his expression. 'Things have changed for me. I've changed.'

He squeezed her tighter. 'I know, but there's nothing wrong with that. You're amazing, Alicia.'

Her vision blurred. 'Thanks, but that's not just what I mean. I ... care about you. I'm not sure you and I can keep doing this.'

She swallowed back the lump in her throat, but knew she couldn't hold herself together for long – the weekend had been a rollercoaster of emotions. Sebastian released her, then turned her around. She hoped the tears had gone, she didn't want him to know she was crying over him.

He cupped her face and ran his thumbs under her eyes, swiping away the traitor moisture. 'Blondie, I care about you too, but that doesn't mean we have to give up anything. We only have a few weeks, why not make the most of them?'

Maybe she'd not been clear enough. The extent of how *much* she cared about him didn't come through in her words, but his offer was tempting. Too tempting, and exactly what she wanted. She couldn't go back to pretending there was nothing between them. It would surely hurt more than staying with him until he left for France.

Alicia sucked in a breath and then let it out. 'You're right, I just didn't want you to go on thinking I don't.'

Chicken. That's what she was. The biggest coward ever. But this couldn't be the end. She didn't want it to be. And more time together might have the opposite effect. She might get sick of him always dumping his clothes where he stripped, or pissed off that he always left the toilet seat up.

'I know you do, and I hope you believe I feel the same.'

She saw the truth in his eyes, and that damn hope got all bright and sparkly. 'I do.'

'Good.' He kissed her forehead. 'How early do you think we can escape from this party?'

Alicia forced the last of her doubts away and grinned. 'Half an hour, tops.'

Taking her hand, he led her through the patio doors and back into the house. 'Enough time for another whirl on the dance floor.'

She followed, the uncomfortable buzz in her stomach a constant nag whether this was the right thing to do. It didn't matter, because she was on the road to a broken heart either way and she couldn't seem to turn back.

'He seems to have wormed his way into Mother's affections,' Sylvia said, handing her a glass of champagne.

Alicia's heart gave out a painful throb as she watched Sebastian whirl Juliette around the dance floor. It was odd to see her mother smile, odder to see the two getting along after what her father had uncovered.

It really did seem like there was no woman on the

planet Sebastian couldn't charm.

'I think I'm falling for him, Sylvia.' It wasn't the whole truth, she was probably already head over heels but she wasn't ready to admit that yet. Not even to herself.

'Then it will work out.' Her youngest sister sounded sure.

Pity she wasn't. 'There's so much working against us: Father, the drama with Mai, and to top it off, he doesn't believe he's worth it for the long haul. He thinks women are better off without him in their life.'

'So show him how important he is. Do something that makes him see you really are in it for ever. You said you wanted to travel, here's your chance, Licia.'

She'd thought about starting up on her own, hadn't she, just that morning? So why were her palms damp and her heart humming just thinking about handing in her notice? Alicia shuddered. 'Still, Father and Mai …'

Sylvia's glare had her trailing off. 'You can't keep letting him hold you back. And as for the skinny peroxide skank, she shouldn't even rank as being someone who keeps you from being happy. She's in the past, a blip, and the press will get bored of her when the next scandal comes along.'

She blew out a breath, then took a larger-than-necessary gulp of the bubbly liquid. Her head was already feeling fuzzy and Sylvia's words were starting to ring true – or did she just have a few too many drinks? Alicia couldn't be sure and she wasn't about to do anything rash until she was certain.

'Mai's not really the issue. I'm terrified I'll make the wrong choice again,' she whispered.

Her sister wrapped an arm around her back and pulled her close. 'We've all done things we regret. But it's the past, you have to move on. At the time we made the best decision for us, now we have to live with that.'

Her vision got blurry again but she refused to cry.

She'd done enough of that this weekend to last her a lifetime. Time to suck it up, find her courage, and go after what she wanted.

'Licia, what's going on?' Sylvia asked, looking past her.

Alicia turned and her breath caught. She'd never seen her father look so livid in all her life. His face was crimson, his jaw and fists clenched so hard she thought his bones might shatter. At his side, two men in black uniforms were speaking too quietly for her to hear. When her father pointed in Sebastian's direction, her stomach fell to the region of her feet.

Glancing at Sebastian, she saw his brows push together as he registered the police. Her mother covered her mouth with a gloved hand, then backed away from Sebastian like he carried the plague or an AK47. She wanted to tell Juliette not to be so ridiculous, that the police weren't there for him – it was someone else – but the music died down and one of the men stepped forward.

'Mr Collins, we'd like a word if you have a minute,' he asked.

She didn't realise she'd been holding her breath until it gushed out in one go There were no handcuffs waiting to slap on his wrists and the men asked for a word. They weren't arresting him, but this was still bad. There were journalists everywhere and all of them had heard the request.

Sebastian nodded, then made his way across the dance floor to her father and the policemen.

'Go!' Sylvia whispered, then shoved her a little.

Alicia did, almost running to him. She took his hand, tried to gouge from his expression what was happening, but he looked as perplexed as she was.

'My study,' her father commanded and then left, expecting them to follow.

The two men shared a glance then shrugged. All three

followed him through the house she'd grown up in but had never much cared for. It was too cold – chillier even than the frost lining her veins just now.

Sebastian didn't speak – no one did – until the door to her father's study closed behind them.

'Why do you want to speak with me?' he asked.

She tightened her hold on his hand.

'We're investigating an allegation of assault, Mr Collins. It might be better to do this at the station.' The man who spoke was heavily built, but it wasn't muscle. Still, his presence was intimidating.

'Who?' Alicia asked. She had an idea, but would the bitch really go as far as to hurt herself?

The shorter man held out a picture and she didn't recognise the woman at first. Mai's face was swollen and bloody. Alicia gasped and Sebastian took it.

She could see his expression change from guilt to anger in a second. 'I didn't do this, but I'd like a word with the bastard who did.'

Her chin dropped. Of all the things he should care about at the moment – his reputation being highest on her list of priorities – he wanted to reap payback on her assaulter? She dropped his hand, feeling a twang of betrayal. Had he lied to her when he said he'd gotten over Mai?

That day at the park … what if it *was* Sebastian who'd kissed her? Nausea rolled in her stomach until she swayed. An arm steadied her, but it wasn't comforting. She looked into her father's eyes and hated the gleam there that said he'd won.

'Mr Collins, we don't want to arrest you if you didn't do this, but any more threats and we'll be forced to take you in. Now, can you tell us where you were around nine o'clock yesterday morning?' The intimidator asked.

Sebastian laughed, but it held no humour. 'You're really going there? Look, my hands are fine – bruise free.' He held them up to show the men. 'Maybe you should be out there finding the guy who could mess up a woman's face like that.'

'Answer the question,' Intimidator continued.

'He was with me,' Alicia said. 'We were driving here.'

'Alicia,' her father scorned. 'Don't make excuses for him!'

She whirled on him, sick of the falsity he was putting on just to break them up – if anything would, it was Sebastian. She was sick of being forced to live her life the way her father wanted her to.

'I'm not, and you know fine well where Sebastian was too.' Turning to the police, she said, 'He's had him followed for weeks by a private investigator. He should be able to clear this up with a phone call.'

'Alicia,' her father warned.

'Tell them, Father! After all, withholding evidence is a crime, isn't it?' If she thought he'd been livid before, he was beyond that now. No doubt she'd run out of chances with him, but she was too angry to care.

'He had me followed?' Sebastian's voice was so cold she winced. 'And you knew?'

'No! Not until we got here.' The disgust twisting his lips hit her like a knife to the heart.

'And you didn't tell me? You've known for over a day and said nothing.' Sebastian shook his head.

She was about to protest when the intimidating policeman asked for the name and number of the guy. Her father crossed the room to his desk, no doubt still fuming at her. She wondered if there was anyone left who cared about her and wasn't mad at her.

'I'm sorry,' she said, even though it sounded pathetic.

Sebastian didn't acknowledge her, just waited until the officer dialled the private investigator. When the call ended, they apologised for wasting his time and left.

Sebastian turned to her father. 'You and I need to talk. Alicia, wait outside.'

She didn't argue, figuring she'd be better off away from the testosterone radiating from both men. When she opened the door, a flash went off and one of the journalists stuck a mic in her face, asking if Sebastian was being charged.

She didn't know if it was the impending doom crushing her will or the unfair judgement Sebastian was placing on her shoulders or even the way her father expected her to believe her lover could actually hit a woman, but anger built up until she couldn't hold in her frustration a second longer.

'If you must know, Sebastian's ex, Mai, went to the police yesterday with a swollen face and accused him of assault – just another lie to grab attention and make money-selling stories like the media whore she is. And it's people like you who encourage her – but I wouldn't be surprised if she's charged this time for false allegations. If it was me I'd sue the shit out of her.'

'Alicia! Get in here,' her father demanded.

The journalist ignored Arthur's command, as did Alicia. '*Another* lie? What do you mean?'

'Do you honestly believe any self-respecting woman would sell stories about her ex when she was trying to move on with a new relationship? She wants payback, probably because his cash isn't there for her to spend anymore. And the only way to get decent revenge is to fabricate the truth.'

She knew she was messing up her plan – so much for denial being the wrong way to go. But it wasn't Sebastian denying anything.

'Sebastian, what do you have to say about the allegations?' the journalist asked, shoving her mic into the room.

She turned to him, dreading seeing whatever anger or disgust he was feeling, but he just smiled a little and said, 'I think Alicia has it covered.'

She let a cautious grin spread across her face, even

though she knew she had a lot of explaining to do and she wasn't completely happy leaving him there with her father. But they had issues to air and she had to get rid of the media. 'Goodnight, Father. Sebastian.'

She closed the door, not wanting him to say goodnight and make it final, but she had a feeling she'd be sleeping alone tonight. Now she was surrounded by journalists and every one had a question for her. She answered as many as was appropriate, then sought out help from the security her mother had hired. As they were led out, Alicia climbed the stairs to her room and settled in for a long, lonely night, wondering if he'd even stay long enough to take her home.

Chapter Twenty-two

Sebastian waited until the door was closed before he turned to Arthur. He tried to reign in the betrayal from Alicia, the anger at what he'd put his daughter through, and do this calmly. 'Call off the private investigator. It's an invasion of our privacy.'

Arthur sat down on a chair better suited to a king than an earl and smirked. 'Why? Are you worried something might be uncovered?'

Pacing across to the desk, he faced off against the man who seemed to have his family too scared to speak up. He didn't get it. Arthur was old, cruel, and long past the age he could cause them physical harm if that was the reason. Plus, her sisters weren't children anymore. If he disowned Alicia, she'd still have them.

'The only person I'm worried about is Alicia. Are you going to do this every time she finds someone she cares about? Keeping this shit going is just going to drag up what happened when was fifteen. She doesn't need that in her life.'

Arthur's scowl was as livid as his voice. 'I have no idea what you're talking about.'

'Yes you do.' Sebastian took a breath, tried to beat down the rage welling up inside. 'What you did gives her nightmares. She still wakes up crying, even now. I'm surprised she hasn't washed her hands with you already, but she wants your approval.'

Something else he didn't understand. If *his* dad had pulled any of that shit he'd have left and never went back.

'How dare she tell you that!' Arthur snapped.

'She didn't, I guessed. It wasn't hard to figure out when she relives that night over and over again in her sleep. You're nothing but a sick control freak.'

Arthur shot out of his chair, slammed his hands on his desk and shouted, 'What about you? Do you think you're any better for her? Can you give her all this?'

He swept a hand around the room. 'Can you keep her safe, protected, and leave her reputation untarnished? If you can look me in the eye and tell me you can, then you'll have my blessing to marry her. I'll even release her trust fund and pay for the wedding!'

Swallowing, he staggered back a step and his eyes dropped to the desk, which was no doubt an heirloom. Everything in this manor had probably been passed down by the older generations, as well as the title and wealth.

Arthur was right about one thing, though his reasoning was probably way off. He knew Sebastian couldn't give Alicia a proper home – not in the monetary sense, but the security and attention she deserved. His past had proved that and so had his upbringing.

And even though he couldn't agree with Arthur's way of providing that, he couldn't do what the guy had asked. He couldn't look him in the eye and make promises he would never be able to keep.

'I didn't think so,' Arthur said.

Sebastian fisted his hands, but it wasn't anger pushing him. It was the way his chest tightened to the point he struggled to get a decent breath into his lungs.

'Perhaps you should leave now, before you ruin her for anyone else. Her heart will heal. This won't be the first time it's been broken by someone unworthy. I only want what's best for her. For my family.'

The logic wasn't lost on him, and the last thing he wanted to do was break Alicia's heart. She'd already faced too much in her life. Was he really going to stay with her, because he was too selfish to walk away?

He didn't reply to Arthur. He just left and returned to his own room. His mind spun with questions and his ribs constricted tighter as the hours went on. Sleep wasn't going to be possible, neither was making the hardest decision he'd ever made.

After an evening out with the editor of *Taylor Made*, Mai got home a little after ten. She expected Jack had long since fallen asleep on the sofa after too many drinks. It was his usual routine and she didn't mind. Over the last two days, they'd talked a lot. Mai was touched at how attentive he'd been to her injuries and how much he'd opened up. They'd even talked about the wedding and she'd withdrawn everything in her accounts to give him so she didn't go on a spending splurge.

Since their fight, she'd discovered he hadn't been with another woman since she'd left him – but understood he had needs. He'd turned to porn, so much so that now he struggled to get aroused without it.

After trying to understand what she'd put him through, she'd agreed to help as much as she could. This morning they had sex while watching it together, and it had been the best, most caring sex she'd had with him in a long time. Before, she'd convinced herself rough meant passion which meant love, but he'd shown her how careful and generous making love could be – even if she had to have the television on with another couple. Plus, it excited her a lot more than she thought it would. And the best bit – it gave Jack stamina to rival Sebastian's.

She hung her coat in the closet and made her way to the living room. It wasn't until she noticed the lack of empty beer bottles or sound of a television that unease slithered down her spine.

'Jack, babe. Where are you?' she called out.

No answer. Her heart took off on a mamba and Mai ran through the house, checking every room. When she got to her bedroom and saw the wardrobes open and devoid of his clothing, her throat became thick. He wouldn't leave, not out of guilt. Would he?

She pulled her phone out of her pocket and dialled his mobile. A voice came on telling her the number had been disconnected.

'Jack, where are you?' Wandering through to the kitchen, she had an awful feeling in her gut. Something was off, way off, and she was about to dial the hospital when she saw a piece of paper attached to the refrigerator.

Pulling it off, she caressed her thumb over her name, written on one side in his handwriting. When she turned it over, her eyes watered.

Did you honestly think we'd last? I'm sorry for what happened, really I am. There was only ever one way I wanted to hurt you and that's the way you hurt me. This is it, Mai, my ultimate payback.

Knowing you and your need for revenge, you'll understand why I've done what I have, but you'll never find me or touch me like you did Collins. I've had to live with you for months, I know how you think and how your mind works. You'll never have anything on me, bitch. Not ever.

Her legs gave out. As she hit the tiles, she dropped the note, not caring where it went. Her heart felt like it had been torn in two, and not the way someone ripping a bandage from a wound felt a quick jolt, but like it was happening slowly. Agonisingly.

Karma wasn't something she'd believed in – not until this backlash happened to her.

Alicia woke alone, just as she'd guessed. Sebastian hadn't called, despite her texts. He hadn't stopped by, despite promising to before he found out about the private investigator.

What had she expected? A warm welcome even though she'd hid things from him?

Instead of showering, she pulled on a pair of jeans and a sweatshirt then jogged down the hall, all the way to his bedroom. Her heart was pounding from more than the exercise and she definitely couldn't put the moisture beading on her forehead down to exertion. It was fear. Fear that she'd screwed up everything, that he'd left her there and she'd never see him again.

She pushed open the door, but froze when she saw him stuffing his clothes into a case.

Sebastian turned to her, his frown and the tension emanating from him a clear warning to stay away. 'I can't do this now, Alicia.'

She couldn't either. In fact, she didn't want to do it ever. 'You're leaving?'

'I've got to get back into training, I've missed enough already.' He turned, going back to stuffing things in his bag.

Alicia stepped into the room. She couldn't help it. Her mind didn't seem connected to her body. 'You're mad at me for not telling you when I found out. That's why you're leaving.'

He sighed but didn't look at her. 'I haven't opened up about everything, not as much as you have. But I tell you things that matter *now*. I told you what happened at the park.'

'Because you were caught. If there wasn't a risk of it getting into the news, would you have told me?' she asked, folding her arms more for warmth than because she was annoyed.

After all, she had no right to be. She'd hidden something from him.

He pivoted round to face her. 'I should have told you first, I get that now. But yes, even if she hadn't set me up I would have told you.'

'And I should have told you straight away, but I didn't because I knew you'd be pissed off at my father. I was going to tell you when we got back to London. I didn't to give you more reasons to hate my family.' He had enough already.

He shook his head. 'What I don't get is why you don't hate him. He's done nothing but rule you since you were born. He threatened you when he found out about us, didn't he?'

There was no point in lying, so she nodded. 'He's my father. I used to think that meant I had to be the kind of daughter he wanted, but now I've realised that it's not me who can't be proper and respectable, it's him who can't understand the way the world's changed since he was young. I can't hate him for it, no more than you can hate Mai.'

Sebastian sat down on the bed and scrubbed a hand through his hair. 'I can't help thinking that if I treated her differently that she wouldn't have done any of this.'

Alicia crossed the room until she was in front of him. Kneeling on the floor, she took hold of his hands. 'You might have hurt her, but that's no excuse for what she's doing to you now.'

He leaned forward until his forehead rested against hers. Squeezing her hands, he said, 'I thought if I could just stay in one place long enough, make proper friends and have real connections with people, that I wouldn't feel so empty inside. Mai was everything I'd ever dreamed of and she wanted the same things – a home, marriage, and babies. But I was too far into my career and was never around. She didn't want the travel since she'd been passed around from foster home to foster home all her life, never knowing what love was. I couldn't give her that. Shit, I can't give anyone that.'

He looked at her then, with eyes as shiny as her own probably were. 'That's why I need to leave. Arthur's right, you deserve better. What we have is going to end soon and it was selfish to insist we keep it up. You mean more to me than a casual fling and I don't want to hurt you.'

She meant more to him. As much as he meant to her? Alicia swallowed against the lump in her throat. 'Then don't walk away. You'll regret it.'

He cupped her face with his shaking hands. 'I'll regret it whenever I do, but now will be easier for us.'

She needed more time with him. The thought of him leaving now was almost as painful as the day she had walked into the clinic all those years ago. 'For you, maybe. What happened to making the most of what time we have left?'

He sighed, squeezed his eyes closed like he was in pain.

'Don't,' she said, then rose up on her knees and pressed her mouth to his.

Sebastian kissed her back warily, like he didn't want to hurt her feelings by pulling away. The need to prove him wrong, to keep him with her, rose until she was threading her fingers through his hair and tugging him closer.

When his lips parted she took the lead, putting everything into the kiss, into their connection. With a groan he surrendered and dragged her onto his lap, trailing his lips down her throat and squeezing her to him.

'I don't want to hurt you,' he said against her collarbone.

Alicia wriggled closer, gasping when she came up against his erection. 'Then don't, just stay … for now.'

He stripped her sweater off over her head, then met her gaze with grave eyes. 'I'll stay for as long as I can. I promise.'

She nodded, accepting that though she had fallen he might not be there yet. But she'd try to convince him that he wasn't the man he thought he was. She had to.

Otherwise she'd live the rest of her life regretting this too.

It was long past time she started fighting for the things she loved.

'Thank you,' she said, then pulled his polo shirt over his head. 'Kiss me.'

He did, and for a second she wondered if she asked him to stay forever, would he? But then he slid his hands under her bra and she was lost to the burning chemistry that had been there since she'd met him.

His promise would have to do, for now at least.

'You were fantastic with those kids today,' Alicia said, a grin spreading her lips wide.

He tugged her closer and wrapped an arm around her shoulder as he led her into a side street away from the main road. The days and nights since they returned to London had flown by with more of the same. Training and Alicia. Despite what he'd been planning to do at the manor, leave her while he still could, he wasn't able to walk away after she'd asked him to stay. Enough people had broken promises to her, and hadn't he promised he'd give her what she wanted when she asked?

Plus, he was glad he had this chance to give her one afternoon and night just the two of them, which was probably as much for his benefit but it was what she'd wanted. They'd spent the morning at the charity, working with local kids and she'd even helped out when he'd been training them.

Now it was time for some one-on-one fun – and not the bedroom kind.

'Another one of your bright ideas. I should hire you full time.' He was teasing, sort of.

She really was doing a great job with the charity, had lots of gyms on board and a few fundraising events in the works. And she did seem to love helping out. It was all she talked about most nights.

The idea to ask her to keep working for him was tempting and as the week had gone on, their end date seemed to make everything more urgent. There was so much he wanted to show her, so much he still wanted to see with her. Another few weeks weren't going to be enough.

But if there was anyone he wouldn't wish his hectic life on, it would be her. Arthur Simpson had been right, he couldn't give her all the things the deserved. The time they'd spend apart would drive a wedge between them and long-distance relationships never worked. His failed engagement to Mai proved that.

'The traveling is definitely a perk, but the price would have to be right.' She raised an eyebrow at him, the twinkle in her eye saying she was hinting at more than monetary.

'You'd take payment in sex?' He tried to keep his tone light.

'It's certainly better than accepting money for sex.'

Laughing, he shook his head and led her past a few backstreet shops until the arcade came into view. Lasers was somewhere his mum had brought him as a kid when they were in London and his dad was focused on training.

'Is this what I think it is?' she asked.

Nodding, he stepped forward and opened the door for her. Alicia just stared at him. Hell, had he got it all wrong? Of course she wouldn't be interested in this, it was a guy thing. 'We can go somewhere else.'

'No, I want to go in. I've never been to an arcade before.' She skipped through the open door, stopping inside until he entered behind her. 'This is so cool.'

Sebastian couldn't believe how little had changed about the place, and even his favourite fighting game was still where it had been. The dark blue walls had seen a few coats of paint over the years. The Pacman transfers had been joined by more updated characters and the lighting was a bit brighter, but it was the same place he remembered.

'I can't believe you've never been to an arcade. Not even at carnivals?'

Alicia rolled her eyes, but still grinned as she took in the room. 'You've met my parents. The only thing we got to visit were parades and snooty parties. I never even had a bouncy castle on any of my birthdays.'

He linked his fingers through hers, a bit shocked at her revelations – despite having met her rigid parents. Well, that hadn't been entirely true. When her mother loosened up and got out from under Arthur's thumb, she'd been a different woman than the cold one he'd met when he arrived. He reckoned it was Arthur who curbed their passion, and he was glad he'd at least got the chance to give the old goat a piece of his mind.

'I bet Juliette would love it here, and your sisters,' he said.

Alicia grinned. 'Sylvia definitely would. She has a thing for geeks.'

'So I'm a geek for enjoying a little time out?' he asked.

She laughed a little. 'Definitely. But you still bring the sexy.'

Pulling her close, he dropped a quick kiss on her mouth. 'Glad you think so.'

Alicia glanced around the arcade again, her eyes bright with excitement, and he knew then that bringing her here was one of his better ideas.

'When did you find this place?' she asked, probably expecting him to have done a Google search.

Sebastian debated whether to tell her, but it wasn't a government secret. After all, his parents had tried to make sure he got his share of kid stuff growing up. And Alicia had confessed more about herself than this.

'My mother brought me here whenever we were in London.' Her mouth dropped, like his admission was the last thing she expected. He shrugged. 'We travelled a lot. While Dad was training, Mum always found places like this for me. She didn't want me to miss out on fun.'

Alicia nodded her acknowledgement and turned quickly, but not before he caught the shimmer in her eyes that said she felt sorry for him. He didn't want that, not from her or anyone. Time to take it back to the fun day he'd planned. No more confession time.

'Since this is your first time, you can pick what game I beat you at.'

That earned a smile from her which made his heart skip a beat. She took his hand, then dragged him around the room, checking out every game the place had. Her smile grew wider until she stopped beside one of the newer seated racing games, pulled out her mobile, and with her back to the machine, snapped a picture with the front camera.

He lifted an eyebrow in question. Alicia wasn't usually one for selfies.

'Instagram, Collins. The game I'm going to whip you on.' She fiddled about with the mobile for a second and he laughed.

'Better hope you do or it'll be embarrassing Tweeting the retraction. And, of course, the grovelling apology.'

She slid into one of the chairs. 'I'm not worried, I've seen you drive.'

'That's it. I was going to go easy on you but you've ruined it by insulting my driving.'

'My devious plan worked.' She grabbed the steering wheel and frowned. 'Do we need change or something?'

'I'll get it.' He left to cash in a fifty, his smile still in place. Even when his mother had brought him here he couldn't remember having a constant grin or this much fun.

When he got back to the game, Alicia was wrapping up a call. He slid into the chair next to her and put a few coins in the slot. 'Good news?' he asked, because her grin got wider.

'The best. Don't you have your mobile?'

He shook his head. 'I wanted to spend time with you without work interruptions.'

Alicia turned to face him, her green eyes almost glowing with excitement and a jolt in his chest made his heart skip a beat again. Ever since they'd got back from her parents', she'd been a different person – all light, smiles, and happiness. Just being near her was enough for her glow to rub off on him.

'That was Mr Maine. Tony called to say you've been made three offers by different sports companies *and* Bentley are putting together a proposal package!'

It took a minute for the words to sink in, and her grin slipped. 'Sebastian, I thought this was the end game. The companies see the effort and focus you're putting in, your work with the charity and –'

He took her face and kissed her hard. Heat instantly zipped to his groin and before he could think about where they were, he hauled her onto his lap. Her lips were still at first, immovable against his, but then he forced them apart. Alicia melted against him, her mouth softening and her fingers threading into his hair.

She was the first to break the kiss, gasping for air and laughing. 'That's some thank you.'

'You're incredible,' he said, then nuzzled her throat. 'You're gold. You're my lucky charm.'

'Um, there are kids here,' she whispered, her voice thick with the same scalding lust burning him inside.

Sebastian sighed. 'True. We should probably stop.' Still, as she rose, he gave her backside a squeeze for good measure. 'Later I'll thank you properly.'

She hit a few buttons on the control pad, throwing him a quick grin. 'When you get lapped by a girl and can't take it, I'll remind you of that.'

'I can take it, Blondie, if it's you.'

'You're on, Collins.'

Chapter Twenty-three

Alicia didn't lap him. In fact, there wasn't much they tried that she beat him at, but he didn't gloat, even when she was forced to tweet her defeat and buy the hotdogs after he all but wiped the floor with her. She didn't care either. There were no memories from her childhood that were ever this much fun, so she conceded to buy him lunch.

Even laughed at herself when she got mustard on the breast of her white blouse. It soon strangled in her throat when Sebastian leaned forward to mop it up with his tongue, going way wide and flicking over her nipple instead.

She batted him away. 'Kids, remember?'

But she couldn't be annoyed at him, not when the day had gone better than she dreamed it would. Especially after last weekend when she almost let him slip through her fingers. But she'd made a promise to herself to take each day as it came and savour every moment.

Then she'd fight for him when the time came.

She'd also started doing things for herself. The almost see-through blouse and skinny jeans she wore were step one of her action plan. But the harder step, big number two, wasn't as easy. Not when she'd lived her whole life trying to make her parents happy, and quitting her job didn't fit into that category.

Still, it was what *she* wanted and that's what she had to focus on.

He flashed a grin. 'I'll try to behave.'

She didn't really want him to, but she'd have to wait before she could get her hands on him. Opting for a topic that wouldn't give the kids and geeky-looking teen behind the counter an eyeful, she asked, 'How often did you come here?'

'Every chance I got. I think my mum felt bad for moving around a lot, and didn't want me to miss out on all the things a kid should experience.'

'It must have been tough,' she said, pity for him swelling up inside again. He'd had a harder life than he admitted, and she got the feeling deep down his old dreams were still there, but after Mai, he was just too afraid to wish for them.

Not that her childhood had been easy. She had a hard enough time fitting into the private school she attended, refusing to engage in chat about boys or anything inappropriate that her mother said young girls shouldn't talk about. But to never be in the same place long enough to make proper friends? That was rough.

He shrugged. 'That's why I really proposed to Mai. I wanted a connection that would last.'

Her heart stuttered. Here she was, back to hoping. But he'd said *wanted*. Things had changed and she needed to remember that – prepare herself in case he still wasn't ready to take their relationship further no matter how hard she fought.

Even if he did still want those things deep down, she might not be the right woman for him. He might not even be ready to open himself up like that again.

Sebastian polished off the rest of his hotdog. She forced herself to eat half, but her stomach felt heavy and a bit uneasy. All week she'd managed to convince herself she could live in the moment.

It wasn't easy. Her wardrobe was full of his polo shirts, jeans, and shorts. The closet by the front door now had a hanger for his racket and all his tennis balls. It was like their lives were merging, and despite his obvious exhaustion every night, he still gave her the most toe-curling orgasms, even if the sex wasn't as athletic as it had been last weekend.

Still, she meant what she'd said to him. The sex wasn't the most important thing – just a delicious bonus. Spending time with him was just as fun, as today had proved. He'd brought her here because it was a place he had good memories of. Untainted ones when his life was moving from country to country, and though she tried, she couldn't not feel touched.

'Your mum sounds fun. All our mother taught us was how to be reserved so we'd be more attractive to men of good standing.'

He made a face. 'In this case, I'm happy to be in the bad standing category. You're much more fun without all the snobbery.'

She threw her napkin at him, pretending to be miffed and put on her most proper accent. 'I am not a snob.'

Laughing, he tugged her chair around the table and threaded his fingers through her hair. 'No, you're not. You're perfect the way you are.' The amusement fled from his eyes and his expression became serious. 'Don't ever change. Promise me.'

Her heart fluttered as his breath brushed against her face, making the room around her sway. Even though his words stung, she could tell from the strain around his eyes that thinking they'd be over soon was affecting him too. Maybe she wouldn't have to fight too hard for them.

'I promise,' she said, holding on to his wrists to keep him close.

For a second, pain crushed his expression, but a huge smile soon wiped it away. Her stomach ached for him, she could see he wasn't ready to talk about the serious stuff and today had been too fun to ruin by pushing him.

She untangled herself. 'I think it's time I beat you at something.'

His brows rose. 'Want me to go easy on you now?'

'No. Bring your A-game. You're going to need it.' Taking his hand, she led him towards the old arcade games. 'I've got this in the bag. Highest score wins.'

Sebastian slipped some coins in and watched as she took hold of the joystick, her thumb rubbing suggestively over the top as she steered Pacman away from the ghosts. Sebastian swallowed, his gaze riveted on the way she used both hands to do indecent things to the stick. With any luck, she'd get him so hot and bothered he wouldn't be able to focus on the game.

A few pulls and twists later, she noticed him rearrange the front of his pants and the thought he was turned on from watching her play shot her concentration to bits. Her breasts got heavy, oversensitive, and every suggestive shift of the joystick made the material rub against her.

Soon she lost her last life, but didn't care since her score was pretty good and she was going to play dirty the second he started. They switched places, Sebastian's attention staying on her chest until she cleared her throat.

His grin was wicked. 'I'm going to blow your score out of the water, then we're going home.'

In his dreams. 'How about we make it more interesting?'

'I'm listening.' His gaze roved over her body and she felt totally naked, rather than in jeans and a top.

'The winner gets whatever they want from the loser, all night long.' As far as she was concerned, either way would be a win because Sebastian would want to be inside of her.

'You got yourself a deal, Blondie.'

He started playing and she moved to stand behind him, a little to the side, pretending to focus on the game. His shoulders were tense, the muscles beneath the polo bunching every time he moved the stick, and she was getting hotter just watching. But that wasn't conductive to him losing. This time she wanted to win, had the incentive, and after all these weeks with him she knew he couldn't resist her.

Alicia slipped her hands beneath his polo and around, dipping her fingertips beneath his jeans and boxers. Pacman lost a life and Sebastian cursed.

'Doesn't look like you're trying very hard, Collins.'

'It's not easy when you're playing dirty.' But he returned his focus to the machine and she guessed he was upping the ante.

Time to up hers. Alicia slid her hands along, until her index finger brushed the tip of his erection. He hissed and his penis jerked, but he kept his attention on the game and played with infuriating skill. She swiped the bead of moisture that had already formed on the crown, and pulled her finger away to taste it. She moaned and exaggerated a sucking sound with her digit in her mouth, fighting back a laugh when Pacman died again.

'Alicia, I'm going to spank you if you keep this up,' he whispered.

Her cheeks flushed, but it wasn't embarrassment. 'Maybe that's one of the things I want you to do.'

Going for the win, she waited until he'd forced his attention back to the game, then grabbed the length of him. Sebastian trembled and his knuckles whitened around the joystick but he didn't let that beat him.

Alicia glanced around, her frustration growing as he pulsed in her palm. There was no one close, but she was positive someone would catch her if she stroked him properly. Instead, she ran her nail gently down the vein on the underside and he grabbed her wrist, but still played with a focus that was becoming a little insulting.

She squeezed him hard, smiling when he gasped and muttered a filthy promise. But the score kept rocketing, and getting more desperate to touch him, she slid her free hand up the front of his polo, across the tight muscles on his belly until she came to his nipple. She plucked it, feeling his erection swell under the onslaught, and forgot to pay attention to the screen.

Sebastian ended the game, then pulled her hands off

him. She was worried she'd taken it too far, until he turned and the lust in his expression nailed her feet to the spot.

'I win,' he announced. 'Now you're going to pay.'

Taking her hand, he practically dragged her out of the arcade.

He'd never been so turned on or strung out in his life.

If Alicia had kept up the teasing and he wasn't so close to winning, he'd have had to take her in the middle of the arcade, with whoever watching. Luckily, a shred of sanity prevailed and he spent the journey home plotting all the ways he was going to make her pay. The fact that her skin was rosy and her breathing so hard it was like he'd just made love to her only spurred him on more.

When they reached her apartment, Sebastian pinned her against the wall in the entrance, grinding his erection into her. She gasped and tried to reach for him but he caught her wrists and held them above her head, smiling down at her. Though his teeth were about to crack with the effort of not taking her right there. He had to reign in some control first.

'What are you going to do to me?' she asked.

Her eyes were huge, but they'd darkened and her face was almost pink with arousal, so he knew she wasn't scared. She trusted him, and that knowledge made his chest swell and glow. *She* did that to him.

Kissing a line from her earlobe down to her chin, he shifted his grip so he held her in one hand then slid the other down the front of her jeans. She was more than ready for him. Her delicate flesh was burning and sliding his fingers inside was easy.

She gasped, then ground her hips. 'This doesn't feel like making me pay for teasing you.'

'There are lots of ways to tease, Alicia. You're about to find out which one I prefer.' But even as he said the words, his erection pulsed.

She squirmed against him as he kept stroking where she needed him, then pulled away. He rubbed his thumb over the little nub until she was almost there, then plunged his fingers deep again.

She let out a frustrated sound and her brows furrowed. 'This isn't teasing. It's torture.'

Sebastian built her up again, till she was almost at the edge. 'Trust me, it feels that way now but it will be better.'

Her head shook from side to side, but not in disagreement. Her muscles were pulling him deeper and his erection was so hard and aching he wasn't going to be able to keep this up much longer. Just as her body began to clench around him, he tugged his fingers out. She focused on him, her eyes wide and betrayed. His heart ached like it'd been sliced in two.

'This time, I promise,' he said.

He undid her jeans and pushed them to her knees. While she kicked them off, he freed himself from his trousers and lifted her. Kissing her hard, he wrapped her legs around his hips and pushed in all the way.

Alicia clung to his shoulders as he gave her what he'd denied, swivelling his hips and watching the sweat bead on her forehead, her upper lip. Her eyes glazed over, occasionally focusing on his, and the ache in his chest was barely overshadowed by the pleasure ripping through him.

She bit her lip just as her body started to convulse around him, and he couldn't hold on. He thrust through her orgasm while she panted his name and his own release came so hard and fast he thought he might pass out from ecstasy.

He hugged her close, catching his breath with his face against her neck, revelling in the citrusy smell of her shampoo. A smell he was so used to going to sleep with and waking up to that he'd probably have to wash one of his pillows with a bottle of the stuff. His heart felt like it was being constricted, and he pushed the thought away.

'That was … intense,' Alicia said.

He pressed his lips against her neck, then worked his way up to her lips. Kissing her slowly, thoroughly, he carried her through to the bedroom and laid her down. After cleaning them up with a cloth, he stripped the rest of her clothes off.

Alicia's eyebrows shot up. 'Again?'

Shaking his head, he said, 'This is for you.'

She was about to argue. After all, he'd already given her the most intense orgasm of her life, but his teeth did something wicked to her nipple and her protest was cut off with a moan.

He worshipped every part of her body with his tongue and lips, working her up to a carnal frenzy which shocked her a little after what had happened in the hall. She tried to think through the pleasure, but then he settled between her legs, pulled her calves over his shoulders, and kissed her *there*. Right where she needed him to. Alicia was lost.

Sebastian was merciless with his tongue, building her higher with lazy strokes, but it wasn't like in the hall. She didn't think he'd pull away now, and she had a feeling that was what this was about. He felt guilty but shouldn't. If she'd trusted him and waited instead of letting the hurt break through her expression, he wouldn't feel like he had to do this now.

Emotions punched her in the chest as he drove her higher, stilling her breath with their intensity. Love. There was no way to lie to herself anymore. She'd fallen for him, hard. More than she'd felt for Darrell, more than she'd felt for anyone.

She'd had the best day ever and it had all been because of him. The panic that should have come was cut off as he slipped his fingers inside her and every sensation doubled. The orgasm stirred beneath her skin, sweeping through her body like a spreading forest fire, just as intense as before, but hitting her in every erogenous zone she had.

Sebastian didn't ease up. He kept going and going until she erupted again and this time biting her lip didn't stop the scream from breaking through as she convulsed for what felt like forever.

The next thing she knew, she was limp and in his arms while he stroked her hair and face. Alicia closed her eyes, snuggling into him and listening to his heartbeat.

'I'm sorry,' he whispered, 'for before.'

She shook her head. 'Nothing to be sorry for.'

He stilled, his whole body tensing and her eyes opened. Worry creased his brow, made the chocolate swirls of his irises hard. 'Sebastian, it's OK. I didn't know what the teasing would come to. If I did I wouldn't have been so impatient.'

'I …' He looked away. 'Every time I think about how that guy used you, left you … I don't know if something I'm doing crosses a line. I don't want to bring it up, but how else am I going to know if I'm hurting you?'

Alicia held her breath. The emotions that had suckerpunched her earlier came back and she couldn't shy away from it now. He was so worried about the past, but even though she'd been too young, suffered horrible consequences, she'd made those choices and couldn't keep regretting them.

'I wanted it at the time. Darrell didn't pressure me into anything. It was after. He made me believe we'd be together forever.' She pulled his face back so she could look at him.

Regret was clear in his expression and she knew it was because he didn't want to treat her the same as her ex. She couldn't hear the words though, thought she'd break if he ended their relationship again.

'I think my father found out the same way he got those pictures of you and Mai, but I didn't ask. Honestly, that part of my life is in the past and I can't keep regretting it or I'll never move forward.'

Sebastian started stroking her hair again, his gaze focused on hers – serious now. 'I don't want to be like Darrell, Alicia. That's one of the reasons I should have left on Sunday.'

'You're not. You won't ever be,' she said.

Sebastian couldn't ever be swayed by her father's bribery. He had a backbone, made his own decisions, and he hadn't promised her the world – he didn't think he was worthy of more than a bit of fun. She hoped one day he'd learn to forgive himself for what happened with Mai, but that was clearly a long way off.

He looked up at the ceiling, a pulse pounding hard in his jaw. 'I won't make promises I can't keep – not to you or anyone else.'

She hugged him hard, hiding her face in his shoulder in case the pain in her heart was clear on her face. Just when she thought things might get better, that he might change his mind, hope was stolen away. He lifted her hand, kissed her palm, then placed it on his chest. She melted and the tears threatening to overflow made her vision blurry.

They made love again. Though it probably shouldn't have happened, he couldn't keep his hands off her. And it was making love this time, not just sex or a way to release tension. It had never been just that with Alicia. Now he was afraid it was more, his feelings had changed. But it still wasn't enough.

It could never be enough.

He could never be who she deserved, and that realisation hit him hard, for the first time. He'd any day take the last few months of stress over this.

As he held her after, listening to her breathing deepen

and her heart slow, Sebastian's stomach churned. They'd gone beyond casual to somewhere that terrified him despite the fact that a few years ago it would have been the one place he wanted to be.

But he couldn't give Alicia the life she deserved. She should be treated like a queen and shown what love really was. His career would make her feel left out, lonely, even – just like he'd been growing up. With parents like hers, she should have so much more. A lump formed in his throat at the thought that it would be someone else who'd give her all those things, and he had to swallow against the urge to weep.

She stirred, her arms constricting around him and he tightened his hold too.

'I love you,' she mumbled against his chest and he froze.

His heart pounded in his chest and a cold sweat broke over his skin. He waited for her to laugh, maybe even realise what she'd just said, but Alicia only sighed a little. His chest felt like it was caving in because now he knew he'd let this get too far. Out of control. Hurting her was the last thing in the world he wanted to do but now, what choice did he have? There was no way to get around it. The only question left was is it better to prolong the inevitable, or make the break as fast and painless as possible?

Chapter Twenty-four

Alicia woke alone, which wasn't unusual for a Monday morning. Fighting sleep, she pulled herself out of bed and headed for the kitchen. The coffee pot was on – even though Sebastian never drank the stuff, he always made sure she had some ready. And she needed it for today.

Working at Maine PR wasn't where her heart was. She loved doing charity work with Sebastian, and so far she'd been pretty good at it. She also loved public relations, and had put together a big folder full of the contacts she'd need to start out on her own.

Daria and Sylvia were right. Her father never visited London and all he'd know was what he heard on the end of the phone. She didn't like lying to him but after all these years she realised that she was never going to make him happy. He was immovable, held onto grudges, and was rigidly set in his ways.

It was her job to make sure she was happy, which made it time to get on with step two. She picked up the envelope containing a letter she'd typed for Mr Maine. It wasn't easy making her feet carry her to the door, but after considering all her options she saw this one making her happiest in the long run.

For the first time in her life, she'd have all the control.

Her resistance to get this over with had more to do with step three of the Make Alicia's Life Better Plan. It dampened her palms and made her stomach too flippy to drink much of her coffee. She picked up her phone and sent a quick text to Sebastian, asking him to keep the night free as she had news, then went to work to face her boss.

'Are you insane?' Sebastian asked the second he'd closed the door to her flat.

She looked up from her spot on the floor, surrounded by the research she'd been doing since she got home. 'That's not the greeting I was hoping for.'

He ran a hand through his damp hair. Sweat made his polo cling to every delicious muscle he had, setting a fire burning through her veins. He usually showered at the gym, but not today, and it was disturbing how much that made her want to jump him.

Him being miffed about something only made the urge worse. She'd never had angry sex before …

'Alicia, why did you leave Maine?'

Oh, he'd heard already. 'I'm going to start out on my own. I've already secured a few contacts. Don't worry, I'll finish up your contract before I leave. Honestly though, things are going great for you right now. After you win the French Opens, you'll have anyone you want signing up.'

He paced across the room, his muscles locked in place and an expression she'd never seen before on his face. She frowned, thinking sex was way down the list of his priorities just now.

'Is this because of me?' he asked, but didn't look at her.

'No, it's what I want to do.' She shuffled papers together and closed her laptop. There was no more ways to stall. Now it was time to throw step three out there. 'But it will make being together easier. Now I can work my own hours.'

Sebastian stopped dead. 'We can't be together, Alicia. I thought that's what we agreed a few weeks ago. I thought that's what we both wanted.'

Rejection made her wither, but she got up, determined to fight for what she wanted. 'So did I, until you moved in and made me see what I'd been missing all these years. I've never been this happy, Sebastian. And I know you think you'll never make me happy but you already have. Please believe me.'

He didn't speak at first, just ran his hands through his hair and turned away from her. His shoulders slumped and she knew then that something was very, very wrong. He couldn't even face her. 'Sebastian –'

'I'm leaving tomorrow. I'm going to stay with my parents before the Opens.'

His words knocked the breath out of her. She slumped back on the floor, unsure her legs would hold her. 'Why? I thought James would –'

He faced her again, his expression more serious than she'd ever seen on him. 'This thing between us can't last. Why kid ourselves and keep it going any longer? You should go back to Maine, tell them you've made a mistake.'

'I thought we …' Her words choked off. She cleared her throat, tried again. 'Why can't we? You care about me and I –'

'Yeah, I do.' He came close and hope swelled her heart. She could still change his mind. But his voice softened, like he pitied her. 'But it wouldn't be fair to string you along like that. I always thought I wanted something steady in my life, a home to come back to. I was wrong. My career comes first and it always will. It's not fair to ask you to hang around.'

His career comes first. He doesn't want anything more.

All hope sucked out of her until there was nothing left. She loved him, thought he still wanted all those things, but when it came down to it he loved his job more. There was no competing against that – she'd never want to take anything away from him.

He didn't even want more – with her, or anyone. She must have imagined the way she thought he felt. She was inexperienced when it came to relationships – look how wrong she'd been about Darrell! She knew that putting her heart out there could end this way, but it still split her in two nonetheless.

There was no way she could hang around now, and watch him go. Blinking back tears, she picked up the handbag and coat she'd left over the sofa in her excitement to get started with her new business.

'I have somewhere to be. You can pack in peace.'

She got to the door before he spoke again. 'Are you going back to Maine? If he's mad I can –'

'That's not really any of your business, Sebastian. Not anymore.' She closed the door and headed for the staircase, determined to hold it together until she was somewhere more private.

Though his dad had retired, training with him was always more challenging than with James. Probably because the guy still played every day, but Sebastian's heart hadn't been in it since he arrived at his parents' home in the South of France a week ago.

'Son, I think you need to hire a new trainer,' his dad said when half-time came.

Sebastian didn't comment, just picked up his water bottle and took a long drink. He wasn't even out of breath, he had barely put any effort into the game at all. There was a huge Alicia-shaped hole in his life and he missed her like crazy. It was like she'd taken custody of his motivation, the love of the game, and his desire to win.

'Leave him alone. This isn't about tennis.' His mum came out of the house, a sad smile on her face. 'Is Mai still harassing you? There hasn't been a story for a while.'

He shook his head. 'Not since she tried to have me arrested.'

Of course his mother had found out about the

282

incident – the whole world had. The press took Alicia at her word and now everyone was on Team Sebastian. But that wasn't fair either, he didn't want Mai being painted as the villain. She was just another woman whose heart he'd ripped in two. He hoped the backlash didn't last for long.

'Then why are you hitting the ball like your racket's made of dough?' his dad asked.

Scrubbing a hand over his face, he knew coming to France had been a bad idea. His parents would pick at him until they got the full story, but he didn't want a lecture on how stupid leaving Alicia had been. They wanted him to be happy, and she made him happy. Problem was, he could never do the same for her. Not until he retired, and by then she might have woken up and realised she deserved better than an absentee partner.

Sebastian pulled himself together. 'I'll play better this time.'

He did, but only through force of will, and even then it wasn't enough to beat his dad. Dinner that night was torture, watching his parents fawn over each other like they were in the first throes of love. Maybe they were. After all, they didn't have much alone time that he could remember growing up. He was almost ready to call it a night and give them some privacy, but after a hushed conversation between the two, his dad beat him to it.

Curiosity got the better of him. When his dad left, he asked his mum, 'How did you cope when he was training?'

Her brows pushed together like she was figuring out he wasn't just there for a visit, but she didn't press him for information. 'I love your father very much. Leaving home and travelling with him was the best decision I ever made. It meant I could stay close to him always.'

'But didn't you feel … rejected? Like he was paying more attention to his career?'

She sat next to him and took his hand. 'If that was

true you wouldn't be here, would you?'

He cringed. That was a bit too much information, but then his mum said, 'She must be very special to you if you would rather hurt yourself by leaving her than risk her feeling like you don't care.'

Sebastian couldn't answer straight away. All he could think about was waking up next to Alicia, hearing her laugh at one of his jokes, and seeing her hot and flushed beneath him, her gaze shining with more than pleasure. It had been love, real love. Not what he had with Mai – that had been two people desperate for a connection trying to make it work. With Alicia, everything was genuine.

'She is. She's amazing.'

She squeezed his hand. 'Does she love you?'

He remembered her in his arms, probably asleep, declaring her love. Then the next day, giving up her job. Despite what she claimed, he had no doubt she did it so she could be with him. Would she do that if she wasn't trying to really make a go of it?

If he was honest, he'd seen her emotions long before that – the night at her sister's engagement party when she admitted she cared for him. If he'd been paying attention to his own feelings, he'd have realised the way he felt then was more too.

'She does.' He swallowed hard. 'And I've never loved anyone the way I love her.'

It was true. At this point he was considering giving up on his career. What would be the point in doing something if he didn't love it anymore? She was the only person in the world who made him feel he'd rather have nothing and her than have everything in the world except her.

His mother sighed. 'Then what are you doing here with us? Go get your girl.'

If only things could be that easy.

Sebastian was glad he opted for a suit as he was shown to a chair in a hall he never thought he'd walk through again. Either there was a door open somewhere or the place really was haunted and the goosebumps on his arms were caused by the snobs of generations past conveying their disapproval.

Taking in the artwork – no doubt genuine – the marble floor, the high, arching ceilings, he knew why the house had no warmth at all. The place looked more like a museum. There weren't photos of the family who lived here, only the respected men throughout the bloodline had a portrait – not their wives.

If there was one thing he was sure of, this wasn't the home he'd want to raise a family in – he was pretty sure Alicia would agree with him on that score.

The door to the study opened and Henry appeared in the hall. 'Master will see you now.'

Sebastian had to bite his tongue before he scoffed at the way Henry called him 'master'. It was no wonder the old earl had a God complex. Instead, he made his way into the study and closed the door behind him.

Arthur was already seated on his throne, wearing a scowl that was becoming familiar. 'I see you're still with my daughter, at least publicly. There are measures I can take that I've been reluctant to so far, but you are pushing me to my limits.'

The icy threat didn't faze him much, but he had a feeling Arthur would follow through if he messed this up. Luckily, Sebastian had prepared for worse.

'You told me if I could look you straight in the eye and promise I can give Alicia everything she needs then I'd have your blessing.'

He waited while Arthur chewed that over like a bulldog sucking on a wasp. 'You could not, I believe.'

'I can now,' he said, keeping eye contact.

Arthur leaned forward on the desk. 'Had enough of a break with the French trollops, have you? Now you have the audacity to ask for my blessing?'

He ground his teeth, ignoring the jibe about the women. 'If your PI followed me to France you'll know I spent all week with my parents.'

'Until the next temptation comes along, then you'll bring embarrassment onto this family.'

Now he slid into the chair and leaned in. Waited until he had the older man's full attention. 'There won't be anyone else. I love Alicia and I'm going to spend the rest of my life making her so happy it overshadows the agony of her childhood. And though I don't need or want your blessing, deep down Alicia does. So what's it going to be, Arthur?'

Chapter Twenty-five

All things considered, week two of her new life was going better than expected. She'd just had a meeting with a new potential client who would end up being her third if he signed. All of them were giving her on-going work if she did a good job, and that would make her a steady income. She'd barely have to touch her savings for a while.

But now came the hard part of her plan. She'd been putting it off for so long but she couldn't leave it any longer, not when the media were speculating Sebastian's abrupt departure to France three weeks early. She had to write a press release announcing the break-up before the rumours got out of control. Or worse, Mai got back on the media bandwagon.

But putting 'the end' in print made it too real and she'd been avoiding thinking about him as much as she could. It was either that, or curl up in her bed letting the misery wash over her.

A knock at her door broke her out of the awful thoughts. She crossed the room, glad of the distraction, and opened it wide. She frowned, not recognising the woman in front of her until she smiled.

'What are you doing here?' she snapped.

Mai looked different: her hair was coloured chestnut and shiny, and there was barely any make-up on a face that looked fuller, healthier, even with the hint of bruises beneath her foundation. Still, there was no denying who it was.

'I want to give this to Sebastian.' Mai held up a small envelope.

The way she said his name made jealousy burn at the back of Alicia's throat, but she couldn't feel that way. He wasn't hers anymore. He'd never been hers. 'He's not here.'

'Can you give it to him?' When Alicia scowled, Mai hurried on to explain, 'It's not what you think. It's an apology, for what I've done since the break-up. He can even give it to the media if he wants. All the lies are there and I want to set things right.'

'Why not give it to the press yourself?' she asked, her suspicion rising.

Mai's head dipped for a second. 'They're already twisting every word I've said. And anyway, I've made so much off his misery then lost it all. I don't want to drag it all up again but Sebastian deserves his revenge, if that's what he wants.'

'Drugs will drain your cash faster than most things,' Alicia guessed, not quite ready to feel sympathy for a woman who'd hurt the man she loved.

Mai pursed her lips. 'I deserved that, what I did must have been hard on you too. I'm sorry. But no, not drugs. I got a taste of my own medicine when my partner left me and took every penny I'd made.'

Alicia felt a pang of sympathy, but she wasn't going to let herself be played. 'And you're really sorry, or were you hoping Sebastian would help you out?'

Her eyes widened. 'No! I just want to make things right so we can move on. There's nothing I want from either of you. Not even your forgiveness.'

Alicia couldn't doubt the sincerity in Mai's voice, so she took the offered note. 'I'll see that he gets this.'

She had his parents' address somewhere – passing it on didn't mean she'd have to see him and have her heart ripped in two all over again. And Mai's apology might be the thing that makes him forgive himself for what happened. Not that she had any hope it would make a difference for her.

'Thank you. I really mean that,' Mai said.

Alicia didn't know what to say, so she just smiled.

'I can see why he loves you. You're kind and beautiful, without make-up or fancy hairstyles. For a long time I thought that's where I was going wrong, but I wanted money and adoration more than real love. It's time I traded in the falsity for something that matters.'

She didn't correct Mai's assumption that Sebastian loved her – and not because she couldn't trust the skinny brunette as far as she could throw her. But because the pain that hit her in the chest was too much to bear.

'I'll leave you now. Thanks again.'

Mai walked off and she closed the door behind her, squeezing her eyes tight in case the waterworks started again. But, like Mai, she had to put the past behind her so she could move on. Arming herself with a glass of wine, she settled on the sofa with her laptop and decided to get the final part over with.

Pulling up a word document, her eyes brimmed over and her chest hurt so much she struggled to breathe. *Get a grip and focus. You need to do this.*

By the time the first draft was finished she was proud of herself for not shedding a single tear, though she was sure she'd rubbed her eyes raw. Didn't matter, she'd done what she had to and the pain in her heart would fade with time. Time made everything more bearable. She'd learned that, if nothing else, over the years.

She called a takeaway – pizza, not the fancy Italian she'd shared with Sebastian – then got down to working on her business. By the time her door knocked again, she was more than ready for a break, but it was a pity her appetite hadn't come back yet.

Grabbing her purse, she made her way to the door and opened it wide. Her jaw dropped a little and she had the urge to slap herself to make sure she wasn't dreaming. After all, the day had been long and he was the last person she'd expect to see. Mai returning would

289

be less of a surprise.

'Can I come in?'

Mai stopped for a coffee at a shop around the corner, wondering why the pain inside hadn't faded yet. Wasn't that how karma worked? She did something nice then she was supposed to feel better. Cleansed or whatever.

Instead her stomach was full of bubbly acid and her heart throbbed painfully. All she had to do was think of her shift at the bar later, where all week customers had gotten drunk and asked inappropriate things about her relationship with Sebastian just to tease her. She was beyond misery.

When would it end?

After paying way too much for a skinny latte, she moved to a table near the back, facing away from the entrance, and slipped her oversized shades back on. The last thing she needed was to bump into more of the horde on Team Sebastian. She just wanted to enjoy her coffee in peace.

But a man slipped into the chair across from her, almost making her drop the cup. She scowled, noticing his snappy shirt, trousers, and hair that was far too well-styled to belong to a man who enjoyed women. Gossip columnist? That was the last thing she needed today.

'I have an offer for you,' he said.

'Not interested.' She made to get up, but he grabbed her wrist. 'Let go of me!'

He smirked and the way his eyes gleamed scared her a little. 'Keep your voice down. Nobody knows you're here. Do you want to let the whole café know?'

She didn't and suspected this stranger knew. She sat down and asked, 'Who are you?'

'Just think of me as your new best friend. The name's Kevin.'

He held out his hand for her to shake, but she just stared at him, waiting for a further explanation. She had a feeling this meeting wasn't down to chance.

He sighed, pulling his hand away. 'I have a proposition for you.'

Mai shook her head. She'd been right with her first impression. This man was a journalist. A snappy dressed one, she'd give him that. But she was done with the media. 'I'm not interested in selling anymore stories. That part of my life's over. I've moved on.'

He cocked an eyebrow. 'To a grimy bar in the East End? *Dahling*, a woman like you should be spoiled with riches, not serving cheap beer to degenerates.'

Her gaze dropped to her mug while she fought against the urge to have more, to get out of there once and for all. But at the cost of dragging up the past and risking humiliation again? No, what she'd done was wrong and she was paying the price.

'It's honest work,' she said, glaring at him.

He shrugged. 'What I want your help with is uncovering the truth. No lies required. And I'm willing to pay you handsomely. With expenses.'

Frowning, she tried to make sense of what he was saying. 'Why would I need expenses if you want to buy a story from me?'

Kevin laughed. 'No, that's not what I want from you. That ship has sailed, don't you think?'

Maybe, but then, 'What do you want then?'

He leaned forward and whispered. 'You know the kind of dirt that sells to the press. That's what I want from you. I need you to dig up whatever you can on a woman. I'll let you know her location, fly you wherever it takes, and pay your living expenses until there's enough there to put an end to her engagement.'

Flights, living expenses, was this guy for real? 'You want help to break up a couple?'

The smirk was back, and the gleam was evil this time. 'Don't worry, it's not what you think. They're not in love. It's all a sham.'

She doubted that. People didn't have marriages made on paper these days. There had to be something else he wasn't telling her. 'Why does it matter to you? Aren't you –?'

'Gay?' he asked, then laughed. 'Very. It matters to me because the woman in question is marrying my fiancé.'

Mai gasped, putting a hand over her mouth. 'Why is he doing that?'

'Blackmail. So you see? I want enough dirt on her so I can get him out of the engagement.'

Mai nodded. She did see, and this would not only pay her bills and maybe give her some savings, but she'd be doing the right thing by helping. The proper thing. Maybe then her life would turn around and karma would give her a slice of something good.

'Who's the woman?' she asked, curious now.

Kevin sat back, linking his fingers on the table in front of him. 'I believe you know her sister already. The woman marrying my fiancé is Sylvia Simpson.'

Alicia stared, unblinking, until her eyes stung from the lack of moisture. Her heart pounded to life like it had been waiting for him, missing him as much as she was. But every thud hurt a little more than she could take.

'No,' she said and shook her head for good measure. She couldn't survive another rejection, and she wasn't sure she'd be able to keep from telling him the truth. That she was in love with him and he'd broken her heart when he left.

'Then I'll say what I came to say.' There was no bluff in his eyes, only determination and his voice echoed in the hall.

What would the neighbours think? Before she'd have cared more, but now she couldn't bring herself to.

'What do you want, Sebastian?' Couldn't he have emailed? That would have been easier to deal with.

'Mostly to apologise –'

'Well, now you have.' Her heart hurt, everything hurt, and his spicy smell brought a barrage of memories back, only intensifying the pain. She tried to shut the door, but he stuck his foot in the way before she could.

'Wait!'

He shoved hard against the door, and her irritation won over the hurt. She pulled the thing wide. 'So you can patronise me some more like you did last week? Why don't you bugger off and leave me alone, Sebastian? You've made it perfectly clear where I am on your list of things you care about.'

'That's not …' He glanced over his shoulder at her neighbour making her way up the stairs, then forced his way inside. She backed up, too angry to speak. When he shut the door, he said, 'It's you. You're the reason I thought I had to end it.'

'So we've moved from patronising to being mean. OK, if that's what you need to ease your guilt –'

He grabbed her shoulders. 'Will you let me finish? Please.'

Shrugging out of his hold, she glared at him, determined not to let him see how much this was killing her.

Sebastian stuffed his hands in his pockets and stared back, waiting for her to agree. For the first time she noticed his eyes, full of pain and underscored with dark smudges like he'd barely slept all week.

Her anger cooled off a little as sympathy took its place. He was training hard, he really wanted to make a go of his career and thinking they could make it work had been a pipe dream. She nodded for him to go on, though she'd rather curl up into a ball and let misery have her for a few hours, maybe even days.

'I'm sorry, Alicia. Sorry because I was wrong, sorry because I pushed you into being with me, and I'm sorry because despite knowing you'd be better off with someone else, someone who doesn't have a hectic training schedule, I can't let you go.'

She blinked back tears, her head spinning and her heart racing. 'I don't understand.'

He stepped closer, so she had to crane her neck to look at him. He wasn't smiling, and that serious expression was back. 'I told you my career came first. All week without you I've not cared about any of it. I've been too busy missing you like crazy.'

She backed up into the living room, too scared to hope and still too hurt from the last time he left to believe this was real.

But even if it wasn't a dream, they were finished. She had the press release all drawn up. She was getting over him. 'It doesn't matter anymore.'

The pain crumpling his face took her breath away. 'You love me, you can't just ignore that. I thought –'

'What?' How did he know?

'The last night we were together, you said so. Just as you were falling asleep.'

She made it over to the armchair before her legs gave out. No tears came despite the way rejection and pain sliced her heart in half – again and again. He'd known. When he walked away from her, told her they could never be together, he'd known exactly how she felt and left anyway.

'I want you to leave now.' Her voice was surprisingly steady, even though she was shaken to the core. 'I never want to see you again.'

Chapter Twenty-six

Sebastian knelt in front of her, placing his hands on either side of her legs. Wise of him not to touch her. She'd never hit anyone in her life but she was tempted to smack him a good one now.

'I love you too. It's why I thought I had to leave. Life with me is going to be tough. I'm going to be exhausted for weeks on end and I didn't want you going through that. Then you left your job and I panicked, thinking you'd given up everything for me.'

Her lower lip trembled and she pressed them together. She was hanging on by a thread and he admitting he loved her didn't help with her resolve. 'What's changed?'

'Watching my parents. They're so happy, Alicia, and my mum doesn't feel cheated at all even though I did growing up. I'd rather have a home base. Somewhere we can stay and raise a family when the time comes, but you have holidays at Maine, don't you? We can haggle for more so you can come with me to the tournaments if you want. After each one I'll take a few weeks off and we can go away somewhere or stay at home. As long as we're together.'

'I quit Maine, remember? I didn't go back,' she said, because she couldn't think of a way to respond to the rest of what he'd said.

'That's OK. I'll support you through whatever you want to do. I just want you close, with me, and I promise to pay you all the attention you deserve.' His eyes were sincere and her heart swelled.

She believed him and wanted what he had to offer. It

wouldn't be perfect, but she'd known that for so long and a part of her had come to accept it. But first she had to give him Mai's note and hope that once and for all he could forgive himself, otherwise how was he ever going to believe that she wasn't going to up and leave him at the first bump they faced?

She pulled the envelope from her pocket and handed it to him. 'Mai came here and asked me to give you this. She says it's an apology and admits all the lies she's told to make money from your misery. She did this so you could have your revenge.'

But Alicia knew him better than that – Sebastian wouldn't be so callous. As she watched him read the note with a slight frown creasing his brow, she just hoped this gave him the same closure Mai wanted.

When he finished reading, he ran a hand through his hair. 'You didn't have to show me that. Most people wouldn't have.'

Unease skittered up her spine. Had Mai lied, begged in the note for another chance along with the apology? 'I thought it might let you forgive yourself if nothing else.'

He looked at her then, really looked at her, like he'd never seen her before. 'It has, really. I just meant that you had no idea whether that's what it said, but you gave it to me anyway and believed in me enough to trust me. There's not a jealous bone in your body, is there?'

Since he was being so honest, she told the truth. 'I do, sometimes. Today, when she came by and said your name like she missed you, I was jealous of her.'

'But you thought I didn't love you then,' he said.

Alicia nodded. 'There might be times when I feel jealous, Sebastian, but I know you love me now. I won't jump to conclusions without speaking to you first.' She remembered what Mai did after Wimbledon, and wanted to reassure him she wouldn't do the same thing.

'I know you won't, and I'm going to prove to you every day that you have nothing to worry about.' He took her face in his hands and kissed her like she was adored completely.

What she said to him at her sister's engagement party was true, it wasn't all about sex for her. But right now her body roared to life again and she wanted him for more than pleasure. She wanted the connection. Alicia pulled back, her breath coming too fast.

'I'd like a demonstration of how you plan to pay me attention. It might help me make a decision.' Though her heart had made up her mind for her, and she didn't hide the love she felt from him – instead let it shine through with her smile.

Sebastian tugged her to the edge of her chair, then hugged her waist hard. 'Thank God. I was ready to beg. And I thought going to see your father would be the hard part.'

'You went to see my father?' she squeaked.

He kissed her thigh, then looked up with a smile. 'After the police left at the party, he told me that if I could look into his eyes and promise I'd take care of you and protect you then I'd have his blessing. Then I was too hung up on making false promises and worrying about hurting you that I couldn't do it. I went back yesterday and convinced him I'd love you forever, just not in his way.'

Tears leaked from her eyes and her breath caught. 'Thank you. You didn't have to do that. We shouldn't have to live our lives the way he wants us to.'

'We won't have to, not again. He doesn't understand it, but he accepts that.'

Threading her fingers through his hair, she said, 'Good. Now enough about my father. I'd like to see what else you can do with that mouth of yours.'

He looked up at her, his cheeky smile flashing briefly but then the serious expression came back. 'Is this what you really want?'

She cupped his face with her hands, her heart melting

at the worry in his gaze. 'I've told you over and over that sex isn't all that matters. Neither is what other people think. I love you, Sebastian. I forgive you for being an idiot.'

His grin came back, the one that suggested he had a few ideas she'd like. 'Let me make it up to you properly.'

Sebastian carried her through to the bedroom, kissing her nose, face, and lips as he went. She didn't want slow and sexy, not now she had him back and everything was right. She stripped him like it had been years instead of days and she was starved for him.

He quickly got with the program, teasing her with his mouth as he removed her clothes, and by the time she was naked she was ready for him. Alicia dragged him to the edge of the bed and wrapped her legs around his waist, pulling his head down for a kiss. He entered her immediately.

His thrusts were slow, sensual, and almost drove her mad. The kissing was equally languorous and had her more worked up than if he'd continued with the hard and fast. As she trembled with pleasure, his lips brushed her jaw and neck, and all the while he told her how much he'd missed her in his life. Before he found his release, she managed to assure him she felt the same.

When they were both sated, he pulled her close. 'Is it too soon to go house hunting?'

She grinned. 'You're that desperate for a ball and chain?'

He looked at her seriously. 'I've been coming home to you for weeks. I don't think we should change that.'

She thought about how much she liked having him around, having his stuff in her space and had to agree. 'OK, I'll agree on one condition.'

He raised a brow.

'You let me keep working on the charity. I miss it.'

He kissed her slowly at first, almost reverently. But

then she opened to him and pulled him closer. As their breath sped and his body grew deliciously hard against hers, Alicia forgot all about her condition.

He pulled away, gasping for air. 'I think I can allow that, but have a condition of my own.'

'You're giving a volunteer worker conditions?' she asked, baffled.

He kissed her softly. 'More of a request, actually. I'd like you to marry me.'

She grinned, her heart full to bursting. 'Don't guys usually get down on one knee and hold out a ring when they say that?'

Shaking his head, he said, 'I don't want us to get engaged, I've done that before. I'll buy you whatever ring you want as a wedding present. What do you say?'

She grabbed his hair, pulled him down an inch or so, then said, 'I like the sound of that. Do you have a date in mind?'

'No, but sooner works for me.'

'Me too,' she agreed.

Trailing a finger along her jaw, he said, 'You really are amazing, Blondie. Or should I start calling you Mrs Collins to be?'

She laughed. 'You're not half bad yourself, Collins. But I think Mr Blondie has a better ring to it.'

Cariad Titles

For more information about
Aimée Duffy

and other **Cariad** titles

please visit

www.accentpress.co.uk

CARIAD

Lightning Source UK Ltd.
Milton Keynes UK
UKOW01f0258020816

279738UK00001B/20/P